JON RIC.....

Disturbing Works

Volume Two

A Collection of Dark Stories

by Jon Richter

To Louise,
I hope you enjoy this!
And that there are no
mistakes this time 😬
Have a great Christmas,
Jon R

For everyone whose book is still trapped inside them.

Get writing!

CONTENTS

THE PIT

Some movement, down in the Pit.

Probably rats. Perhaps a squirming sackful of maggots, about to burst into a cloud of bluebottles that would gorge themselves until they were swollen and dizzy. Maybe a seagull that had swooped and become entangled, dragged beneath the surface of the festering heap.

An orgy of filth, just a few dozen feet below him.

He tossed another bin bag into the foul abyss, watching as it split open upon landing, scattering plastic milk bottles, chicken bones, beer cans. Everything had been squashed and condensed to fit as much inside the black plastic liner as possible, but even if everyone in the whole town adopted this approach, it wouldn't be long before the disused quarry was completely overflowing with garbage.

The gulls wheeling overhead screeched and cawed as though excited at the prospect.

Walter grabbed another bag from the back seat of the

car. He knew it was disgusting to use the family's only vehicle for this purpose, but what other choice did he have? The streets were choked with rubbish, including a reeking mound right outside his own house. The heaps of decaying trash had been dubbed 'rat hotels' by the media, the ever-growing piles photographed gleefully by the hordes of journalists that had descended on their town like… well, like flies around garbage.

And it really was the flies that were the worst part. After so many weeks without a bin collection, he was almost used to the appalling stink. You could even adjust to the sight of rodents scurrying around in broad daylight while you were walking to work. But those flies… despite closing every window, blocking every crack, they somehow found a way into your home. They buzzed around, bloated and content, jubilant in their dominion.

Then they bit you.

He scratched absently at one of the pustules on his face, thinking about his poor children, the six-year-old twins covered in similar swellings, crying in their beds while he tried to distract them with a story. Begging him to keep the rats away from them.

Another bin bag tumbled into the void.

He wiped sweat from his brow with the back of his glove. It didn't help that it was so fucking *hot*. The record-breaking summer heatwave only served to heighten the town's misery: people slowly roasting inside their homes, unable to open their windows because of the stink, while the trash pile outside also cooked, its fetid vapours oozing out like oil from cooking meat. Every day, the town woke up to a brand new stench.

And the garbage piles kept growing higher.

It was like living through a divine punishment. A plague of unending pestilence.

He hurled another sack into the hole, spitting the nauseating taste from his mouth, which was still preferable to breathing through his nose. This close to the quarry – or 'the Pit', as the town's temporary and unofficial landfill site had become known – the sickly tang was almost intolerable. He could feel it seeping into him, filling his lungs with something toxic, infecting him from the inside out. This was the third pilgrimage he had made to the dumping ground, and he knew the memory of the odour would linger with him as he drove home. It made no difference whether he wound the windows down, or left them closed; the car stank inside, and the town stank outside, and the stink was inside him, in his nostrils and on his tongue, under his fingernails, which leaked pus whenever he took the gloves off.

He stopped and looked around. He saw others like him, unloading their cars, filling up the quarry with their detritus. He saw misery and anger in their blazing eyes, their clenched jaws. Some had scarves wrapped around their faces, and others wore surgical masks, making them look strange and inhuman. All of them were sweating as they laboured beneath the setting sun, the sky above them lit with a hellish red glow.

The bin men had been on strike for months now. The next round of talks was taking place tomorrow. Surely a breakthrough must be made.

If it wasn't, the town was going to go fucking crazy.

He hefted the next bag, realising as he did so that it was

leaking. He watched the brownish fluid dribble down his T-shirt, and started to laugh, quietly, to himself.

*

"In a weird way, it's almost beautiful. Don't you think, Jonny?"

Adam stared out across the undulating dunes of waste. At night, a strange chemical haze hung over the Pit, catching and holding the light from the moon, or maybe emitting its own malevolent glow. Swathed in this greenish fog, the site looked otherworldly, like the surface of an alien planet.

"Are you joking? This place fucking hums." Jonny turned away from the precipice, coughing, and walked back towards the car.

"Yes, but if you ignore that aspect… my point is that beauty can be found in the most unusual forms."

"Whatever floats your boat, mate. Now give me a hand with this fat loser."

Jonny popped open the car boot, and Mitch immediately started screaming. Jonny cracked him around the head again, and stuck the duct tape back across his mouth.

"For fuck's sake, this tape we're using is rubbish. Lost its stick already. I knew we should have got the proper brand."

He slid his hands under the heavy man's shoulders and glared impatiently at his companion.

"Alright, alright," Adam grumbled, walking over to grab Mitch's legs, which were tied together with more of the substandard adhesive. With a grunt, they lifted their prisoner out of the car, carrying him a few paces across to the quarry's edge before dropping him unceremoniously to the dusty earth.

"You're a biggun, aren't you?" said Jonny, breathing heavily. Mitch's arms were also bound, and he writhed on the ground between them like a salted slug. "Maybe if you didn't spend all your money on kebabs, you wouldn't have had to cut up the boss's drugs, and then you wouldn't be in this mess, would you?"

Mitch squealed beneath the duct tape. Adam reached down to peel it off, an expression of pity crossing his face.

"Don't do that, he'll only start fucking screaming again," complained Jonny.

Adam fixed Mitch with a stern look. "No you won't, will you, Mitch? We're going to be nice and rational and adult about this, aren't we?"

Mitch's eyes squirmed in their sockets, wide and horrified.

"Give me a nod, Mitch, otherwise the tape is going back on."

Mitch nodded vigourously.

"Okay. Good. Now, let's have a conversation. Why do you think you're here, tied up, on the edge of the quarry?"

Mitch's mouth jerked feverishly, but no sound came out. It was as though his lips were dress-rehearsing a list of possible responses.

"Come on, Mitch. I'm genuinely interested to know whether you realise what you've done to incur the boss's wrath."

"Oh, for fuck's sake. Why do you always have to play with them?" muttered Jonny, turning to walk back to the car once again. He left the boot open so that the smell of the sweaty, terrified man could dissipate, although any lingering odour was completely overwhelmed by the godawful reek coming from the Pit.

"I… you… there's been a mistake," mumbled Mitch eventually.

Adam sighed disappointedly. He looked down for a moment, brushing a fly off his plain black hoodie. It buzzed away for a second, then landed on his plain black pants.

"No, Mitch. There's no mistake. Now come on. Jonny even mentioned it already. You know why we're all here. Why don't you at least tell me your side of the story?"

Mitch's eyes and mouth went into overdrive. The overweight man kept blinking, as though he thought this might somehow change the scene on the other side of his eyelids. But it didn't. Each time his eyes opened he was confronted by the same black, starless sky, and by Adam's face staring down at him, clean-shaven and serious. The stink of the Pit was acrid in his nostrils.

"I… I was cutting up the drugs," he stammered. "I was trying to make more money." His eyes closed as the confession spilled out of him. "But I was going to give it all to Mr Bodicker, I swear!"

Adam shook his head and held up a finger. "Shh shh shh… none of that nonsense, Mitch. You were doing so well. Like you said, you were cutting up the drugs, because you wanted to make more money. You weren't happy with the share the boss was giving you, and you wanted more. I understand completely. Hey, I'm an ambitious guy too!" His smile was wide and friendly. Mitch cowered away from him, wriggling backwards, perilously close to the edge.

Jonny was leaning on the car, messing with his phone.

"But, Mitch, that's where you went wrong," Adam continued, the smile suddenly evaporating. "Mr Bodicker doesn't pay us to think. He doesn't pay us to use our initiative. He pays us to do exactly what he asks us to do. Like machines. Like worker bees. Efficient and reliable. And if one of the worker bees starts fucking up, messing with the workings of the hive, do you know what happens, Mitch?"

Mitch just blinked some more, tears stinging his eyes. The fly had landed on his forehead, and was gleefully drinking the sweat that was beading there.

"The other workers get rid of the renegade," said Adam decisively. "For the good of the hive. Because if word gets around that our product is substandard, then all our customers are sure to look elsewhere. And a business without customers is like a hive without... hmmm. I'm not sure I can quite make this analogy work, actually."

"Honey?" volunteered Jonny as he approached, carrying something.

"P...please... don't kill me. I've learned my lesson," stuttered Mitch. "I get it, I really do. I didn't mean to upset Mr Bodicker. Please. I..." Then his words dissolved into a strangled gargle as he saw that Jonny was holding a sledgehammer.

"No… the honey would be the product, wouldn't it?" mused Adam. "I suppose in this case the issue is that we have a worker bee who has sabotaged the honey itself."

Jonny shrugged, and reached down to plaster the duct tape across Mitch's mouth once again. Then he swung the mallet downwards, and Mitch's kneecap exploded beneath it. The tape barely suppressed his howl of agony.

"I was thinking 'a hive without a queen' but that would reflect a scenario where Mr Bodicker himself was compromised," Adam continued, more to himself than to either of the two men. He gazed out across the Pit once again as Jonny swung the hammer into Mitch's other knee. There was another horrific crunching of bone and gristle, another inhuman shriek of pain. "No, I think this whole speech needs a bit more work."

"Shall we do his arms as well?" asked Jonny, breathing heavily once again. "I can't really be arsed. It's boiling."

Adam didn't reply for a moment, still pondering his soliloquy. Then he seemed to reach a decision, nodding and smiling to himself, and hopped nimbly across Mitch's prone body.

"Nah. It's not like he'll be able to haul his fat fucking carcass out of the Pit, is it?" he said brightly, and with a single vicious kick propelled Mitch over the edge and into the putrid chasm below. Mitch, not yet lost to the unconscious oblivion of shock, screamed once again as he fell, a long and harrowing sound, before his head smacked against a jutting rock, and he was silenced. His body plummeted into the festering lake of rubbish and was lost amongst the leaking bin bags, the crumbling polystyrene, the discarded appliances, the soiled nappies, the little bags of dog shit. Watching him disappear, Jonny fancied he saw a great plume of the glowing gas billow out as the garbage was momentarily displaced, like the toxic burp of some irradiated creature that had just swallowed Mitch Scanlon whole. The trash pile shifted and rippled, as though digesting him.

Then it fell silent, and still.

"Well, I'm hungry after that," said Adam cheerily. "Shall we get a KFC on the way home?"

*

Smoke curled around her, like ghosts caressing her skin. She stared at the crumpled-up cigarette packet in the waste bin, painfully aware of the irony.

The man watched her with a smile on his face. Or, more accurately, on his mouth. His eyes were cold and cruel, like two huge hailstones.

"How will you do it?" she said eventually, trying to keep the tremor out of her voice. A fat bluebottle landed on her arm, and she swatted it away disgustedly.

"It's best you don't know."

She could hear the fly buzzing around her office somewhere. It was dark, because this was a secret meeting, so she had felt the need to illuminate it only by the light of her desk lamp. She had thought it would feel intimate, conspiratorial. It meant that all she could see were the things on her desk, and the sinister smile on the face opposite her, and those piercing blue eyes. She scratched anxiously at the insect bites on her arm.

"If I'm paying for the service I want to know what I'm getting." She tried to hold his gaze, to mirror the hard steel she found there, but couldn't. She sucked another long drag from the cigarette.

"He will disappear, as you have requested. No-one will ever find him."

"Okay, but… what if something goes wrong?"

"Nothing will go wrong." The man's voice was a deep monotone, devoid of emotion. Like a machine, for killing. Which was exactly what she wanted.

"But I can't just… my career is on the line here."

"Not just your career," the man intoned. "If I fail, you will go to jail. But I don't fail. I have worked with many clients, and all have been left extremely satisfied."

"Like who?" she asked, trying to catch him off guard. But the smile on his face simply widened, and he said nothing. She finished the cigarette, opening a drawer to crush it out in the ashtray she kept hidden there. The stink of stale tobacco that wafted out was infinitely more pleasurable than the reek of festering waste outside. Her windows were closed, but the stench seemed to seep in through the glass, through the walls, into her clothes, into her hair.

"Okay… but you understand that if we reach a deal tomorrow, the arrangement is off? You can keep the half I've paid up front."

The man nodded, once. "I understand. I will wait for your text. Unless I receive a message containing the code word, I will withdraw."

She nodded, satisfied, lighting up another cigarette. Her nerves felt stretched and frayed, like ligaments on a torture rack. She looked down again at the items on her desk, all neatly arranged, in-keeping with her meticulously organised approach. They looked somehow hostile, like things she could no longer control. She picked up the nameplate, and stared at it as though she didn't recognise the name it bore.

Judith Dawson, Mayor.

Across from her, the fly landed on the man's cheek, but he didn't seem to care.

*

Walter paused at the door, feeling a sudden and awful wave of sadness. No wife, no children, to wish him a good day. They had gone to stay with her sister, which meant they were missing school. But it was the right thing to do. The three of them couldn't continue to live in this shrine of filth. How could anyone?

"Goodbye," he said to the empty house, and stepped outside into the stinking heat.

Their modest house had no front garden, so the door opened straight out onto the pavement. He stared for a moment at the pile of bin bags by the kerbside, which was now so high it was all they could see from their window, not that they bothered to open their curtains any more. He thought about the layers of refuse, about how the upper strata were relatively clean and unspoilt, the shiny new bin bags glistening in the sun. Beneath them were older bags that had started to spread out and burst, spilling into the road and onto the pavement, a banquet for the pigeons and gulls and rats that swarmed around them. And then there was the bottom layer, decayed by now into a liquid mulch that nourished the bacteria and maggots. Like human society, the bottom-feeders, the downtrodden, were crushed at the bottom of the bloated heap.

The council offices were about half a mile away, in the town centre. Walter always walked there, for the exercise, and to save money. Usually he would see other people heading into town, walking or cycling to work, or to do their shopping. But since the strikes had started, the streets had become increasingly barren; the people that hadn't left the town already were either driving to work or just staying at home, trying to avoid the foulness that surrounded them.

Today, Knoxton seemed like a ghost town. There wasn't a soul on the street, other than him and the feasting creatures. He tried to ignore them as he walked, to stare straight ahead, to imagine that everything was normal. But his eyes were drawn inexorably back to the stacks of rubbish, to the animals it was sustaining. He imagined new lifeforms growing inside the piles, the rustling bin bags like grotesque cocoons.

On the corner of the main crossroads, he saw a fox. He knew that urban foxes were a common sight in London, but they were a long way outside the city, and the sight of such a sleek and beautiful animal was still a novelty to him.

Except this one was neither sleek, nor beautiful. Its emaciated frame was covered in scabs and sores, its fur clinging to it in clumps like fungal growths. The creature's flesh seemed to dangle from its carcass as though trying to escape from its diseased bones. One of its eyes was swollen shut, a clump of yellowish abscesses seeming to visibly throb around the inhibited organ. The repulsive thing's lips peeled back in a feral snarl as it regarded him through the other eye, polluted saliva dripping from its mouth. Then it went back to pawing and biting at the pile of trash on the street corner.

Gazing at the forlorn, contaminated creature, Walter was consumed by a sudden and insane urge to join it, to kneel down alongside it and sink his face into the slime. This was the world now, the septic dystopia that his own employers had contrived to build. All the centuries of filth and muck, buried beneath us in the drainpipes and sewers, rising up to reclaim the earth.

He watched as the fox ate its fill.

*

Clive pulled the baseball cap further down, realised he couldn't see where he was going, and lifted it again. He kept his gaze tilted downwards, daring to raise his eyes only occasionally to make sure he didn't blunder into a lamppost or stumble into a heap of garbage. He thought about the Pit, imagined himself flailing and struggling as he sank into the atrocious pile. Poetic justice, they would call it.

He reached the corner where they had told him to wait. He glanced nervously around, but the streets seemed quiet, the trash baking slowly in the sweltering heat. Apparently a black Prius would collect him this time. He wished it would hurry up. With a face so recognisable, he didn't want to be outside in public for a second longer than he had to. He'd already had to dodge a gaggle of reporters who knew the next round of talks was happening today; thankfully the council had lied about the timing, so the majority of the hacks hadn't yet begun to assemble.

Dawson had seemed different in the meeting today; she had been much more cooperative, at one point almost pleading with him to accept her revised deal. And he had wanted to, so very much. He hadn't meant for this to get so out of hand. He looked around again, surveying his empire of grime. The townsfolk held him personally responsible, of course; he'd had death threats, hate mail, Twitter campaigns and Facebook groups threatening to lynch him outside his home. He'd had to send his family away for their own safety. Now he spent most days shut up inside the house, the curtains drawn, trying to fend off the flies while he watched his e-mails and waited for Bodicker to call him.

Bodicker had been *very* unhappy when he'd found out about Clive's family's departure. He had people watching the house, of course, so Bodicker had phoned minutes after the car drove away, ranting and raving, screaming at Clive that if he was planning to double-cross him he would be very sorry. *Wherever you've sent them, I'll find them, and the next time you see them they'll be missing their eyes and fingers*, the crime boss had shrieked. Clive had managed to calm him down, assure him that he wasn't about to do a deal, that the strikes would continue for as long as Bodicker kept paying him. That his family had only gone away to protect them from the angry social media mob. That his loyalty was unwavering.

He wondered again why Bodicker hated the mayor so much. He had always thought he understood politics; those were the skills he had utilised to ascend to a prominent position within the Environmental Department, and become the head of the union. But this was a different kind of politics; the politics of crime and hate and greed, sprouting out of human suffering like poisonous toadstools out of bad dirt.

He glanced at his watch. Where the fuck was this Prius? He knew Bodicker was paranoid, that sending a car to collect him directly from the council offices was too risky.

But the kingpin had been extremely keen to receive a personal, face-to-face update immediately following the latest talks. It wasn't like one of Bodicker's drivers to be late. Clive felt exposed, out here in the open. His bald head was suddenly intolerably hot beneath the cap, like an egg slowly boiling. He took off the hat and took a deep, gasping breath, loosening his tie as he looked upwards at the cloudless sky. Time and space and the cosmos, blue then black, an uncaring void that regarded him no differently than the trash piled around him.

Some movement caught his eye. He turned towards the opposite street corner, and saw a horrible four-legged creature, much larger than a cat or even a fox. It was reaching into the garbage heap, clawing at the polluted mound, shovelling handfuls of filth into its mouth. He squinted into the sunlight, his eyes not what they used to be. Was it a dog?

The creature seemed to sense him, and turned its head. It smiled. A shred of black plastic hung from its mouth, snagged between its teeth.

It was a man.

Clive felt nausea squirming inside him, as though the rats had somehow found their way inside his stomach. He retched and leaned forward, coughing up a gout of vomit into the road. The man watched as the union leader voided his guts, his mad eyes glinting in the sun.

A black Prius pulled around the corner, gliding to a halt alongside Clive, mercifully obstructing his view of the lunatic. He yanked open the door and scrambled into the back seat, still gagging.

The driver stayed motionless, watching him in the rear-view mirror. "Are you alright?" he asked in a slow, monotone voice.

"Yes, I'm fine, just fucking drive please." He knew that the trash-eater was still out there, just a few metres away, and couldn't bring himself to look through the window. He breathed a long sigh of relief as the car moved off.

He didn't notice the driver continuing to watch him with ice-cold eyes, the same colour as the sky.

*

"Just fuck off, will you?"

Adam kept laughing, slapping his thigh and rocking backwards.

"Seriously I'm going to go back in there and shoot the bitch."

Still Adam couldn't speak, tears rolling down his face as he sniggered uncontrollably.

"What can I even do about it? Short back and sides, I said. Not 'shave the whole lot off and leave a random quiff on the top'. I'll have to wear a fucking hat."

Adam leaned forwards, taking deep breaths as he tried to compose himself. Then he looked up at his friend.

"Honestly it isn't actually that bad. It just makes you look like an Iced Gem, that's all." A fresh howl of laughter erupted out of him. Jonny stared at him acidly, then went back to clawing at his hair in the mirror.

The living room of their shared flat was like a strange

amalgam of their personalities. Adam's huge television dominated the clean, light space, his game consoles arranged neatly beneath it in a white Ikea unit. Alongside this arrangement was an old bookcase crammed with Jonny's graphic novels and ornaments, the silly souvenirs and action figures and memorabilia that he had accumulated over the years. Other than Adam's uproarious laughter, the only sound was the whirring of the hamster wheel in the corner as little Claude went about his daily exercise.

"I can't go out tonight. That's it, no women for me until this fucking grows back."

"How much did it cost you?" Adam asked through his tears.

"Thirty quid," Jonny replied sourly, and Adam dissolved into hysteria once again.

Then his phone rang, and he immediately fell silent, the laughter switched off like an electricity supply at the mains.

"Yes, Mr Bodicker?" he answered coolly.

Jonny could hear their boss's voice at the other end, screeching with rage.

"I'm sure Bill wouldn't do that, sir. There must be some other reason." More furious shrieking. "Yes, of course."

The call ended, and Adam stared thoughtfully at the phone.

"What was that?" Jonny asked miserably, continuing to stare at his haircut.

"We've got another job, Jonny-boy. The boss wants us

to find Bill's car. He was supposed to be bringing Clive Halsall to HQ, and he hasn't turned up. The tracking device says he's gone to the Pit instead."

Jonny frowned. "Why would Bill do that?"

"I don't know. I think we'd better take the guns."

He bent down to pull out the draw hidden underneath their plain grey sofa. Inside it was an array of weaponry. He lifted a Glock 18, pondered it for a while, then swapped it for a sniper rifle.

"Go on, I'll take that one," said Jonny. Adam retrieved the machine pistol and handed it over.

"Hair you go."

"What did you say?"

"I said here you go."

Jonny's eyes narrowed. "Fuck off," he muttered, as Adam began to chuckle once again.

*

The sun glared down upon Knoxton as though it was enraged. Its unrelenting heat drew revolting odours from the piles of rubbish that covered the town. The flies seemed lazier than usual, the rats and foxes dazed by the warmth, all of them dozing amongst the reeking heaps.

Yet despite this foul bouquet, the smell of the town was nothing compared to the Pit. It was as though the overflowing quarry was the epicentre of some demonic invasion, a portal straight into a stinking nether realm. The rubbish that had been hurled into it belched out fumes so vile that people had stopped coming to the makeshift dump. The stench was almost tangible, a heavy thickness in the air that seemed capable of eating through clothing, dissolving flesh.

Into this toxic hell came a car. A black Prius, rolling slowly up to the lip of the putrid maw. It stopped, its engine still running, its headlights pointing down into the depths like eyes gaping in disgust. A man emerged from the driver's seat, his movements slow and measured as he donned a surgical mask. The sun did not concern itself with individual human affairs, but if it had focused its gaze on the man's face, it would have seen a pair of intensely blue eyes, as though the man's blood was ice-cold inside his veins.

The man opened a rear door of the car and slid something out from the back seat. It was another man, a bald one, lying comatose. The blue-eyed man left him on the ground beside the car, and circled to the vehicle's back end, opening the boot. If the sun had cared, it could have looked inside the boot, and seen the car's original driver there. The man was neatly folded into the small space, a long needle sticking out of his right eye like a pin in a map. A single rivulet of blood leaked from the wound, as though it was the man's life-force escaping.

The blue-eyed man extracted the needle, wiping it clean with the latex gloves he wore. He squatted beside the other man, and inserted the needle carefully into his eyeball, this time choosing the left, perhaps for no reason other than a sense of symmetry. The bald man jerked, once, and then ceased to be the bald man, and became instead a man-shaped pile of meat and bones.

The blue-eyed man hoisted the overweight body,

displaying a strength that belied his slender frame. No emotion was visible in his eyes as he dropped it over the quarry's edge, watching as it tumbled into the unspeakable quagmire below. When it disappeared beneath the surface, he gave a single satisfied nod. Then he returned to the boot of the car, hefting the other body onto his shoulder with greater ease this time. The sun's gaze was unblinking as the second carcass was thrown into the Pit.

Calmly, the blue-eyed man removed one of the latex gloves, and took out his phone. He carefully typed out a text message, a single code word, and sent it to a recipient stored in the phone simply as 'J'. Then he hurled the phone out across the dump. Like the two bodies, it was devoured greedily. He nodded once again.

Then his head exploded.

*

"Well, at least we got the car back."

Adam and Jonny stared over the edge, their expressions troubled. A gentle breeze had arisen, scattering bits of litter across the Pit's surface, ruffling Adam's hair. Jonny's was hidden beneath a woollen hat.

"I don't think that's the outcome Mr Bodicker had in mind," Adam replied. "Without Halsall, we don't have control over the Union anymore."

Jonny shrugged. "So what? Another worm will crawl out of the dirt to take his place. And then we'll pay him a visit, too. It won't matter."

Adam glanced at him. "Or her. That's very sexist of you, Jonny."

"I hope it isn't a woman. I've never liked doing jobs on women. Call me a gentleman."

"Gallantry isn't dead," murmured Adam, looking over the edge where they had just tossed the assassin's headless body.

He saw movement, and frowned. Yes, it was unmistakable – something was stirring amongst the bin bags and the bodies and the junk. He squinted, trying to work out what it was. It was too big to be a rat, or even a cat. It seemed almost as though a large animal was moving about, just under the surface.

"Can you see that?" he asked.

"See what?" said Jonny.

"There's something down there."

"What, besides the ten thousand tons of shite?"

"Yes. An animal, or something. Look, there!" He pointed towards a bulge that had appeared, close to where they had dumped Mitch Scanlon, less than twenty-four hours earlier.

"I can't see anything, mate."

And then Jonny gasped, because at that moment the thing emerged, bursting up out of the enormous garbage heap like a surfacing sea monster.

It wasn't an animal. It was a matted, stinking, sickeningly entwined *knot* of animals. Cats and foxes snarled and shrieked at each other, unable to pull apart their tails, which had become horribly entangled amongst plastic six-pack holders, carrier bags, drawstrings and cable ties. Rats and squirrels were caught in the chaos too, scrabbling and biting, further antagonising the larger creatures that had become imprisoned in the seething morass. Bits of wood and nails and curls of barbed wire held the creatures together, embedded in their flesh. The whole monstrous tapestry was caked in muck and slime, and despite each creature pulling in different directions as they tried desperately to escape, the thing seemed to have taken on a sort of consciousness of its own, dragging itself across the Pit's surface.

An unbearable new stench drifted up to them, the sort of sickly-sweet fetor that you might imagine belonged only in Hell itself. The animals screeched a maddening cacophony as they fought to free themselves. Adam and Jonny gaped as the biting, scrabbling, clawing, shrieking mass chewed and gouged and hauled and wriggled its way towards them.

Then they heard a scream that was undeniably human, and recoiled at what they saw, right in the centre of the churning heap. It was a man. His arms and legs were caught amongst the enmeshed garbage, pulled and yanked and torn from their sockets, his eyes gnawed out by gulls or perhaps by the rodents to which he was hopelessly attached, a dreadful hybrid of flesh and plastic and bone and rot.

It was Mitch Scanlon.

Adam and Jonny backed away from the edge in horror. Feeling an unfamiliar sense of panic, Adam turned back towards the car, whose engine was still running behind them.

A demonic face peered out at him over the steering wheel. Its skin was smeared with faecal gunge and filthy, knotted hair clung to its scalp; the true colour of either was unknowable beneath the crust of hardened muck. Leering out at them from the centre of the ghastly visage was a wide, crazed smile, the expression of a madman, of a beast, of a nightmare.

Acting automatically, Adam raised the pistol, spraying bullets into that terrible grin. But still the car leapt forwards, ploughing into them.

Adam, and Jonny, and the car, and Walter, plunged into the hideous maelstrom below.

*

Hours later, darkness fell and the ghoulish green glow began once again to hang over the Pit. Its surface was still and calm once again.

THE TRUTH

Ellen's shape beneath the bedsheets. A form made of arches, arcs, curves: inward at the neck, outward at her breasts and again beneath, a new swelling where our baby boy was being pieced together a cell at a time. Next her hips, then the delightful tapering of legs down to impossibly small feet. The woman that I loved: a brain, a spinal column, a nervous system, that wonderful consciousness housed within such an elegant form. A whole, a soul, my wife, my world.

I knew she felt guilty that she was taking an extended break from work. I bent to kiss her forehead, smelt her warmth, her hair unwashed for a few days. Her brow was creased in a slight frown as though her worries had accompanied her into sleep. I watched her for a whole minute, feeling my own guilt twisting my mouth, my heart, my stomach, like a cold hand rummaging inside my body.

I stood up, and put on my tie. A foolish charade, a performance for a sleeping audience. Still I played my part, donning my suit jacket, scooping up my laptop bag, taking the sandwiches she had made for me out of the fridge, smiling sadly at her note: 'Have a lovely day!' There were many words to describe the day that loomed before me, words like 'bizarre', 'disturbing', 'addictive'. But nothing remotely 'lovely' awaited me, in the dark cellar beneath my father's house.

I wrote 'You have a wonderful day too!' at the bottom of the post-it note, added a kiss, and left it stuck to the inside of the bedroom door. Ellen didn't stir as I closed it behind me.

*

I had left my job as a Financial Controller three months previously. I suppose what I'd experienced had been something resembling a breakdown: a feeling like choking, of being slowly dragged beneath the surface of a lake, bureaucracy and corporate politics tangled around me like discarded plastic ensnaring a helpless sea creature. I had known after only a few years that I hated the job, had made the wrong career choice, had been blinded by the juvenile prospect of a higher salary and more beer money; by the time I had realised my goal of becoming a qualified accountant and seen my pay packet begin to bloat, I no longer wanted any of it.

At heart I was a writer; ever since I was a tiny child I had written silly stories, dark fantasy and science fiction inspired by the likes of Tolkien and Donaldson and Pratchett, and the video games I had loved in my youth. I became obsessed with the idea of quitting to become a full-time author, of striding into my manager's office to proudly resign, rejecting their pleas for me to reconsider, their ever more extravagant offers of pay increases and company cars and shares and my own private office falling upon resolutely deaf ears. This became my dream, the fantasy that would help me through the endless procession of monotonous days, ticking by like the monthly columns of a financial forecast. Years passed in a grey blur of budget cycles and tax returns. I hated, *despised* it, this stifling world I had stupidly blundered into, as though I had voluntarily placed myself in manacles.

But I had met Ellen by then, and she surely wouldn't tolerate some penniless loser for a husband, some struggling wannabe who hadn't even published a single short story. So I stuck it out, for her, for us, for the baby we were going to have. This would be my legacy; not a bestselling novel, but instead a happy family, a child raised in an environment of love and worthwhile sacrifice.

Then I'd quit anyway. Perhaps I was just a selfish monster, at heart. Perhaps my mind had been somehow derailed by my father's disappearance. Who knew. There hadn't been any offers of pay rises or bonuses or promotions; just a shrugging, indifferent acceptance that I would be working a one-month notice period and then moving on, 'to pastures new'. I thought about pastures as I negotiated the uneven stairs, about meadows of verdant grass, cavorting sheep and abundant crops, the rising sun drenching the landscape with life and joy and warmth.

I flicked on the light switch, activating the dangling bulb that provided the basement's only illumination. The workshop had a unique smell, somewhere between burning dust, melting plastic and vomit, and it attacked my nostrils gleefully as I descended.

"Ahhh, there you are," said the monstrous thing that lived down there. "I was wondering what time you'd get here. I'm fucking starving."

*

My father had been a troubled man. In equal parts brilliant and utterly inept, his failure to monetise his inspired electronic tinkering had driven him to frustration, anger, alcoholism. When they met, my mother had been awestruck by his mind, his eccentric charm, his enthusiasm; had given birth to me within two years of meeting him at university, after they had both dropped out and before a hasty marriage; had watched him plough through a series of menial jobs, growing bitter and cantankerous as they struggled to make ends meet, watched him transform into a sullen and resentful creature, like milk turning sour.

It was clear to me now that he had viewed us as a millstone, blamed us for his own failures, right up until my mother finally left him when I was twenty years old. Now, in his late fifties, Howard Jackson had all the time and solitude he needed to work on his inventions. And he was more miserable than ever.

Or, he had been. He was missing now, presumed dead, although committing suicide without a note didn't seem like his style. If my father had intended to off himself, he would have poured out every drop of his vitriol onto paper first, letting us all know exactly what we'd done to drive him to this unfortunate end. He wouldn't have simply vanished, quietly and with dignity, into the night on a chill February evening.

And yet that appeared to be exactly what he'd done. I hadn't spoken to him for several weeks – quite a normal occurrence in our fractured, fractious relationship, despite the fact that he lived within a five-minute walk of my own home – when I received a call from the police. My father had been reported missing by his neighbour, who had observed him leaving the house one evening, and had not seen him return for a week. The old busybody had even gone around to knock on the door, finding it unlocked and slightly ajar. Inside, she'd encountered the same scene I would later discover during my own visit: a pandemonium of wiring, tools, motherboards, half-dismantled printers, computer parts and unfinished robotic creations. Synthetic arms seemed to reach out beseechingly, their plastic fingers curled as though in pain, begging to be given life. Crude assemblages were held together by duct tape or makeshift soldering, their components harvested from other appliances and attached like the limbs of a digital-age Frankenstein's monster.

The disordered mess of seemingly directionless creativity was a perfect reflection of his mind. He valued intelligence, hated authority, had respect for no-one except himself and his own ingenuity. What a disappointment I must have been to him: mediocre in every way, with no real achievements to speak of in either sport or academia, risk averse and sensible, abandoning my creative endeavours for a career as an accountant. Even my physical appearance – medium height, not particularly handsome, neither big nor strong – seemed to frustrate him, with his unkempt good looks and imposing stature. Such was the dynamic between us; I would visit him out of a sense of duty, out of guilt, and he would recognise this motivation, and be unable to restrain his spite. Barbed insults were dispensed with increasing viciousness as each swig of whisky passed his lips, until I could stand no more, and left.

"Ellen not left you yet? You know she's too good for a wet lettuce like you."

"Work's hard is it? I remember when you used to come home from school crying all the time. You've never learned to toughen up."

"Today I've built a prosthetic that can be controlled remotely via a neural interface. What have you done? Filed someone's VAT return?"

And so on. The last time I'd spoken with him hadn't actually ended all that badly; the conversation had taken its usual circuitous route around his fury at my mother for leaving him, his sadness that she had died of leukaemia several years ago, his anger that a great visionary like him was forced to live an impoverished life in a grotty terrace, his disappointment that I couldn't 'make something' of myself; but I'd managed to finish my entire cup of tea without him saying anything too unpleasant.

The only unusual element had been the enthusiasm in his words when he spoke of his latest project, the zeal dancing like flames in his eyes, an intense fire that burned away his advancing years and jaded cynicism. Usually, when I asked what he was working on, he would dismiss the question with an air of disgust, managing to convey simultaneously his distaste for the simplicity of his current undertaking, and his contempt for my presumed inability to understand it. But this time he could barely contain his excitement when he told me that what he was working on was a true breakthrough, the endeavour that would finally earn him fame, fortune, a Nobel prize. When I had pushed him for details, he had grinned, almost maliciously, as he asked, "Have you ever heard of the Brazen Head?"

I told him no. He had nodded, as if to say, 'of course you haven't', and fallen silent. Perhaps he thought his cryptic words might encourage me to do some research, to discover for myself this new and secret passion. But instead I'd gone home and forgotten all about it.

I hadn't thought about the Brazen Head again until my father vanished, leaving behind his wallet, his passport, his life's work.

More accurately, I hadn't thought about it until, on my second visit to the house a few days after my first, I had found the Brazen Head in his basement.

*

"Don't look at me like that," it mumbled between slurps. The thick plastic tube was by far the easiest method of feeding the creature, given the volume of baby food it needed to consume. I'd started off doing it with a spoon, but not only was this less efficient, it also brought me into physical contact with it, which I was keen to avoid.

It wasn't just that the sight of a pale, bald head emerging from a dishwasher-sized, transparent box full of grinding gears, spinning cogs, twitching tubes and live circuitry was unsettling. It was the head itself: perhaps its moist, rubbery skin, that looked as though it had been dunked in a bucket of glue; perhaps its plasticky teeth, gleaming white and clacking unnervingly when it spoke; perhaps its wide, staring eyes, lidless orbs that seemed too big for their sockets, as though at any moment they might pop out and roll away.

"I have to eat, just like you. I'd use a knife and fork if I had any fucking hands."

Its voice (Lancashire-accented, like my father) was a guttural rasp, undercut with a vile, bubbling sound as though its throat was clogged with too much mucus. Did it even have a throat? It certainly had a thick pipe, down which tub after tub of baby food would disappear, and from which baleful sarcasm would emerge. The pipe disappeared into the tangle of whirring mechanics that filled the Perspex cube I thought of as its 'body'.

"I'd just like to understand how you work, that's all."

"You've asked me that question already, and I'm pretty sure you're still none the wiser. If you stick a crayon in my mouth I could try drawing you a diagram." It took another gulp of the foul-smelling slop that served as its only nourishment. "Food in this end, wisdom out the same end, shit out the other."

It was right about the process. Whatever alchemy took place within that unholy box, converting the food into fuel for the disturbing automaton, produced a waste by-product that resembled a cross between human excrement and tar. Every few days I had to remove a foul-smelling receptacle from the side of the box and flush its reeking black contents down my father's toilet.

When I'd first found it, the container had been overflowing, and the room had smelled like a sewer. The head hadn't eaten for a week, and was almost dead, if indeed it was remotely alive in the first place, which I suppose it wasn't. I kept reminding myself that it was a machine, a thing my deranged father had constructed from spare parts, from lengths of garden hose and pieces cannibalised from the cars and washing machines whose husks rotted amongst the weeds in his back yard. Yet still it needed sustenance, and I wasn't heartless enough to deny it, not when there were huge tubs of baby food piled just a few feet away, taking up almost an entire wall of the squalid chamber beneath my father's house.

"Help me," it had called weakly, the repeated phrase at first making me think my father was somehow trapped and injured in his own cellar. I had hurried down the stairs, stumbling and almost falling down them due to my unfamiliarity with a room that had previously been kept locked. Down here the chaos of the rest of the house was repeated, magnified, the sheer concentration of clutter like an assault on my eyeballs when I finally found the light switch. Other than the pots of baby food, the shelves on the walls were piled with odds, ends, gadgets, gizmos, parts and pieces; the constituents of the bastard electronic offspring that my dad had spent his life crafting, getting bored with, abandoning, starting again.

A bit like me, I supposed. A project begun, then scrapped. A failed prototype.

After scouring the dingy space for any sign of my dad, my gaze flicking from the rickety wooden table in the centre (heaped with junk, of course) to the lethal-looking circular saw in the corner to the inexplicable tower of microwaves stacked next to it, my eyes settled on the bizarre contraption that was directly opposite me. I'd assumed at first that the head was a waxwork, or taken from some movie-set dummy, genuinely startled by the lifelike face that seemed to be staring back at me, wide eyes mirroring my own expression of alarm.

Then it had said 'help me' again, and I'd screamed and ran back up the stairs, tripping and skinning my hands as I fled from that dark place and its horrifying occupant.

"Please," it had called after me, its voice sounding like someone trying to whine through a throat full of gravel. "If you... don't feed me... I'll die."

For some reason I'd stopped, instead of slamming the front door and dashing shrieking into the street, like I should have done. For some reason I'd slowly turned, and descended the stairs. For some reason I'd followed the creature's instructions as it explained where to find a spoon and which flavour of food it preferred. For some reason I'd nourished that fucking thing back to life.

Once it had recovered from its ordeal, I found out it

knew everything.

Everything.

*

It's hard to explain why I kept going to the house. I ought to have stopped lying to Ellen, confessed that I had left my job, started interviewing for another as soon as possible. My only thoughts should have been of our baby, our future. But instead I donned my suit as though nothing had happened, as if I was heading off for another day cheerily analysing the murky financials of Investalot Capital Solutions. I walked around to my father's house, ignoring the dials and diodes and circuit boards still strewn all over the floor and every available work surface, and headed down into the basement.

I spent the days writing, and talking to the head. Its malign presence had become strangely comforting to me, its toxic wit a pleasant contrast to my father's humourless bile. It would happily watch me while I tapped away on my laptop, sometimes asking me about the plot of my story, sometimes chipping in its suggestions, which were usually appallingly vulgar, making it chuckle its wheezing, throaty laugh. The enigmatic abomination became, in a way, my friend.

Towards the end of each day, I would ask it my one allotted question.

"What are you?"

At first I had tried to unravel the mystery of its existence.

"A computer, basically. With a highly original user interface."

"Do you have a name?"

Gears churned as unspeakable fluids were forced through tubes inside the machine, hammering pistons driving the answer up and out of its obscene, clacking mouth.

"Your dad called me Brazenhead."

"Why can you only answer one question per day?"

"Programmed that way. Don't blame me."

"How can you know everything?"

"Internet connection and advanced statistical probability algorithms."

"Can you predict the future?"

"No. Do I look like Mystic fucking Meg?"

"Are you conscious?"

"It feels like I am. Are you?"

"Do you remember being born?"

"I wasn't born, I was built. I'm like a Lego set but with more personality. But to answer your question in a figurative sense: no, I don't remember it. I was just here, with your dad grinning into my face like I'd just wanked him off, and that was when my universe started."

"How did you learn to speak?"

"Mainly programming, bit of online research, a few chats with yer old man before he fucked off."

Later I had tested it, to see if its supposedly perfect knowledge was as infallible as it claimed.

"Who was Henry VIII's third wife?"

"Really? An infinite sea of information to dredge, and you're asking me primary school history questions? Jane fucking Seymour, you boring bastard."

"What was my grandmother's middle name?"

"Jesus, they're getting worse. On your dad's side or your mum's side?"

"My mum's."

"Ethel. And here's a bonus answer for you: she was fucking ugly."

"Who finished thirteenth in the Scottish second division in 1924?"

"Dunfermline Athletic. They were shit then, and they're still shit now."

Slowly convinced of Brazenhead's strange abilities, I found myself asking it all manner of questions, probing scandals about the world, my friends, my family.

"Who killed JFK?"

"The CIA."

"Who killed John Lennon?"

"Mark Chapman. Nothing to do with the CIA, that one."

"Did my mum really spill bleach on that dressing gown I bought her?"

"No. She hated it so she threw it away."

"Are any of my friends secretly gay?"

"Tim Farrimond. Not so secretly either if you go to the *Eagle* on a Saturday night."

"Did Rachael Edmonds ever cheat on me at school?"

That had given it a good laugh.

"Loads of times, pal. Sorry. Including with your best mate Ben."

Every day I would descend those stairs, stuff the tube into its throat, let it glug its fill, then talk to it for a while before I carried on working on my novel. Gradually I learned its bizarre rules: it couldn't respond to direct questions (unless it was my official question: I'd wasted a few already by asking things like 'how are you today?' and even a sarcastic 'what have you been up to?') but it was more than happy to chat; it couldn't give a response to a question with a subjective answer but was happy to give its own unsolicited opinions on just about everything (for example, 'who is the best looking Spice Girl?' had resulted in 'obviously there's no objective answer to that Josh', but then moments later 'but for my money it was clearly the ginger one with the big tits').

Despite the pleasure of unearthing my friends' darkest

secrets, my questions – perhaps inevitably – would often come back to my father.

"Why did my dad build you?"

"Because he could."

"Why did he disappear?"

"It was his will."

"Where has he gone?"

"I can't tell you."

"Why can't you tell me?"

"I'm sorry, you know the rules, one question per day. You'll have to wait until tomorrow to ask me, sunshine."

At that point I'd become exasperated with it, struck the side of the box in frustration.

"Yeah, that's it Josh, pick on something that can't fight back. I bet you knock your old lady about as well, don't you?"

I think that day, that precise moment, was when our relationship had started to sour.

"How do you know about Ellen?"

"Tomorrow, my friend. There's always a tomorrow, and always a question."

It smiled as it winked knowingly at me, exposing teeth as white as bones.

Over the coming days, I learned to despise my father. Brazenhead knew where he'd gone, but the answer was locked, the creature forbidden to relinquish the knowledge until a certain condition was met.

"What condition?"

"You'll have to ask me tomorrow, matey boy."

"Fuck you, you smug bastard."

But, like my tormentor said, tomorrow always rolled around. My writing project hadn't been touched for weeks; instead my notebook was covered with scribbled questions, avenues of attack, ways of carefully wording my next query to obtain the maximum amount of information.

"What condition do I have to meet in order to unlock the answer to my father's whereabouts?"

"Now you're getting the hang of it. You have to ask me the right question, a question that will reveal an important truth that Howard wanted you to learn. Only when you've learned *that* truth can you be granted the other."

My father had left behind a fiendish puzzle, just for me. His true suicide note.

It wasn't until Ellen said something to me that I realised how little time I'd been spending at home.

"You've been working late a lot lately," she said meekly one night when I collapsed in bed beside her. I grunted a monosyllabic response.

"Is something wrong?" she persisted.

That was when I turned to look at her, considering her for the first time through my new eyes, the eyes of a man that knew *everyone* had secrets.

From then on, the questions got really nasty.

*

"Jesus, Josh, do you really want to know? I'm worried I'm becoming a bad influence in your life." Its voice dripped with barely-disguised, malevolent glee as its said this, its tongue seeming to roll around the words as though savouring a delicious morsel.

"Just do your job."

"Whatever you say, boss. In which case the answer is thirty. Nice round number, actually."

I exhaled slowly. Four, she'd told me. Four sexual partners before me. And I'd specified full penetrative intercourse, so who knew how many others she'd kissed, been touched by, given blow jobs to.

"You don't look happy. Bet you wish you'd never asked." Again its mouth spread into a reptilian smile, clammy lips peeling back like the skin of a flayed animal.

"Never mind," I said eventually. "Today, you're going to let me have two questions."

The smile remained in place, the neck using whatever mechanisms granted it some limited mobility to tilt the head quizzically to one side. "Oh really? And why is that?"

I walked across to the jumble of tools my father had

hanging from hooks on the opposite wall, calmly selecting a pair of pliers. Brazenhead's eyes followed me, unblinking.

"You told me once that you don't feel pain. That's good, because it means it won't hurt when I start to take you apart."

I studied it for a reaction, for any sign of fear. Did I imagine its eyes growing even wider than usual? Did I see it swallow nervously before it replied?

"Seems a bit of a shit plan, Josh. If you break me then you won't be able to access my knowledge any more. And you'll never find out what happened to your dad."

"You're right. But as long as I don't damage you too badly, you'll keep answering, won't you? It's what you're programmed to do."

I crossed the room slowly, realising how tall and imposing I must appear to the disembodied head, whose brow was level with my chest.

"So what would be the point?" it said carefully, eyeing me with what seemed to be a mixture of curiosity and apprehension. "You can't hurt me, and you don't want to break me. So I'm intrigued to see what you plan to do with those."

Brazenhead's eyes were fixed on the pliers as I raised and opened them.

"Like you told me, you're not alive. You're just a computer." My heart was beating faster and faster in my chest, every nerve in my body seeming to squirm and writhe in horror at what I was planning to do. "So doing this isn't immoral. It's more like... fixing a broken radiator." I knew

I was trying to convince myself. I watched Brazenhead's lips moving soundlessly, as though it was trying to figure out a way to dissuade me.

I didn't wait to hear it. Instead I drove the pliers into its left eye.

The worst part was that the mechanoid didn't make a sound as I wrenched and tore and finally yanked out its eyeball. It took me over a minute to dig out the organ, which felt disturbingly soft and lifelike when I held it between my fingers. I was breathing heavily, almost hyperventilating, while Brazenhead seemed completely calm; even as viscous fluid, dark enough to be almost black but crimson enough to still look disconcertingly like blood, oozed down its face from the hollowed ruin of the eye socket.

"Well done, Josh. Very creative."

"You're... going to give me... another question. Otherwise..." Vomit fountained up inside me, and I turned to spew it onto the floor. I expected some mocking comment from the monster as the bile dribbled through my teeth, but it remained silent, watching me through its one remaining eye. I wiped my mouth on my sleeve, and turned to face it again, setting my jaw in grim determination. "Otherwise the other one's coming out too, and you'll be fucking *blind*."

If I thought the threat would have an impact, it didn't. Brazenhead just nodded solemnly. "I thought that might be your play. It's pretty good, Josh. All credit to you. But what you don't seem to realise is this: *I don't give a shit if I can't see*." For just a second, its expression twisted into one of pure, concentrated rage, of absolute vehement hatred of the world and everything in it.

In that moment, it reminded me of its creator.

Then it grinned evilly, and the thick dark goo dripped onto its clacking teeth. "What is there to look at anyway? This shithole of a workshop, and your ugly mug? If it makes you feel better, blind away, mate. But know this: *it won't change the rules.* You'll be in exactly the same situation you are now, except with the guilt of having taken my eyes from me. And I know you, Josh. I know you couldn't live with it."

I didn't know if Brazenhead was calling my bluff. I didn't know if it was in agony, somehow suppressing the pain to convince me of its cold reasoning. I didn't know if it was secretly afraid, if sweat would be beading on its forehead if it only had the requisite glands.

But I did know that it was right. I couldn't stomach the thought of ripping out another eye. I choked down another wave of nausea, hurled the pliers and the repulsive, bloodshot orb into the nearby sink, and stalked out of the cellar.

*

I starved it instead. I didn't go back into that basement for two weeks. I told Ellen I'd booked a surprise fortnight's holiday to be with her, to show her how much she meant to me and to apologise for being so busy at 'work'. We even managed to get away together for a weekend in the Lakes. We relaxed, ate lots of food, talked like we used to, laughed about baby names.

I tried, so very hard, to forget about that accursed *thing*. How I longed for it to be a delusion, the product of a mind under extreme stress; indeed, I would happily trade what remained of my tattered sanity for a return to the crushing dreariness of my former life.

But I knew it was still down there, hungry, half-blinded. Was it in pain? Was it afraid? Was it angry? The time away from it only served to highlight just how symbiotic our twisted relationship had become.

And what was this torture even achieving? I'd missed out on *two whole weeks* of questions. I thought about the things I wanted, *needed*, to ask it. The questions chewed at my mind like brain-dwelling parasites.

Has Ellen ever been unfaithful to me?

Does Ellen have secret money that I don't know about?

Does Ellen love me?

The day we got back, I told Ellen I had to go straight to bed, because I needed to be up really early to go and get a head start catching up on the e-mails I'd missed in the office. I pretended to be asleep when she clambered in next to me, huffing and groaning with the pain of carrying our boy around. I lay there, staring upwards into the inside of my eyelids, my mind spinning like a rotating cog, or the whirling blade of a circular saw.

I left the house at four thirty, not even bothering to keep up the pretence of putting on my suit. I almost sprinted to my father's place, breathlessly fumbled the key into the front door lock, tugged open the basement door, mashed my palm into the light switch.

The light didn't come on. The bulb had blown, perhaps. I stopped at the top of the stairs, staring down into a void as black as the pupil of an eye. Cold, sickening dread squeezed my heart. Brazenhead didn't breathe, so I wouldn't hear it unless it chose to make a sound. A fetid smell made me wrinkle my nose, and I thought of the bucket of excrement that would need to be emptied, its contents maybe spilling over into the creature's internal mechanisms. Perhaps the monster had drowned in its own shit.

Then I heard a whimper. An animal keening, high-pitched and inhuman, that gradually trailed off into a single, choked sob. My guts lurched in horrified guilt.

I turned the house upside down in my search for a torch. Drawers were yanked out and tipped onto the floor. Mechanical crap piled on top of mechanical crap, the detritus of my dad's life tossed into a growing heap as I hunted. Eventually I found one, a heavy-duty device that he'd left on top of the refrigerator of all places, and after a couple of sharp smacks the large bulb came on.

I returned to the basement doorway, listening again for that awful mewling sound. Only silence and darkness greeted me. As though its light would protect me, I aimed the torch into that abyss, and descended into a hell of my own creation.

Brazenhead remained silent until I reached the foot of the stairs, and turned the beam towards it. I almost screamed. Somehow, the foul machine had hauled itself halfway across the room, then toppled over, the head landing tantalisingly close to the stacked tubs of baby food.

Illuminated in the torch's harsh glare, Brazenhead squealed and hissed like a trapped animal.

Like something alive, and in pain.

Its skin seemed to have changed colour, the pallid fleshy

hue now a rancid grey, and mottled with dark spots as though it was rotting. The ravaged eye was a swollen horror, blackened and gangrenous, yellow pus dribbling from the hole into a putrid pool on the floor. Its lips had receded from its gums as though all moisture had been sucked out of them, making its expression resemble a deranged grin. It gnashed its teeth at me, spitting and snarling, and I stumbled backwards in shock, landing heavily on the stairs.

"I'm sorry," I managed to stammer, but this only seemed to intensify its frenzy. "Please... calm down. I'm here now. I'll feed you. I'm sorry."

Its remaining eye spun dementedly in its socket, but the mention of food seemed to at least partially penetrate its delirium. Its teeth began to clack, its tongue snaking out like some shrivelled eel, reaching hopelessly towards the plastic pots.

Before my revulsion overcame me, I found a spoon, and used it to pop open the lid of a fresh tub. I shovelled the sweet-smelling slop into its mouth, trying to avoid being bitten as it snapped ravenously at every mouthful. After several minutes of feeding, I realised that I was stroking its head with my other hand, muttering soothing platitudes as though it was a household pet that had come home injured.

I stood up and, grunting with exertion, bent to haul the casing that housed Brazenhead's guts back upright. When this was done, I found its plastic feeding tube, and moved one end towards its lips. Its good eye watched me suspiciously, but it allowed me to insert the apparatus into its mouth. As soon as the other end entered the tub, it began to suck and gargle, draining the entire contents of the vessel with alarming speed. I opened another tub, connected the tube, watched as it ate, trying not to focus on the horrific wound I had inflicted.

I sank down onto the steps, feeling exhausted. I didn't even notice it had spat out the tube until it spoke to me, in a voice that sounded cracked, broken, ancient.

"So… you came back."

I jerked upright, unsure how long I'd been asleep. The torch was slung across my knee, so Brazenhead was just a shadow before me, like something carved out of my nightmares.

"I… yes. I'm… I'm glad you're alive."

I could hear mechanical sounds coming from inside the box, as though the thing's components were reaching breaking point.

"Don't ever do that again, Josh."

"I won't. I didn't mean it. I just… I want to know what happened to my father."

Brazenhead made a strange sound then, a single syllable forced explosively out of its throat, and then repeated. I realised it was laughing.

"What… what's so funny?" I asked, pointing the torch at the hideous contraption. Still it laughed, the head rocking backwards as the sinister cackle grew louder and louder. After a while, I found myself chuckling too, and before long we were both laughing uproariously, down there in the dark, immersed in noxious air.

"Is that your question for today, Josh?" it said eventually.

"I suppose it is," I replied, still giggling.

"It's just... if you'd asked me to tell you what happened to him in return for the food... I'd have said yes."

I stopped laughing then, and just stared at the creature. *The rules...* I thought my father had programmed it, had forbidden it to break the constraints. Was Brazenhead telling me that all along it had had a choice, that it could have told me what I wanted to know months ago?

Its eye met mine, two flawed beings regarding each other in the torchlight. Two broken machines.

Then we burst out laughing again. Within seconds I was hysterical, tears streaming down my face, feeling as though something inside me had collapsed. The relief I felt that Brazenhead was still alive was inexplicable, intoxicating.

"Josh? Josh, what's going on?"

Ellen's voice was somehow there, intruding upon that toxic pit, that place of shit and gore, and my laughter was replaced with horrified disbelief. I stood and whirled around, pointing the torch up the stairs to find her standing in the doorway.

"Why are you laughing, Josh? Who's down there with you?"

She started to descend, and I heard the mania in my voice as I screamed at her to stop. The devastation in her face broke my heart.

"What's happening, Josh? Why are you here?"

"How did you find me?" I heard myself hiss, remembering the sound the Brazenhead itself had made, just hours earlier.

Tears were dripping from her eyes as she answered, one hand clutching her distended belly, perhaps in pain, perhaps protectively. "I just had a feeling... I've suspected for a while that you haven't been going to work."

I bared my teeth in a snarl. How dare she distrust me, the cock-sucking *whore*?

"Hello Ellen," came another voice from behind me, in a mellifluous tone I'd never heard it use before. "You look ravishing."

"Who... who is that?" A note of fear had entered her voice, and she was starting to back away, up the stairs.

I knew, then. The suspicions that had filled my mind like hornets, had bled from my fingertips into the pages of my notebook, whose tendrils had reached out to infest and infect everything in my life; they coalesced in that moment into one question, *the* question, the great truth my father had wanted me to find, in his absence.

"Brazenhead," I said, my tone commanding, my gaze still fixed on my wife. "Who is the father of Ellen's baby?"

Behind me, Brazenhead gave a deep and euphoric sigh, as though released from a terrible curse. The sound sent a shudder through me, and I wished in that moment that the thing would just die, that I would never hear the question's answer.

Then it spoke, in a low whisper that sounded like earth being shovelled into a grave.

The torch went out then, leaving my anguished howl to

echo in the darkness as Ellen stumbled out of the cellar, and ran from the house.

*

I never saw her again. We communicated only by text messages, stiffly civilised, and within a week I had moved into my father's house while she hid at her parents'. I didn't care. She was welcome to her life with the bastard child that was both my stepson and my half-brother.

Brazenhead wears an eyepatch now. He still claims that he can only answer one question per day, that he was just joking with me, that he was only permitted to break the rule that one time because I figured out *the* question. I am not sure if I trust it. Programming a sadistic streak into his creation is exactly the sort of thing my father would have done.

It kept its promise, though, and told me what became of the old monster. It really was suicide, after all. They found the body, bloated and rotten, at the bottom of the canal, weighted down with pockets full of old engine parts. The police believed me when I told them I'd found a clue in my father's diary, and left it at that.

There were many more questions I wanted to ask, of course. The next one was why he'd fucked my wife.

"Because he could," had been the machine's reply, in a strangely sympathetic tone.

The others will come in time. Why did my father end his life? Why did Ellen sleep with him? Was she planning to tell me? How is the baby doing?

Eventually, I know I'll run out of days. Everybody does.

But for now, there's always a tomorrow, and always a question.

POLARIS

She gestured to the pack at her feet, from which the barrel of a .375 Holland & Holland Magnum rifle protruded menacingly. "I don't care how fuckin' big it is – when I shoot it full of premium buckshot, it'll bleed just like everything else does."

I'm no gun expert, and hailing from a quiet village in Lancashire the sight of a real firearm still strikes me with a kind of unnerved disbelief, but Meryl had talked about little other than her intimidating arsenal since we arrived, so I felt as though I knew the specifications of her gear by heart. The coldly malevolent, sniper-scoped rifle; the ballistic-tipped ammunition she favoured; the separate sidearm she kept 'just in case something got too close'; the night-vision goggles she'd bought for the trip into the mine. I'd noticed that she kept the pack by her side at all times, as if she didn't yet trust the three of us not to try to steal it from her; an implausible prospect given that the muscular Texan was by some distance the biggest of the group, and given that we were solely reliant on her proficiency with the guns for our protection.

What did we need protection from? Establishing the answer to that question was the reason the four of us were out here.

"I hope you're right," replied Jack, his earnest but friendly Inuit features illuminated in the soft glow of the camping lantern. "Whatever killed those bears… it must be a monster." His voice was gentle, almost reverent, his breath misting in front of him as though threatening to give form to his haunting words.

"Oh, stop talkin' horseshit," sneered Eddie, sucking another deep drag of poison from his cigarette and emitting a hacking wheeze that was part laugh, part cough. "It was probably just a really big walrus, or something."

"I hope not," grinned Meryl. "I want something that looks nice when I'm wearing it."

I forced a smile in acknowledgement of her bravado, and glanced around our drab surroundings. Despite the layers we were wearing, it was still bitterly cold in what had once been a staff canteen; but my discomfort was an infinity away from what I'd experienced earlier, outside, on the short walk from Eddie's plane towards our modest accommodation. Out there, without the proper clothing, I'd been told that a human could die of exposure within seven minutes. It didn't seem believable until you set foot in it yourself, and felt the vicious grip of the Arctic air squeezing your chest, freezing the marrow inside your bones.

The tiny island community of Resolute had seemed like an outer limit, a last bastion of humanity clinging to survival even as it was battered by formidable elemental forces. But we'd journeyed far beyond even that final outpost, boarding Eddie's plane and crossing the inhabited boundary of Canada's northernmost territory, deep into icy desolation.

Inside that rattling plane, surrounded by an expanse of snow the colour of stripped bones, I'd felt like I was losing my mind.

Then Polaris B had appeared on the horizon.

The two Polaris sites were abandoned zinc mines. Polaris A had stood empty for more than fifteen years, while the second site's stores had run dry just a few years later, meaning that it too had been deserted for over a decade. The mining company had been bankrupted by the end, and so had neither the money nor the will to decommission them properly; as a result, the sprawling facilities still stood to this day, gradually rusting like monstrous, slowly decomposing carcasses. The entrances to the underground quarries gaped like the tortured screams of colossal, dying things as we approached, and the cheerful maple leaf painted on the roof of the main building seemed to mock my mounting horror.

Like Meryl and Eddie, I was there because I had responded to Jack's social media post. Unlike those two – the ferocious predator, the grizzled pilot – I'm a cryptozoologist, which meant that I was not there to hunt big game, or to make money flying a tiny plane in conditions that no-one else was insane enough to attempt. I was there to find, catalogue, and photograph the creature that had caused the devastation captured so compellingly in the pictures Jack had shared online.

I wanted to see what sort of monster could tear four polar bears – a mother, her cubs, and a 1,000-pound male that had presumably been harassing them – into dismembered chunks of flesh. I saw that picture behind my eyelids when I blinked, that pool of crimson sinking slowly into the snow, the heaped body parts like some sort of grisly monument. Arms, legs, torsos: the powerful animals had been pulled apart like insects by a callous child.

And only their heads had been taken.

Silence settled on our peculiar group for a time as we each chewed our energy bars. I studied the faces of my companions, wondering if their imaginings were as dark as mine; if they were secretly reading my own expression, discerning there the potent mixture of fear and excitement that warmed my frozen blood.

Fear of the hulking beast I visualised, lurking underground amidst a pile of bones: a ten-foot-tall behemoth, a muscled slab of hair and teeth and talons, a prehistoric giant that knew only hunger and violence.

Excitement that I might finally track down a creature known around the world by countless names: Mirka, Kang Admi, the Abominable Snowman, the Yeti.

This trip to the Polaris sites – first B, then A as we worked our way around Little Cornwallis Island, theorising that whatever had slaughtered the bears had made its home down in the mines themselves – had been my idea. I looked again at Meryl's rifle, which suddenly seemed very small.

"Ain't there any heating in here?" she muttered.

"No power, and it's too dangerous to start a fire indoors," Eddie replied. "This is as warm as you're going to get, until we're inside the mine." He inhaled another deep pull from the cigarette, chuckling hoarsely once again. "Or should I say, until y'all are inside the mine; I ain't risking my neck down there for no amount of money."

"Pussy," Meryl retorted.

"Say what you like, ma'am, but I'll be waitin' up here with the plane, and if y'all ain't back on time, I'll be flying outta here solo, and you can stay down in that fuckin' cave forever."

Their gazes locked, and for a second I caught a glint of rage in the woman's eyes. Then she laughed. "Better get some sleep then. We'll set out at 0600 hours tomorrow." She turned her head to Jack and me. "That okay with you, monster hunters?"

We nodded obediently, watching as she hoisted her pack and turned to head to the sleeping quarters. We'd already selected beds in four separate dormitories; plenty of space was the one luxury we were going to enjoy during our stay here.

Another hush descended. Eddie held out his pack of Marlboros; Jack took one, but I declined. The smoke that curled upwards from their cigarettes seemed to be tracing the bizarre outline of an animal, briefly imagined. I thought about Meryl's words, about the things I chased across the globe, about the family life I had sacrificed in pursuit of creatures most people didn't believe existed. Many times I experienced feelings of doubt, of regret, the awful sense of a life foolishly wasted.

But not today. Today I was certain.

"I think I'll take a cigarette after all, Eddie," I said. He handed one to me, and the silence and the smoke hung around us like a pall.

❄

Icy oblivion stretched away around us, vast and

merciless and utterly indifferent to our presence. We were minute details on a panorama of pure white, three dotted lines extending from the comparative comfort of the welfare facility towards the mine's entrance, as insignificant as krill drifting towards a whale's jaws. The sun stared down in mute, futile outrage, succeeding only in dazzling us with the reflected glare from the snow.

Eddie, wearing a battered trucker's cap on his head and a filigree of ice in his scruffy beard, had told us tersely that we would fly to the other site at 1700 hours. Perhaps in response to this deadline, Meryl was setting a punishing pace across the tundra, even Jack struggling to keep up with her. Every few metres they had to stop and wait for me, and I felt feeble and useless as I scrambled to catch up to them. The climate meant I was already struggling for breath, and these added exertions were making me gasp, the frigid air cutting into the back of my throat as though I was inhaling tiny razorblades.

I caught up; we pressed on; I fell behind; they waited; I caught up, coughing and wheezing; and so the cycle repeated itself as gradually we ate up the yards of a half-mile journey that felt more like a gruelling marathon. *Seven minutes*, I kept thinking, looking down with renewed appreciation at the bulky layers of protective clothing that shielded me from the malevolence of the conditions.

Of course, when the mine had been in operation, the workers would have been spared this arduous trek, instead transported to and from the mine at the beginning and end of their shifts by contraptions that resembled miniature snowploughs. We had seen these vehicles scattered around the site, their rusted hulks jutting out of the snow like half-unearthed bones. I wondered what other apparatus we would encounter inside the mine itself, what state the excavation had been left in, and started to worry about hazards other than elusive snow-monsters: collapses, cramped tunnels, slippery rocks underfoot. I imagined a nasty fall, a splinter of bone jutting from a shattered leg, an agonising wait for a rescue helicopter.

I imagined dying out here, in the pitiless cold, at the edge of the world.

"Toby, if you don't stop dawdling, I'm going to use you for target practise," Meryl snarled at me, although a good-natured smile belied her harsh words. I hurried to draw level with the pair once again, trying to dispel my disturbing thoughts. "If Jack's monster lives in this mine, shouldn't we be seeing some tracks?" she asked as I approached, having to shout above the wind's vengeful howl.

I shrugged. "A fresh snowfall would cover them. Once we get inside we'll know if something's living there: there'll be droppings, bones, an animal smell."

"And you're convinced this is where it's living?" she said, raising a sceptical eyebrow.

"Call it a hunch," I replied.

"The blind leading the fuckin' blind," she murmured, turning to press on towards the mine's entrance, which yawed open before us like an expectant throat. Jack remained silent throughout the exchange, looking towards the opening with mounting dread etched on his face.

We forged ahead, and the Arctic wind shrieked around us as though incensed by our intrusion.

An hour later we reached the mine.

❉

We abandoned our parkas after a few hundred yards, the temperature inside still freezing but not as bitterly hostile as the surface. We draped the thick coats on the side of a train carriage, which had perhaps once ferried personnel deeper into the mine, or maybe transported the quarried zinc back out again; none of us had a clue, but the rail tracks gave us an easy route to follow, Meryl taking the lead with a torch mounted to the end of her rifle.

I had expected featureless tunnels, claustrophobic and oppressive, but instead this main passageway was surprisingly spacious. Sturdy wooden supports and unlit fluorescent tubes lined the walls, and the stone itself was decorated with strange, colourful mineral growths; streaks of blue and green bled into swirling, entrancing shapes at our feet, and here and there calcium carbonate deposits bulged outwards like an otherworldly fungus. Stalactites hung, slender and misshapen, like the fossilised tentacles of some inquisitive subterranean creature. A clump of glittering crystals caught my eye, and I pointed it out to the others, thinking we might stop to take photographs. Jack turned to admire the structure, but Meryl was uninterested, pushing on ahead so that we had to run to keep up with her disappearing light. I sensed her bloodlust, her determination to make a kill, her rising frustration as we marched on and on along the tracks.

"No sign of anything so far," Jack said eventually. His words were unnecessary, but I was grateful that the reverent silence had been broken; a feeling of distress had been building within me, a sensation I couldn't easily explain. I told myself it was merely the innate horror of descending willingly into the bowels of the earth, of exploring somewhere so remote and isolated.

But in truth, as illogical as it seemed, I had become

convinced that we were being followed. I had a vivid sense of something shambling after us in the darkness, just out of earshot; something that had secreted itself in shadow as we first passed by. I imagined guttural breathing, knuckles scraping along the ground, gleaming eyes that peered out in fascination from behind the mine carts. The eyes of a predator, coldly calculating.

"How long does this fuckin' tunnel go on for?" Meryl grumbled.

"The entire mine is about a mile long," I replied, a nervous tremble in my voice that the walls gleefully echoed. "Soon we should come across a few offshoots from the main tunnel." *Plenty of places to hide*, I thought.

"I'm getting bored, Toby."

"I'm sorry. It's just a theory. I can't promise we'll find anything. And we have another mine to search tomorrow."

She grunted, hunkering down and placing the rifle on the floor while she detached the torch. She pointed its beam at us, and I squinted in the sudden glare.

"Let's eat," she said in a voice that made it clear this was a command, not a suggestion. She rummaged in her pack for energy bars, tossing a couple to Jack and me. Once again, no-one spoke while we devoured the flavourless snacks. I heard the slow drip-drip of water somewhere ahead, like a clock counting down to something; I felt restless, my skin itchy beneath the layers of my clothing. My blood seemed to curdle in my veins as I imagined the sound of sudden footsteps sprinting towards us, an inhuman scream of animal savagery.

"Let's just keep going, shall we?" I blurted, clambering

to my feet.

Meryl looked up at me, her shaved head like a gleaming skull in the harsh torchlight. "Oh, I'm sorry, champ, are we not moving fast enough for you?" She made a point of opening another energy bar, her eyes fixed on me while I fidgeted, pretending to study some of the spirals on the tunnel wall.

You're trespassing in its lair, Toby. Did you think it would just wander out and politely introduce itself?

Eventually Meryl rose, tossing the energy bar wrapper on the ground with disdain. She reattached the flashlight to the rifle and aimed the barrel into the darkness ahead. We walked on, the gun and Meryl's bulk suddenly seeming a woefully inadequate defence. More abandoned machinery emerged from the gloom, seeming tense and potent, like a great serpent lying in wait. Jack glanced at it nervously as we passed by, his confidence seemingly diminishing with every minute spent in this forgotten pit.

I imagined life down here, days spent in endless murk, hewing metal from the earth as though defiling the planet itself. Monotony, repetition, intolerable cold, like Dante's vision of hell: the Ninth Circle, the frozen lake of Cocytus where traitors were trapped and twisted into grotesque sculptures of pain.

You've been working too hard lately, Toby.

A sound, somewhere behind us. A single thump, like a heavy sack being dropped to the floor.

Meryl spun around so fast it was as though she was a character in an old video game, with only a single frame of animation depicting the turn. Within a microsecond the gun was aimed just centimetres to the side of my head, the torch beam blinding me once again before she clicked it off and we were consumed by the darkness.

"What are you doing?" I yelped.

"Shut the fuck up! I'm using the night vision."

We stood like that, frozen in place, for what felt like hours, my mouth suddenly sucked dry of moisture, my limbs trembling. Powerless, blind, terrified, I realised how utterly dependent I was upon this stranger for my survival. My ears strained for any more sounds in the tunnel behind me, but all I could discern was that infernal drip, drip, drip, drip, drip.

The thought occurred to me that Meryl and Jack were both dead, that whatever was stalking us had silently snatched them away in the lightless void. Perhaps it was crouching over their corpses even now, eyeing me hungrily while it prepared to pounce. Perhaps it was standing right behind me, its hot breath inches from my neck, its fanged smile widening. I imagined huge, black, soulless eyes, like tunnels into its head, and suddenly my whole world was pitch-dark tunnels and I just wanted to get out, to run screaming back into the light and the snow. I fumbled in my pocket for my own torch, my shaking hands almost dropping it to the ground before I could switch it on.

A few feet in front of me Meryl cursed, and dropped her rifle.

"Turn it off you idiot!" she hissed as she wrenched the goggles from her head.

"Shit, I'm sorry, are you okay?" I stammered, turning the torch back off and instinctively running towards her. She shoved me away, switching her own flashlight back on as she stooped to recover the gun.

"Yeah, I'm fine; it doesn't hurt, it just whites out the display so I can't see shit."

"What about before that? Did you see anything?" Jack asked timidly.

Meryl shook her head, her gaze fixed on the tunnel behind us, her expression curled into a suspicious scowl.

"Maybe the noise was just a beam falling, or something?" I ventured.

"I fuckin' hope not," she retorted. "This rifle won't be much use against a rock fall." She paused, then continued. "Okay boys, we're doing a one-eighty. Get behind me, and *no torches other than mine*, understand?"

We retraced our steps, the torchlight glittering as it danced across the same stalactites, the same crystals, the same rusted metal husks. On one wall I spotted some writing I'd missed earlier, mysterious letters and numbers that might have been important information for the miners, or perhaps just indecipherable graffiti.

If we'd been quiet on the journey in, on the way back out we were as silent as the dead. Meryl's strides were slow and careful, the gun barrel sweeping the tunnel ahead of us, the torch scything methodically through the darkness; but still my fearful brain conjured a monster lurking behind every mine cart, a simian fiend squatting in every shadow.

An eternity of dread passed, the only sound our footsteps and the dripping water that was somehow always in the distance, never nearby. When we saw the sun's feeble light ahead once again, I almost sobbed with relief.

But my joy vanished as we approached the entrance, and saw a set of fresh footprints leading away from the mine. They followed our own, but in reverse, back towards the welfare facility.

The prints were large and deep, much bigger than any of ours, with long claws clearly extending from each of the five toes.

❋

"You're serious, aren't you?   The abominable fuckin' snowman?"

I nodded.   Meryl cursed and spat, and I watched the saliva turn to ice before it hit the ground, while she peered again through her sniper scope.

"Couldn't it just be a polar bear?" she asked as she squinted through the lens.

Jack shook his head.   "The prints are too large, too deep. These were made by something… bigger."

"Well if it's that big, it moved pretty fuckin' fast," Meryl replied, without a hint of fear in her voice. "The tracks lead all the way back to the welfare facility."

"Where exactly do they go?" I asked, trying and failing to sound as unfazed as she did.

"They disappear behind the plane."

I pictured a great white ape, running at speed across the snowy wasteland, its gait stooped and graceless but effective. "And there's no sign of Eddie?"

Meryl shook her head. "He's probably inside, jackin' off."

"But… what if that thing is in there with him?" Jack's voice sounded choked with fear.

"Then at least we'll have it cornered," Meryl replied, her fingers absently stroking the barrel of the gun, the vicious glint of murder in her eyes once again.

I thought about suggesting we should wait inside the mouth of the cave, so that we could use the scope to watch for any movement back at the site, lay a trap for the monster should it return. But if we truly believed Eddie was in peril, we had an obligation to go back and help him.

And besides, I thought, and immediately hated myself for being so cynical: he's the only person who can fly us out of here.

The journey back across the tundra was even harder than the morning's trek, the wind lashing us ruthlessly as it picked up speed, whisking the snow into a blinding swirl that gradually covered the tracks we were re-tracing; but even as our old prints were obscured, those of our quarry persisted, large and deep and indelible, as if those terrifying claws had scarred the ice forever.

What would we have found in the mine if we had ventured deeper? The skulls of the slaughtered polar bears? Perhaps piled alongside those of a dozen missing fur trappers?

And why did it only take the heads?

As we walked, the wind became a gale, and soon those dark thoughts were sucked out of my head by the sheer ferocity of the unexpected storm.

"Should we turn back?" I shouted into the pummelling elements. I felt as though at any moment I would be ripped out of my boots and flung across the ice. But Meryl either didn't hear or chose to ignore me, her powerful body hunched forward as she battled on, and I had no choice but to follow.

As my field of vision was gradually replaced with impenetrable, roiling whiteness, I once again imagined my companions vanished, dragged into some secret nearby cave where their bodies could be carved apart as I staggered onwards, oblivious. I became convinced I'd lost my way, gotten turned around, wandered off alone into the blizzard's brutal heart.

To die, Toby, out here in this nothingness; frozen and forgotten, chasing your silly monsters.

I called out Meryl and Jack's names, my breathing ragged and desperate as panic tightened its noose around my throat.

Then I slammed into Meryl's back, and fell into the snow.

She turned, hauling me upright with one brawny arm. "The facility's just ahead," she barked above the squall. "Stay right behind me."

"Where's Jack?" I shouted back. But Meryl just turned and pushed forward into the churning maelstrom. For many minutes, her silhouette was my entire universe. A hulking shadow, half-glimpsed, then lost in a jolt of horror, then reappearing, leading me onwards like a lighthouse guiding a stricken craft to shore. I hobbled and lurched and stumbled in her wake, and eventually she was helping me up the few stone steps that led to the facility's main entrance, and we were inside, and I sank to my knees as Meryl heaved the door shut behind us.

"Eddie didn't say anything about a fuckin' storm," she muttered, a slight breathlessness the only sign of her exertions. I, meanwhile, collapsed to the ground, appreciatively sucking in lungfuls of air while my brain rejoiced in its survival. I lay like that for minutes, sprawled on the grubby plastic flooring, until Meryl prodded me with her boot.

"Come on, get up," she chastised. "We need to search the place. But don't go calling out to Eddie or Jack – I don't want to broadcast our fuckin' location if your monster is in here with us."

I clambered wearily to my feet, glancing back at the door. "But... what if Jack's still out there?"

She shrugged. "He's an Eskimo. He knows what he's doing."

I frowned at her harsh words, then imagined the icy tempest raging just beyond that thin sheet of metal, and realised that any lingering shreds of heroism had frozen and died inside me. If Jack was trapped in that blizzard, then Jack was dead; I was going to abandon him to his fate without even a whimper.

I followed Meryl along the corridors, once again protected by her imposing outline and the sleek menace of the .375. She was slow and meticulous, checking every room, pausing to listen intently at each doorway. Peering over her shoulder I surveyed meeting rooms, storage spaces, changing areas, a gymnasium; all were gaudily painted and well lit, the exact opposite of the mine, yet their silence and emptiness somehow made them even more eerie. I felt like I was creeping through a world where all the people had one day been blinked out of existence, as if by some arcane magic or anomaly of quantum mechanics; as though Meryl and I were the last humans alive.

I thought of Eddie and Jack, and those terrible footprints, and realised that on Little Cornwallis we quite possibly were.

We went upwards first, trying to tread carefully so our footfalls didn't echo noisily in the stairwell. Our slow, painstaking search revealed nothing alive on the second floor; just cold, empty rooms, like those of a condemned building resigned to its fate.

By the time we reached the third and final storey, the weather had subsided. The rooms there were offices, full of desks strewn with old documents and mysterious files. Archaic computers gathered dust, the blackness of their screens seeming portentous and striking against the blanket of white visible through the windows. Outside, our tracks were erased, as though the elements had conspired to completely delete us; even the monster's prints had been obliterated by the storm. I saw Eddie's plane partially buried, and a cold lump of dread rose in my throat as I thought about our absent pilot and the prospect of having to dig the precious craft out of the snow. In the distance, the mine's entrance seemed to observe our plight, now looking less like a gaping mouth and instead resembling a cruel, unblinking eye.

There was no sign of Jack, or Eddie, anywhere.

We thought about searching outside for them, but Meryl decided we should first go and check the basement.

The sky was beginning to darken as we descended, but there was still enough light coming through the stairwell's windows to create a horrible contrast with the black void that awaited us on the other side of the basement door. The entrance itself hung ajar, and was covered in ominous warnings: *electrical apparatus ahead; danger of death; only authorised personnel permitted*. Its hinges groaned stiffly as Meryl hauled it the rest of the way open. I shrank from the doorway, half-expecting some slavering horror to loom out of it, but like the rest of this accursed place the space beyond was silent. Just as she had in the mine, Meryl aimed her trusty rifle into the darkness, fearless determination in her eyes and the line of her jaw.

She switched on the torch.

The corridor was long and grey, seemingly overlooked by whoever had chosen the bright colour scheme we had seen in the rest of the facility. Instead, this space appeared neglected and forgotten; cobwebs clung to its corners, and one of the overhead strip lights had at some point fallen and shattered on the ground. At regular intervals, closed doors were labelled with things like 'boiler room', 'generators', 'septic tank'.

But we weren't really looking at those things. Instead, our eyes were drawn to something propped against the wall, about halfway down the passage.

It was Jack.

The Inuit's head was tilted backwards, his eyes closed

and his hands resting palm-upwards at his sides, almost as if he was meditating. A slick, red pool had formed around him, glistening in the torchlight. I gasped as I saw that a set of bloody prints led away from it towards the end of the corridor, where a door marked 'emergency rations' was standing ajar.

"Jack!" I cried out, starting towards him in spite of my fear. Meryl shot out an arm like the branch of a tree, restraining me.

"He's dead," she said, with rare compassion in her voice. "Can't you see how much blood there is?"

I didn't know what to say. Terror and confusion bubbled up inside me, making me feel suddenly nauseated.

"Those prints…" I gurgled.

"They're human footprints," Meryl replied, calmly. "Not your monster."

"But… why…" I stammered, bewildered.

Meryl moved forwards cautiously. I hesitated, but the thought of being separated from my protector was even more unpleasant than the grisly scene before me, so I followed just behind her.

"Eddie?" she called as she advanced. "Eddie, what the fuck happened?"

There was no reply other than the taunting echo of her own words. When we reached Jack, Meryl stooped to examine him.

"See this?" she said, gesturing towards a wound in the

trapper's chest, from which fresh blood was still seeping. "He's been shot."

"But why?" was all I could manage once again. I could see that she was right about the tracks – the crimson smudges leading away from the corpse were clearly shoeprints.

"He didn't tell me he had a gun," she mused.

"You think *Eddie* did this?"

"It's the only explanation. Maybe he was hiding down here, and thought Jack was the monster." She gestured towards the door through which the gory trail disappeared, facing it as she rose and straightened. "Which means he's probably still in there." Once again she called Eddie's name, but the basement remained as still and silent as a tomb.

For a long time she pondered our next move, chewing her lip while I stared at Jack's corpse. In my studies of the paranormal, I had seen countless dead bodies – in photographs and video footage, trampled or burned or half-eaten or poisoned, unexplained phenomena that hinted tantalisingly at predators beyond the realms of modern science or imagination – but this was the first time I had seen a cadaver in person. It seemed unthinkable that this slumped shape could not blink its eyes open and rise to greet us, that what resembled Jack Irquittuq was now little more than a punctured, fleshy sack, robbed of life and movement and the ghost of the shy, quiet man that had first summoned us here. I watched my breath misting in front of me and thought of escaping spirits, of souls expelled from their physical forms, and felt overcome by a crashing wave of sadness.

Then I looked again at the room marked 'emergency

rations', at the bloody footprints leading inside, and the sadness was swept away by fear as sudden and powerful as an avalanche.

Meryl started towards the door. I willed the leaden terror from my legs and followed, like an obedient husky behind its intrepid master. The darkness beyond the door seemed to swallow the torchlight as we approached, and even Meryl seemed apprehensive as we drew near. She stopped to call Eddie's name a final time, then darted suddenly forwards, slamming her bulk against the wall to one side of the door. She gestured with her head that I should do the same on its opposite side, and I did as instructed, heart thrashing in my chest.

"Wait there and don't follow me until I give the all-clear," she growled. I nodded dumbly, my eyes feeling too large for their sockets as they were drawn once again to Jack's body, at the footprints that someone – Eddie? – had made with his blood.

Meryl spun, kicking the door open and aiming the gun into the room in a single fluid movement. I watched, transfixed, expecting to see her blasted backwards by a gunshot, or perhaps dragged inside by a massive, clawed hand; but instead she simply stared into the chamber, and slowly whispered the words, 'fuck me'.

She stepped forwards, out of sight. I tried to wait in place as she'd commanded, steeling my nerves against the blackness and the silence. Hellish images swam in my mind: of a towering monstrosity awaiting us beyond the door; of Jack lurching to his feet and stumbling towards me, his head still lolling hideously backwards. I felt a scream rising in my throat, and clenched my teeth, pressing myself against the cold stone of the wall as though it might absorb and protect me. But my beleaguered mind continued to conjure demons; did I sense a shifting in the air to my right, as though something had just emerged from the room Meryl had entered, passing by me in the darkness? Did I imagine the feel of something brushing against my arm, the sound of scampering footsteps disappearing up the corridor?

I could wait no longer for Meryl to summon me; with a horrified cry I turned and lurched into the emergency rations room.

Meryl had taken a few strides inside, and was sweeping her torch around the dusty shelving that lined the walls. The space was large and the shelves were crammed with provisions: tinned food, MREs, boxes of crackers, bottles of water. If I'd been thinking rationally, I might have celebrated that we'd be able to survive here for months while we awaited rescue.

But I wasn't thinking rationally at all. Because the beam had shifted to illuminate the strange shapes in the room's centre: a bizarre series of scattered, mangled articles that my brain at first simply refused to process. But, as they glistened horribly in the torchlight, recognition forced itself into my consciousness, and vomit pushed itself up and out of my throat.

A half-smoked cigarette.

A rifle.

A pool of bright blood, slowly spreading.

A severed finger.

An arm, without the hand.

A torso, torn in half down the middle, with a single leg

still connected, the foot wearing a snow shoe.

Eddie's cap, upturned and empty.

"His head's not here," murmured Meryl, her voice softened by a kind of fearful awe. I could do nothing but gag and retch, my eyes squeezed closed as I tried to shut out the image of those repulsive hunks of human meat.

Meryl waited for me to stop vomiting, then frog-marched us out of that charnel house. As we stumbled along the corridor, past Jack's seeping carcass, I saw the main door still hanging open ahead of us. The stairwell beyond was completely dark, as though a noxious gas had been released from the basement to flood the entire building.

When we reached the door labelled 'boiler room', Meryl stopped, turning to push against its protesting hinges.

"You want to stay down *here?*" I cried.

She aimed the rifle and torch into the room, sweeping the beam across a tangle of pipes and fat water tanks.

"I need to think," she snapped in reply. "First rule of hunting: don't become the hunted. Eddie had the right idea; find a base, with only one entry point to defend."

"And look what happened to him!" I protested, determined to flee, to escape from this underground hell.

Meryl looked over her shoulder at me. "Look, Mr Cryptozoologist. You were right about the monster. It's real, and it's in here with us. You want to photograph it, and I want to kill it. But right now, we don't know where the fuck it is, and it's dark, and I'm tired, and we're trapped on a frozen island without a fuckin' pilot. So I'm going to hide out in here while I figure out a plan." She stepped into the room and turned to point the torch, and the gun, back at me. "You're welcome to fuck off and go it alone out there."

I swallowed, glancing once again at Jack's body, at the footprints Eddie had left as he walked towards the last room he would ever enter. Had I really felt something pass by me in the dark? Or had the creature been in that room all along, hidden somewhere in the shadows while I moaned and vomited, watching us with malevolent eyes? Had it been afraid, or fascinated? Perhaps it was simply sated, uninterested for the moment in two more scuttling flesh bags.

But it would come for us soon, just as it had for Eddie. And when it did, I would rather be in Meryl's foxhole than alone and trembling, with only my camera to protect me.

I bowed my head meekly, and followed her inside.

We decided to barricade the door and wait out the night. It meant risking losing our quarry, but neither of us had the stomach to face it in the dark; if there were no further storms, we could follow its tracks tomorrow, aided by sunlight. Our first job of the day would be to call for help using the radio we had seen in one of the offices upstairs.

Meryl made a couple of trips back to the ration room to lug shelving units to our hideout, so we could construct a barricade. She patiently showed me how to work the rifle so that I could cover the basement entrance while she worked, and to prepare me for my three-hour stint on sentry duty. I was terrified, sweat trickling down my face in spite of the cold, as I aimed the weapon into the black abyss beyond the door. I am not a religious man, but I mouthed silent prayers as she heaved and grunted behind me; at any moment I expected something to dart through the torch's beam, a blur of sinew and claws and fanged fury. Somewhere inside, a part of me still willed this to happen, yearning to glimpse the miraculous beast before it shredded me like a few sheets of tissue paper.

But nothing came. The only noise was my own heartbeat, which to me sounded as loud and fast as a pneumatic drill, and low metallic scraping as Meryl dragged the heaviest furniture she could manage.

When she was ready, we retreated into the boiler room, closed the door, and piled the shelves in front of it as though we intended never to leave.

Meryl took first watch, insisting that I get three hours' sleep.

"I won't be able to," I insisted.

"Try," was her terse response. "You're no use to me tomorrow if you're exhausted."

We still had our packs with us, and because the disasters we'd planned for included spending a night in the mine, this meant we had sleeping bags and dry base layers. I felt a little strange stripping naked with Meryl only a few metres away from me, but I knew such self-consciousness was ludicrous in these circumstances, and got on with it. Soon I was warm and secure inside multiple sleeping bags, nestled between two water tanks that had long ago ceased to function, but still somehow created the illusion of added warmth.

"If we have to stay here for longer, maybe we can get the

generators switched on and get this place up and running again?" I ventured.

"I'm not planning on staying here for longer," came Meryl's brusque reply. "Tomorrow we're going to kill that thing and get a plane out of here. Now shut up and get some sleep."

Others might have described her self-confidence as impressive, perhaps even delusional. To me it was utterly alien; I wondered where it came from, and realised I knew so little about the woman to whom I was entrusting my life. I wanted to ask her about herself, her background, her hopes and dreams. I tried to imagine why she had wanted to travel out here on this crazy expedition, whether she had a loving family waiting back at home. Or whether she was as alone as I was.

I stared at the reassuring shape of her broad back as she sat facing the barricade, hunched and still, as vigilant as a gargoyle. The rifle rested across her lap, always pointing forwards, always protecting. As I watched, the events of the day began to coagulate in my head and soon snow was falling in the boiler room, and tall creatures like stooped Neanderthals covered in white hair were peering at me from amongst the pipes, which themselves were growing and twisting, sprouting stalagmites and flowers of strange, colourful fungus. My sleeping bag dissolved away and I lay on an endless, empty canvas of frost, and the surface was paradoxically warm and yielding, and the ice became the warm belly of a dead thing, sliced open and raw, and I fell asleep as I was subsumed into its steaming entrails.

I awoke in complete darkness. My brain scrolled through memories of beds as it tried to locate itself, to fathom why it found itself completely deprived of optical input; my flat in Manchester; my parents' spare room; the bed I had shared with my fiancée before our separation years ago. The boiler room below the Polaris B welfare facility.

Meryl. Why had she switched off the torch?

I was warm in the sleeping bag, but still I began to shiver as I felt a presence in the room, something malign and resolute; something that watched, patiently. I felt that same shifting of the air, expecting at any moment to once again feel the brush of fur against my skin. I squeezed my mouth shut, trying to stuff the scream back down into my throat, suddenly convinced that to release it would bring an onslaught of slicing talons down upon me. I wondered what it had done to Meryl, whether I was lying surrounded by quivering, fleshy pieces of my only remaining companion.

The torch came on, pointing at my face.

"Wakey wakey, eggs and bakey," Meryl chuckled as I winced and shielded my eyes.

"I'm already awake," I grumbled. "Why the fuck were you sitting in the dark?"

"I switched to the night vision goggles," she replied. "Trying to save the torch's battery. We've got spares, but no sense wasting it."

"Did you… see anything?" I asked, glancing across to see the barricade thankfully intact.

"Not a creature has stirred. Our friend doesn't seem interested in us tonight."

I nodded, clambering to my feet, keeping the sleeping bags wrapped around me as I blinked and rubbed my eyes. "I guess it's my turn to watch?"

"Sure is. Time three hours on your watch and then wake me up." She handed me the rifle, then removed the night vision goggles from her head. "Use these. Look, here's the switch to turn them on."

She turned off the torch first, then demonstrated the goggles. There was a low hum and a flash of white filled my field of vision, quickly coalescing into a view of the boiler room, but coloured an outlandish green as though I'd been transported to some bizarre alternate dimension.

"Now put the torch back on while I get ready for bed," she instructed. "Just remember to turn the goggles off first, or you won't be able to see."

I did as I was told. She seemed to have no problem undressing in front of me, but I averted my eyes nonetheless, unsure whether I found her muscled figure attractive or intimidating, or a bit of both.

Then she clambered into her own sleeping bags and within minutes was snoring heavily, and I was alone, trying not to think about how insane the situation was. I wondered about the monster; where it was, what it thought, what it wanted. Did it sleep? Was it frightened? What did it even look like?

And what did it do with the heads?

I stared, and my fingers twitched against the rifle's cool plastic, wondering if I'd be able to wield this unfamiliar power if – when – an attack actually came. And how would it come? Footsteps outside, a slow but determined pounding at the door as our blockade was gradually battered away? I thought about the storm that had nearly ended us yesterday. I had read accounts detailing the yeti's ability to summon such blizzards, to conjure freezing blasts of wintry air right out of its mouth; I had thought them fanciful, but now I could vividly imagine the barrier smashed aside by such dark sorcery.

Hours passed like ice ages. My eyelids drooped, and I tried to find other things to stare at, any scant stimulus that might keep me awake and alert until my shift was over and the sun rose again. I glanced at Meryl's sleeping form, her expression surprisingly childlike and feminine; I peered up at the ceiling, worrying about ingress through the suspended panels. I looked at the red smears around the base of the barricade, where Meryl had dragged the shelves through poor Jack's blood.

I saw marks, leading out from beneath the heaped furniture, following the line of the wall. They led into a corner of the room, disappearing behind one of the water tanks. Feeling the heat drain from my arteries, I stood and moved to take a better look.

My mouth dried instantly, like a dead thing shrivelling on the tundra. My stomach seemed to open like a trapdoor.

They were large footprints, made in Jack's blood. Much larger than a human's, each had five long claws. They led behind the tank and around the perimeter of the boiler room, stopping at the rear corner, just behind where Meryl was sleeping. There the final pair of prints faced out into the room, as though their owner had propped themselves in the corner to watch, and wait.

But there was nothing there.

I opened my mouth, but only a horrified croak could emerge. I stared into that dreadful corner, not understanding how, but certain that the creature had been in the room with us all along.

I had to escape. I had to warn Meryl. I had to kill it. I had to do too many things, and my splintering brain could not decide which, or how.

I turned and began to tear down the barricade.

The crashing woke Meryl instantly.

"Toby, what the fuck?" she yelled, her torch coming on and immediately blinding me. I tore the goggles from my head, not stopping, focused only on escaping from what I now knew was our coffin.

She shouted my name again and I turned as she rose to her feet; then she *kept rising*, seeming to suddenly possess the power to levitate. Her face wore a scowl of confusion as she floated up to the ceiling, her arms clamped to her sides as though encircled by invisible ropes. Her torch fell to the floor, and I switched mine on, aiming the rifle towards her as she struggled and grunted, her legs flailing wildly as she hovered in mid-air. Her eyes locked on mine, and I saw fear there for the first time, a little girl who found herself in the body of a powerful woman.

A body that was suddenly pulled apart.

I watched, aghast, as Meryl's arms and legs snapped off like twigs, limbs tumbling to the floor as blood geysered from the wounds, and she began to scream. I gaped as her head twisted violently backwards, the scream choked off as her skull completed a full 360-degree rotation; then another, then another, as though it was being slowly *unscrewed* from her mutilated torso.

I waited for something inside me to snap, but it didn't. I waited for insanity to preserve me, for blissful catatonia to settle upon my senses, but such a reprieve was not granted. I was acutely, painfully aware of what was happening, that Meryl was dead, that I was alone in that room with a monstrous creature that could somehow conceal itself from sight.

I yanked and struggled and tore at the barricade, my bones chilled by the knowledge that, for hours, the monster had been quietly standing in the corner, watching us. A monster I had come here to witness, to photograph, to study. Even in my frenzied horror, the irony was not lost.

Sickening sounds came from behind me as I worked, of splintering bone and separated flesh, and I found myself screaming just to drown them out. My body tensed, expecting to be seized at any moment, but still I was spared, and somehow I made it to the door, jerked it open, and stumbled out into the passageway beyond.

Light spilled in from the stairwell, illuminating Jack's body and the criss-crossing tracks that we had doodled in his spilt blood. We, and the creature we had foolishly imagined we were here to hunt. I ignored the macabre tableau and sprinted towards the daylight, taking the stairs three at a time before hurtling headlong down the main corridor. I almost pulled the front door off its hinges – the final door, in my world which seemed to have become nothing but doors, doors with darkness and horrors on the wrong side of them – and stumbled out into the snow, my legs still working feverishly, propelling me forwards across the ice as I continued to shriek like something driven finally mad.

When my screams subsided, I became aware of the crisp, cool tang of the breeze in my throat, and gratefully swallowed deep breaths of air that was mercifully unlike the stale brume of that underground mausoleum. I continued to run like that for many more minutes until my legs began to tire, and I slowed to a stop.

It was only then that I realised I was out in the snow, woefully under-dressed, and suddenly very, very cold.

Seven minutes, I thought, as my teeth began to vibrate. I looked around frantically, trying to get my bearings; I had travelled a staggering distance in my bewildered fright, and the welfare facility was perhaps a mile behind me, the garish maple leaf daubed on its roof reminding me of patterns made in blood. To its left was Polaris B, where we had begun our hunt, before realising too late that we were not the hunters at all. Beneath me were my own prints, made with bare feet that had been insulated from the cold only by adrenaline and terror. Now those extremities felt encased in pain, the cold like a thousand nails driven simultaneously into my toes, heels, soles.

I gasped, but not at this sudden agony. I gasped because I noticed tracks running parallel to my own, stopping a few metres behind me. As I watched, another pair of prints appeared, the snow rearranging itself before my eyes.

Large footprints, each with five claws.

My eyes bulged, and I took a step backwards. The footprints followed suit, another taloned paw imprinted in the frost. Calmly keeping pace, as though watching me.

I began to shiver violently, hugging my arms around my chest as I turned to run. After a few more metres I crumpled to the ground, icy pain seeming to bloom within me like a tree sprouting from inside my ankles. Kneeling, folded over, wheezing like a man twice my age, I looked back over my shoulder once again.

The prints had matched my steps. Following me. Observing, at a distance.

"What are you?" I screamed at my tormentor. "*What do you do with their heads?*"

The monster did not reply. It only watched, silently, as the cold gnawed hungrily at my skin.

EPHEMERA

The sage drew deeply on his pipe, his expression darkening as he pondered the question. Exhaling a cloud of blueish smoke, he eventually replied, "Because I fear another uprising."

The torches on the walls sputtered as though in shock, mirroring the murmurs of concern and outrage around the table. I watched Patrician Beaumont carefully. His once-proud frame was stooped with age, and perhaps by the weighty adornments of his rank; jewelled medallions hung from his neck and robes, heavy bracelets encircled his wrists, and the gold rings on his fingers glinted in the flickering light. When he moved, it was accompanied by the soft tinkle of precious metals.

Yet still he carried a gravity about him, an inner resolve that commanded the respect of the assembled councillors. His words were softly spoken, yet as incisive as the blade of a Lordsguard. When he responded, the chamber immediately fell silent.

"Why?"

Jarvis Mortimer, trusted advisor to the F
longer than I had been alive, held his m..
"Beneath us, they have been digging for years. Exiled trom
the surface, the Inferior spawn and multiply, breeding like
vermin. Sealed as they are below the impenetrable Plate, the
only way for them to expand is downwards, seeking ever
more space for their degenerate progeny. Their detestable
mines delve ever deeper even as we speak; this we know,
and this we abide."

"But the plague, Councillor Mortimer," cut in the
whimpering voice of Foljambe, head of the Merchants'
Guild. "You told us of a great sickness, spreading through
their denizens. Won't that wipe them out?"

Mortimer took a deep drag from his pipe once again,
eyes closing as the potent blend of his tobacco granted
momentary respite from his worries. When his eyes
reopened, his face seemed suddenly very old indeed. "Their
people, diseased and crippled though they are, are proving
hardier than I thought. My spies speak of catacombs deeper
than we could possibly imagine, and of a great power
rumoured to have been unearthed."

"Your spies!" scoffed Brigadier Gascoigne, slamming a
fist angrily into the table top. "Their misguided forays
beneath the Plate threaten to bring the plague right to our
doorstep!" Across the table, Beaumont's bodyguard eyed
the Brigadier coldly. The Lordsguard were independent
from the army, meaning Gascoigne had no influence over
the lean and capable-looking warrior at the Patrician's side.

Beaumont ignored the outburst, eyes still fixed on
Mortimer. "And what have your spies told you of the nature
of this power? Are we to believe that the ravings of the
Subterraphiles are true – that there is ancient magic, buried

deep underground?"

Gascoigne gave a snort of derision, sinking back in his chair and shaking his head. Smoke curled around Mortimer's gaunt face, like the rumours and deceit with which he surrounded himself.

"I'm afraid, my lord, that my people have been unable to ascertain that information."

"Then what bloody use are they?" Gascoigne cried in exasperation. This time the Patrician held up one finger to silence his general, its tip ending in a pointed, silver nail ring like a sharpened talon. The other nobles and officials around the table had the good sense to stay quiet, not sharing Gascoigne's brash confidence. I could feel the tension in the room reaching a critical point, the air seeming to thicken like clotting blood. Even the City's forefathers, whose portraits surrounded us in this grand and storied dining hall, observed the proceedings nervously, eyes peering out from fading canvases across the gulfs of time and death.

"And why not, Councillor Mortimer?" the Patrician said. A note of anger had slipped into his tone, like a knife slid between shoulder blades. "Is the ample budget with which I finance your activities no longer sufficient for you to do your job? Why are your well-paid agents 'unable' to find out what is happening down there?" His tone seemed brittle, ready to snap. I thought about our City, where all was ephemera; a job, a reputation, a life, all hanging by delicate threads. They were so deeply entangled that a tiny rustle on one side of the web could set them all swaying.

Sometimes they broke, and faces disappeared from around this table, never spoken of again.

I thought about my own position, held for nearly four years, as understudy to the Minister of Technologies. It was old Grimwald's infirmity that had granted me my seat upon this committee, elevating me to become its youngest – and only current female – member. Such attributes were of course far from beneficial; they made my tenure the most fragile of all, my grip on power the most treacherous. At times, when I dared to speak, the hostility radiating from some of my supposed colleagues was palpable.

But if Mortimer felt under pressure, he did not show it. He seemed uninterested in the other people in the room; indeed, I felt the rest of us fading away, an audience of cutthroat politicians and backstabbing careerists slipping into shadow as the two wily old villains conversed. Mortimer's expression was neither fearful nor defiant as he met his master's eye, and replied evenly.

"Because, sire, those that descend that deep do not come back."

*

I hurried through the darkness, gathering its anonymity about me as I clung to Lodehearth's alleyways, backstreets, wynds and ginnels. Above, the stars peered down like accusing eyes, glittering with indignation. I ignored them, like I ignored the drunks that occasionally shuffled past, or the homeless vagrants with whom I briefly shared the City's gloomiest alcoves. The air was tainted by their vomit and shit, reminding me of the torrents of muck that seeped daily down the cobbled streets, the stench as nauseating as it was strangely comforting. Metal grates set into the kerbsides carried the worst of it away, of course, draining the City's waste down into its ailing bowels, where the Inferior were condemned to dwell amongst our effluence.

The thought made me gag and cough unexpectedly, and I resolved to concentrate on keeping quiet for the remainder of my nocturnal excursion. At least there were very few Watchmen for me to disturb, and those that were making the rounds were sticking to the well-lit roads, avoiding the danger of the shadows like…

Like the plague.

After what felt like an interminable journey, darting anxiously from nook to cranny like a scuttling rodent, I slipped into the overgrown passage that I knew would lead me into the old graveyard. The Watchmen never ventured there, believing – like the rest of the townsfolk – that the cemetery was haunted, still beleaguered by the same spectral malevolence that had once turned its ire against the church and set the great building ablaze. Others, like me and my true master, knew the truth: that the fire, and the subsequent relocation of the Subterranic Order to a crumbling ruin on the City outskirts, had been deliberate strategies, the means of the Order's castration at the hands of the Patrician.

Having won the civil war and sealed the usurpers in their own mines, Beaumont simply couldn't afford to tolerate a religion whose sacred texts spoke of a mysterious power he had buried with them.

I crept uncomfortably through the tangle of thorns and weeds that choked the passageway. In some places the vegetation was so thick that I thought about using my falchion to hack a way through, but I needed to minimise any evidence of my incursion, and so tolerated the rips in my clothes and the tears in my flesh until I emerged with some relief into the church grounds. A full moon hung over the desolate scene like a bright, motionless pendulum, its inertia matching the stillness all around me; gravestones sagged like disciples bent in worship, the blackened ruin of the church a carcass torn open and left to rot in the darkness.

I hurried towards it, feeling the familiar sense of dread that clung to this wretched necropolis, and not wanting to keep the Hieromonk waiting. As I slipped amongst the tombstones, I thought about the coffins buried beneath me, the skeletal occupants that slept peacefully within. The power that Mortimer had spoken of, the buried mystery whose disturbance had so perturbed the Patrician; what was its nature? Would it simply fuel our furnaces, replacing the coal from which we had annexed ourselves? Or would it drag those slumbering bones from their caskets and raise cackling death to wander Lodehearth's streets?

Nonsense, of course. As a woman of science, I did not believe in magic… but still, I feared it.

And I feared my master. As I slipped through the crack between two partially collapsed walls and heaved open the trapdoor at the centre of the scorched antechamber, I felt gooseflesh prickle my skin, and cold sweat sheen my brow. The ladder was not long, yet as usual I felt as though I had descended into another world altogether. I turned to face the single passageway that led from the dusty storeroom, walking towards its flickering, blood-coloured light.

*

"And then?"

"Attention turned to the report of Sheriff Cunningham. He thinks the stores of coal will run out in the next five months."

A slow exhalation of breath, like the wind sighing along the City streets. "And what does the Patrician propose to do when that happens?"

"He said the matter would be discussed at the next Committee meeting. Brigadier Gascoigne pushed him for an answer, even suggested venturing out into the Afflicted Lands in search of more fuel, but Beaumont said the matter was simply not on this month's agenda."

"Gascoigne is an impetuous buffoon. The Patrician recognises the military's loyalty to him, but he thinks that makes him indispensable."

Hieromonk Grey's voice was barely louder than a whisper. I could see his lips moving beneath the shroud, and wondered again what he looked like under the white cloth that covered his entire body. The standard garment of the Order represented the winding sheets in which corpses were wrapped for burial; his religion embraced and exalted mankind's inevitable reunion with the earth, seeking answers and meaning in its endless depths. Unlike Beaumont, Grey wore no accoutrements to symbolise his rank, nothing to differentiate himself from his followers or the putrefying dead in the graves that surrounded us.

"However, the Patrician's problem is the threat of revolt from his own people, when they realise the severity of the fuel crisis. Add to that this new peril beneath the Plate, and he cannot contemplate destabilising his army."

My master was doubtless correct. He was a skilled politician, as exhibited by the deft manoeuvring that had returned him to the Committee's meeting hall, despite the Order's removal from the Council.

That manoeuvre was me. Grimwald's ongoing frailty was no coincidence. I almost laughed at the irony: a man of science tricked and poisoned by a man of the church. I had asked in the past why Grey did not simply kill the old fool outright, but the Hieromonk had explained that my place on the Council was more secure as Grimwald's pet; the rest of the 'gibbering hyenas', as he called them, would tolerate me only as long as I had their colleague's endorsement. This made my job a many-faceted deception: devoted assistant to the bed-ridden and lecherous Grimwald (tolerating his lectures and mood swings and insistent groping at my buttocks); attentive and compliant member of the High Council; and worshipful disciple of His Reverence, the Grand Hieromonk.

In reality, I am simply a scientist. My pursuit is one of knowledge, not power.

But sometimes one facilitates the other.

"So," Grey said, in a voice like sand slipping through an hourglass. "Mortimer spoke of the Great Truth, the Secret Interred." I glanced around the room, the crimson flame casting a hellish glow across the bookshelves and the arcane tomes and scrolls with which they were crammed. Grey tilted his head, following my gaze, and reached out a sinuous arm to point towards the Order's emblem, daubed on the wall behind him.

"That symbol appears many times in the Texts. Its significance is still debated to this day, even by the most ardent members of the Order. Do you know what I think it means?"

He turned to face me, and I realised how unsettling it was to be studied by someone that had no visible eyes.

"I... do not know, Your Reverence." I lowered my face, feeling suddenly frightened by this slender thing that resembled an exhumed corpse.

"The small circle, surrounded by three large outward-facing blades," he continued, his tone containing a note of awe. "I think it depicts an artefact. Something that exudes great puissance, despite its small size. Something, perhaps, that could be acquired. Wielded."

I realised that, despite his position and the resources that the Order could still command, this man was just like every other member of his sect: a zealot, grasping for power and truth. Reaching downwards, into the earth, scrabbling amongst the worms and the muck. I almost laughed at him.

But... what if he was right?

"The Patrician will doubtless be preparing a secret expedition to retrieve the relic. It will be a raiding party, large and formidable, and slow to assemble. To outmanoeuvre him, we must strike quickly."

I lifted my gaze, and an eyebrow. "Then you propose to send your own group beneath the Plate?"

There was a subtle movement of the cloth across his face.

"Not a group. A single agent, skilled at clandestine operations."

I couldn't see beneath the fabric, but I was sure that the Hieromonk was smiling.

"You."

*

Who built Lodehearth?

Why did the City exist when the world around it was a wasteland of ashen ruin?

Such mysteries permeated our lives, and the origin of the Plate was yet another.

The Patrician claimed to have built it, of course, to act as a great and impregnable barrier between the surface-dwelling populace and the brutish savages that lurked beneath; but many suspected it to have been yet another artefact recovered from the mines. Believed to be forged from lead and requiring a whole battalion of men to move it into place, the weighty disc bore no markings or any other evidence of its true purpose. Ironic that the Inferior had unearthed the strange object, only for their masters to use it to entomb them.

But of all the riddles surrounding the Plate, the most pressing was how I would bypass it. The Patrician's paranoia had led him to increase the garrison that monitored the great spiral stairwell, supplementing the usual gaggle of drunken Watchmen with capable soldiers from the ranks of Gascoigne's army. And even if I could somehow get close to the disc without my intentions being challenged and discovered, how would I move it? Such a feat would be impossible for even the brawniest strongman of a circus troupe.

The only way, therefore, was around it. But could there possibly be a second entrance, a back way that Beaumont left unguarded?

The answer, against all probability, was yes.

That was why I found myself, after three decades willingly incarcerated within Lodehearth's imposing walls, venturing out into the Afflicted Lands. It was surprisingly easy to escape the City's perimeter: all I had to do was masquerade as a wandering lunatic and allow myself to be rounded up and tossed into a wagon with various other undesirables. Before I knew it, the Watch had escorted us beyond the City Gates, dumping us unceremoniously without trial or provisions as soon as we had crested the horizon. I was worried they would beat me, or confiscate the map I had secreted inside my ragged costume, but their attention was occupied by the ravings of my fellow outcasts, some of whom seemed only now to be realising their fate. One of the men, a filthy beggar whose drunken stupor had begun to dissipate, was screaming for mercy, pleading to be allowed back through the Gates where he would atone for his uselessness and vagrancy. The Watchmen left him sobbing in a ditch with two broken legs.

I watched them leave, waited for the clattering of their terrible carriage to fade into the night, then struck out in the direction Grey had indicated on my map. Soon the other seven souls were left far behind me. I tried not to contemplate their future, suspecting they would attempt to return to the City where people would gather atop the ramparts to laugh as they were showered with arrows and boiling oil. As I trudged across the barren, slate-coloured terrain, I tried also to forget my new status as an exile, trusting that my master would fulfil his pledge to somehow smuggle me back into Lodehearth to report to him, and to enjoy his promised rewards.

I had tried to object, of course. To explain why I was unsuitable for such an important mission. But the Hieromonk is nothing if not insistent. He had given me four dawns; just over three days in which to keep time in a land without sun, where I must somehow identify and steal the enigmatic boon rumoured to have appeared in that forsaken kingdom.

This first phase of my quest ended with me scrambling down a steep shale slope to the edge of a fetid lake, its black waters bubbling with foul, sulphurous emanations. It was as though all the darkness and ruination of these lands had flowed down to congeal here into a murky, leaden quagmire, drained of all colour; how ironic, I thought, that I should be banished here by someone named 'Grey'. A strange feeling rose in me, something halfway between a laugh and a sob, and I choked down my despair as I scanned my surroundings for the cave entrance he had scrawled.

Sure enough, it was there, on the other side of the rancid pool: a secret known only to my master and to Mortimer, and to those of the sage's spies who had been lucky enough to return from their subterranean excursions. I made my way around the gurgling water, wondering if I was soon to join the ranks of those he had lost, those whose espionage had led them to their nameless doom, somewhere deep beneath the earth.

As I entered the mouth of the cavern, trying not to think of the hanging stalactites as teeth within a hungry mouth, I sucked in one final lungful of outside air, but the stink of the lake was so bad that I almost vomited.

*

It had been years since they had performed any such function on behalf of Lodehearth, but people still called them the Mines: a cavernous, labyrinthine warren that had been chiselled into the earth in the City's frenzied pursuit of coal. That black harvest, along with an occasional deposit of other precious minerals, was extracted and funnelled upwards, always upwards. The Inferior toiled until their bodies buckled, and not a penny of their excavated wealth ever flowed back down.

One day they had grown tired of their lot. They had revolted, and been brutally defeated.

Then buried.

Grey had people stationed down here, a sort of rotating cell of agents of the Order, integrating with the people to monitor them while subtly stoking the fires of their malcontent. With no way to contact his disciples aside from sending in their replacement, and no reliable way to smuggle equipment out of the City, the Order maintained a cache of supplies close to the cave entrance, whose location my master had explained in precise detail.

"Without light, you'll be helpless down there, stumbling about in the void until you're reduced to sucking water off the stones," he had intoned gravely, in a voice like rustling parchment.

Panic began to wriggle in my stomach as I searched in vain for the very specific rock he had described, but I found it eventually, and followed the trail of similar stones that would be unnoticeable to anyone lacking the Hieromonk's guidance. When I located the final boulder and heaved it aside, I almost cried out with gratitude at the sight of the torch, tinderbox and water canteen secreted in the crevice beneath. I drank deeply, too deeply, almost giving in to the urge to drain the flask's entire contents in a single gulp; then I remembered that I knew nothing of this place, of the plight of the Inferior, of the nature of my errand.

For all I knew, this might be the last drink I would find for days.

I remembered also the Hieromonk's strict instructions to replace the stone, and to later seek out Brother Millis, informing him of my quest and of the need to once again restock the supply. Millis had been stationed down here for nearly six months, and might be expecting to be substituted; I wondered if the priest would be aggrieved to learn he must continue at his long and solitary post, or delighted to remain in the depths that he so revered.

But, first, a long descent awaited me. This cave was unknown to even the Inferior themselves, leading down into a network of tunnels from which the Hieromonk's map was my only hope of escaping. The carefully-drawn diagram looked less like an abandoned mine than the construct of some demented spider, and I shuddered as I thought of what I might encounter inside its tortuous expanse.

The answer was: nothing. Left turn followed left turn followed right, the map leading me ever onwards under the torch's amber glow. There was no breeze down here to stir the flame, no smell except for the faint clammy odour emanating from the walls themselves, nothing to see except for the bleak disaffection of cold, endless rock. Of the other souls that had navigated these tunnels before me, of those that had become lost and died down here, losing their minds as they starved in the darkness, I found not a single trace.

On I went, shivering in the chill of the grim catacomb, terrified that I would take a wrong turn and be cast adrift forever. But the Hieromonk's diagram proved fool-proof, and after hours of patient progress I emerged from the hellish maze into a large cavern. It was eerily quiet, the only sound the soft crackling of my smouldering firebrand.

My map pointed the way to exit this great chamber, and there its assistance ended. I was utterly alone, so far beneath the Plate that I felt I might awaken at any moment as if from a bad dream.

*

The cavern was roughly circular, and fluid dripped from its roof to form a shallow pool covering most of the floor. Stalagmites reached upwards from the water like the wasted fingers of a submerged, fleshless giant. All around me were dozens of other passageways, and I realised just how impossible it would be to find the way to the surface from this end; the people that dwelt in these Mines would never know that an escape route was within their grasp. A vision flitted through my brain, of a general leading a great army of the downtrodden to their liberation, unleashing their vengeful horde on the City like a great crushing tsunami.

First things first, Annora. You haven't met a single soul down here. For all you know, the plague has wiped these people out altogether. And you, with no protection or antidote to speak of, might be blundering into its pitiless embrace.

Yet I could do nothing but continue, splashing through the water towards the largest cave mouth as indicated by the map, which I then stuffed back into my ragged clothing as securely as possible. Never had a scrap of parchment held such value to me. Almost as precious was the torch and its blessed illumination, and I began to worry that it would burn down before I found any signs of civilisation; but after a short while, I beheld an amber glow at the end of the tunnel. Extinguishing my own light, I hurried towards it, and was shocked when I stepped into a huge cavern, large enough to dwarf the previous chamber.

The space was dark, barely lit by the few flickering torches mounted on the walls, but it was clear that it was a living area. Cramped hovels were chiselled into the walls, in many areas stacked on top of each other all the way to the cave roof. Scraps of wood and metal, doubtless reclaimed from the previous mining operations, had been crudely lashed together to create ramshackle walkways between these homes, and other repurposed fragments spoke tragically of the life these under-dwellers were trying to recreate: strips of fabric hung in redundant windows, and the outline of a children's game had been scraped into the jagged ground at my feet.

Yet despite these signs of life, my excursion remained a solitary one; no defensive garrison appeared on the rickety scaffold, and no-one emerged from the stone shacks to confront me. I had to make a choice: was I a silent interloper, skulking in the shadows as I had done so often in the streets of Lodehearth? Or a friendly visitor, announcing my presence and trying to win the trust of the denizens of this dismal enclave?

Just as I decided there was no hurry to reveal myself, I heard a cough from a nearby shelter, a wet and feeble sound that suggested severe ailment. My mind raced with thoughts of the plague; perhaps that was what had decimated this place, reducing it to this sepulchral state? Dare I risk contact with a contagion that I knew nothing about?

I sighed, asking myself a different question, one that I had been led back to over and over again since that fateful meeting with the Hieromonk countless hours ago.

What other choice did I have?

I approached the source of the coughing, grimacing as I heard the noise once again; it lasted longer this time, tinged with the desperation of someone unsure whether their breath would return. Cautiously I approached the ground-floor building, whose flimsy wooden door hung ajar, and peered inside.

The tiny space was barely large enough for the two beds that occupied it, sandwiching a small brass cauldron that was presumably used for cooking whatever these people subsisted upon. I tried to resist the urge to speculate whether this was moss scraped from cave walls, or the flesh of their weaker companions, unsure which was worse. Instead, my attention was drawn to the figures occupying the stone cots. One of them was the poor fellow I had heard coughing, an emaciated creature with a few strands of hair clinging wretchedly to his skull-like head.

The person in the other bed, a woman, was dead. That the place reeked only of vomit and shit suggested she hadn't yet begun to decay, but that time would come. I wondered if they were partners, and realised I did not know whether the Inferior even celebrated the holy union of marriage; either way, to share a hovel like this with the mouldering corpse of a loved one, too incapacitated to mourn her... even savages like these deserved better.

The man saw me and attempted to sit up, drawing another spasm of coughs from his cadaverous chest, and I grimaced as he spat bloody phlegm into the cooking pot.

"Who are you?" he growled.

A lack of sunlight, I thought suddenly. Perhaps this rumoured plague was no more than the effects of years below ground, starved of the sun's life-giving warmth and energy.

"I'm... an outcast, from above," I replied, not too concerned about the plausibility of my tale. This man might not last the next hour, never mind raise a guard against me. "I seek another of my kind, who has been here for some time. You may know him as Brother Millis?"

At the sound of that name, the enfeebled old man seemed possessed by a sudden impossible vigour, and leapt to his feet like a puppet jerked upwards on a string. The movement was so swift, so unexpected, that he was upon me before I could retreat from the squalid tomb.

"Millis," he hissed, drawing out the final consonant into a long, snakelike sibilant that sprayed my face with mucus. I closed my eyes and mouth lest the man did indeed bear an infection, desperate to prevent his fluids from polluting my own. He bent forward, gripped by a bout of demented cackling that culminated in another dreadful cough, but still his spindly fingers burrowed into each of my shoulders with surprising strength. He brought his face up to mine again, and I was horrified by the terrible grin he wore, and by the toothless wrecks his age or his affliction had made of his gums.

"Your *Brother* brought this ruin upon us. We had a plan... a leader... a hero that would lead us to victory. But instead of uniting to dig our way upwards, outwards, bursting forth to glory like the great green trees once did across this accursed land..."

He sagged into coughing once again while I reflected on his words. Despite his foolish belief in childish fables like 'trees', he was surprisingly eloquent for a brute, and I decided to let him speak his piece instead of making my escape.

"Who was this leader?" I probed as his convulsions subsided. His sunken, yellow eyes widened with apparent enthusiasm at the question, and I noticed that there was a dark hue to his skin, almost as though he had been toiling above ground rather than imprisoned beneath it. An obscure symptom of his illness, perhaps, or a surprising effect of prolonged sunlight deprivation, which I had always assumed would render a man's skin as pale as the maggots that wriggled out of the city's sewer grates.

"Our keeper, Protector Cotton," he replied. "A fair man, strong and just, who rejected the title of Lord to remind us that all men are made equal in the eyes of the gods. After months of abjection, searching in vain for escape, fighting over dwindling food supplies, it was the Protector who formed us into an army, a legion capable of overrunning the City and raising the Patrician's head on his spear." He seemed almost rapt as he spoke, as though this fanciful story was what had kept him alive this long, giving him something to hope for even as he rotted in his bed.

"But how could Lodehearth possibly be overrun?" I asked gently. "Did you seek to break through the Plate?"

Once again, that sulphurous fire in his eyes. "No, fair lady. We were going to dig *around* it. To emerge simultaneously from a dozen breaches, to swarm the City's defences before they'd even had time to assemble. The bloodshed... the righteous wrath of reprisal... oh, it would have been the greatest day of my life."

His eyes were wide, his expression ecstatic. I, meanwhile, was reeling, his pronouncements making me sick to my stomach. How had Mortimer's spies failed to unmask such a scheme? Were these the ravings of a madman, or was the old seer really so far lapsed in competence?

Or, worse... was Mortimer conspiring to *support* such an uprising?

"What... where..." I stammered, my mind still awhirl. "What became of this army?"

The blaze faded from the man's eyes, leaving only milky orbs that seemed suddenly unable to focus on me. He sank down onto the edge of his bed, willowy legs buckling beneath him. I noticed the sores on the skin of his arms and thighs, and wondered again how he could possibly have summoned the strength to stand.

"Dead. Fallen. Stricken by this same scourge that now chews the flesh from my bones."

"How can you know this?"

"Because..." he wheezed, pausing to draw in a great gasping breath that I felt sure would trigger another seizure, but mercifully did not. "Because I was among their number. I was the only one that made it back here alive. Such a catastrophe... after we had hacked, and scraped, and clawed, and burrowed, like animals in the dirt... to be so close and then to succumb, to whatever that bastard Millis had dug up beneath us."

I frowned. "I don't understand. With respect, sir, you are surely far too old to have participated in such an undertaking?"

Another smile carved open his face, this time wry and remorseful. "My years number only two dozen, milady," he rasped. "I daresay if you'd glimpsed me a fortnight ago, you'd have found my form more pleasing to your pretty eyes." A mirthless chuckle escaped from his cracked, swollen lips. I stared, wondering at his words; could this wasted thing really be a boy younger than me?

"This plague... you say Millis is somehow responsible for it?"

"Some of the Minefolk didn't think we could succeed,"

he murmured, scarcely louder than a whisper. "They feared another defeat. They were weak, hungry, unambitious. They abandoned the Protector's course and followed another. A charlatan, eschewing practical solutions in favour of senseless proclamations of paradise, of the answer to our prayers, deep below."

"What did they find?" My voice too had fallen, as though in reverence. I had the strange sense that I was communing with a ghost.

His head lifted slowly towards me as though his neck was barely able to support it, as if all his strength had been utterly drained by his earlier outburst. His cloudy eyes were streaming; perhaps with disease, perhaps with incalculable sorrow.

"A door," he said, before sinking back onto the bed, staring upwards, seeming not to want sleep to take him.

I thought about trying to encourage him to come with me, to at least leave that house and the horror of his lifeless companion; but in the end I just left him there, stretched out as though on a mortuary slab.

*

That was how it was for miles. The village was in fact a town, almost a city, a sprawling settlement hewn into the rock and strung with walkways, ladders and rope bridges; a marvel of human ingenuity, I had to admit. Somehow, the thousands that we had defeated and discarded had endured, had built something amazing from nothing at all, had created light from darkness down here in the abyss.

But now that hardy populace had been devastated. The Minefolk, as the invalid had called them, were reduced to a motley rabble of survivors, those that weren't bedridden tending to those that were, the rest dead and slowly decomposing in their homes; occasionally I found their bones littering the high-ceilinged tunnels that passed for streets. It was the survivors that kept some of the wall-mounted torches lit, a sad and futile act of defiance.

That accounted for maybe half of the town's original population. The others had left, pursuing the twin expeditions of their would-be saviours; both leading to the same calamity, if my tragic acquaintance had spoken the truth. I thought about Millis, about the toxic combination of fanaticism and greed that must have driven him; surely he can't have expected the Hieromonk to approve of such a drastic reinterpretation of his role?

Whatever the truth, I was now destined to follow his path, for better or for worse. Little point pursuing Protector Cotton, only to find a dead-end full of corpses. I didn't allow myself to consider that the decision might be irrelevant, given that whatever evil had been disinterred might already be coursing through my own veins. I didn't allow myself to admit that I had begun to feel rather queasy, and that a headache had begun to throb right in the centre of my forehead, like a burrowing insect.

Besides, either way I first had to find my way out of this endless succession of silent dwellings, hidden bones, invisible death.

The first thing I found was the Plate.

The cavern was enormous, palatial in comparison to the others, its roof stretching upwards far beyond the feeble torchlight. The walls were curved, making the chamber into a huge cylinder, with a vast spiral staircase encircling its perimeter and leading upwards into the black void. At the top of these steps, I knew, rested the Plate, heavy and heartless, as undeniable as a death sentence. Even if I ascended the stairs and hammered on it with all my might, the ancient thing would absorb and deaden the sound as though I didn't exist at all. I thought about the guards patrolling above it, oblivious to the suffering and drama unfolding mere miles below.

If I escaped this hell, I thought, I would make it my mission to move that hateful thing, to emancipate at least the memory of the people that had lived beneath it, even if their physical bodies had long since passed on. Then I remembered the foul miasma that the dying man had spoken of, and realised that moving the Plate would release its doom into the City above. But did I believe him?

A door, he had said. What could that even mean?

As if on cue, my body was racked by a sudden fit of coughing, and I covered my mouth as I stooped, hacking like the old man who had claimed to be my junior. I recovered and continued my wandering, hurrying to the other side of the gargantuan plaza, trying to ignore the flecks of blood I had seen spattered on my hands. Soon I found a tunnel mouth that was much more roughly-hewn than the others, its jagged edges suggesting a path carved in haste, perhaps in excitement. Young men and women, their bodies bent but not yet broken by years in the Mines, their passion ignited by a charismatic leader. Their vengeful bloodlust demanding to be slaked.

And yet, somehow, Millis had conspired to alter their course. To plant seeds of doubt amongst their number, to sew them into enough discord that Cotton's regiment had splintered into two. Perhaps he was merely seeking to stop the invasion, and the blight that had consumed this place – this buried metropolis whose size had astonished me, whose unforgiving bedrock walls housed more people than I had thought possible – had some other cause entirely.

Or perhaps he had found something he had been unable to ignore.

I proceeded along the tunnel, holding my torch aloft as the faint illumination of the main chamber faded behind me. Its light caught something in the distance, a glinting circle that at first had the unsettling appearance of a hideous eye, watching me from the shadows. I approached cautiously, and realised as I proceeded that the main tunnel curved away in a coarsely-chiselled arc. The glowing thing, hovering in the air like a polished coin, was straight ahead of me, down a separate fork that led straight ahead. I continued, frowning as I realised that this new path had perfectly straight walls, as though a lot more time and care had been taken in its construction. But why would Millis, or Cotton, suddenly decide to do that?

Unless this second tunnel had *already been here.*

I continued towards the floating light, perhaps another eight hundred yards, realising eventually that it was in fact a metallic disc, jutting out of the floor. It was scarcely larger than a shield, and at first I could make no sense of it, until I saw that beneath it was a narrow cylindrical shaft, with a metallic ladder leading downwards into the black void beneath. It must be some sort of trapdoor, whose appearance and craftsmanship suggested similar origins to the great Plate itself.

Even more unsettling was the emblem carved into the face of the mysterious hatchway.

A circle, with three outward-facing blades.

The symbol of the Subterranic Order, here in the bowels of the earth.

*

My feet clanged against the ladder's steps as I climbed, the sound echoing up and down the shaft like the toll of a church bell. I realised how quiet this place was, how starved of sound I had been for many hours, save for the soft drip-drip of distant water and the ever more frequent rattle of my own worsening cough. The light from my torch did not extend further than a few steps beneath me, revealing a seemingly endless series of rungs. I fought to concentrate on the laborious descent despite the pain of my worsening headache, feeling occasionally dizzy and nauseated, worried that I might lose my grip. But I focused on the cold reality of the ladder, and on the systematic movements of my hands and feet, moving as rhythmically as one of the Inferior's mining machines. Eventually, with a deep sigh of relief, I felt my foot strike solid ground.

I turned to find myself in a narrow passage; like the tunnel above, it seemed painstakingly precise, its edges perfectly straight, its ceiling smooth and indented with clear strips that served no obvious purpose. The walls were painted an off-white shade the colour of bad teeth, and the floor was covered with a sheet of metal that bore a repeated criss-cross pattern. It sloped downwards as I proceeded, my footsteps echoing once again in the tight space.

What had Millis found, buried deep beneath the city? Was this some sort of lost temple?

The passage led onwards for maybe a hundred yards before curving around to the left, as though skirting the edge of something circular. Soon I began to see evidence of digging, the smooth cream–coloured wall on my right chipped away to reveal iron or steel beneath, like the exposed bone of some terrible mechanical monster. I stared, baffled, momentarily gripped by another fit of wheezing. To my left, the wall had been breached, this time not hiding solid metal but smashed wood and brick, and a dark void that led downwards into the guts of this perplexing structure.

A short way past this cavity I found a door, set into the right-hand wall. A rectangular plane of metal, whose edges seemed to have been somehow melted into the surrounding surface. All around it, the paint had been scraped away, but no way past the impenetrable portal had been found.

I reached out to touch it, almost expecting to feel the power of whatever it concealed; heat, or the pulsating hum of something ancient and malign. But instead I felt only the chill of hard metal, thick and enduring.

With my fingers, I traced the icon engraved on the door's surface: the sign of the Order, once again.

Not just any door. This was *the* door, of which the dying man had spoken.

*

In the chamber below I finally found them.

Their corpses were appalling. Dozens of men and women, virtually indistinguishable from each other, sitting or lying around the edge of the large rectangular space. Their hair had fallen out, their rotting skin sloughed from the putrefying flesh beneath. The stink of their accumulated shit, vomit and decay was almost unbearable. This room was like Hell, compressed into a cube.

Resting in its centre was a large metal lozenge, about the length of two men lying with their feet pressed together, and about a quarter of this in width. Behind it, the floor was heavily scored, the marks leading through an open doorway to suggest the thing had been dragged from beyond. It looked heavy, and must have taken an immense effort by those that had hauled it this far, before they all inexplicably lay down to die. My torchlight sketched frightening shapes on its curved surface, which was flat and smooth apart from one raised symbol: an embossed emblem, now familiar.

I coughed violently, ejecting a crimson lump of sputum onto the floor. My tongue sensed the coppery taste of blood, and I reached upwards to feel inside my mouth; my tongue and lips felt swollen, my gums tender and receded. When I tugged at my front teeth, they were alarmingly loose. I realised how itchy and inflamed my entire body felt. This thing, this unfathomable capsule, was undoubtedly the epicentre, the source of whatever unseen evil had been unleashed.

It didn't take long to find Millis among the bodies. He was lying on his back close to the bizarre object, as though he had lay down to ponder its mysteries. The funereal robes of his religion covered his head and body, as if he had known his fate long before setting foot in this grisly chamber. A sudden urge compelled me to remove the veil from his face, half-expecting to find him wearing a beatific smile; instead I saw a young man, not much older than me, with a vacant look of bewilderment in his eyes. His lips were swollen, his skin the same darkened shade as that of the dying man.

I vomited then, but not in horror or disgust. It was as though simply being near the priest's obscene trophy was enough to mangle your innards. I felt like an invisible hand was reaching inside me, squeezing my guts, prodding at my brain like an inquisitive child. My head began to swim, and I reeled towards the capsule, reaching out to steady myself but then pitching sideways at the last minute so I did not touch its baleful, gleaming surface. Instead I collapsed to the ground, overcome by nausea as I gagged and retched, my stomach attempting to unmake itself.

When the sickness abated, I clambered woozily to my feet. I felt exhausted, more so than ever in my life. But what could I do? There was no way to go but onwards, into the hole through which the infernal device had been dragged. Like an apparition, I drifted towards it, ducking through the open doorway. Another metal walkway led downwards, my steps faltering as my weakening legs threatened to betray me. I saw the tracks left by the capsule's passage, marvelling again at the determination that had brought it this far. More coughing conspired to tear the lining from my throat as I followed the tunnel through another door and out into a large chamber.

I stopped, frowning in puzzlement. If I had expected some grand cathedral, an ancient shrine where the artefact was worshipped by our long-buried ancestors, then this was not it. Instead I found myself in an empty room, its low ceiling latticed with pipes like the hub of a factory. At the centre of the roof was a huge, ragged hole, as though something had burned through from above. The tracks led towards this fissure and stopped beneath it, amongst heaps of strange, grey dust. I walked towards the breach, the peculiar ash deadening my footsteps as though I was plodding through a desert. I stopped twice to cough, feeling bile rise in my gullet once more, and wondered at the source of this heaped substance that looked like grey sand.

I reached the hole and looked upwards, finding it a struggle to even lift my torch. Beyond the ruined ceiling was another chamber, apparently much larger than this one, its own roof far beyond the range of my light source. I saw the outlines of steps and criss-crossing walkways. Machines were mounted on the walls, their circular dials seeming to stare back down at me. This was a place that spoke of technology far beyond anything we had conceived of in Lodehearth. *My wildest dreams, made real.*

But that could wait, for now. I was tired. I reached up to clutch my pounding head, so groggy that I barely registered surprise when a large lock of hair came away in my hand. Sleep. That was all I needed. It was so clear to me now.

I lay down in the dust, and closed my eyes.

SOURCE

Sometimes, when you first awaken from sleep, there's a strange moment when your surroundings feel fluid, undecided; as though the universe is trying to figure out which of the things in your head it's going to retain, and which it's going to discard, to consign to the barely-remembered abyss of dream fragments. But, just for that moment, *anything* could be real. That lottery win; that horrible disfigurement; that incredible rendezvous with your workplace crush; that devastating public humiliation; all of them become, fleetingly, the truth. And then they aren't, because normality is restored.

But not that night. That night, it was as though the dream had leaked out of my head and permeated our house. Because, instead of lying in bed next to me, Katie was gone, and there was a loud banging sound coming from downstairs. Banging, and shouting.

I squeezed my eyes together as though willing these last remnants of my dream to dissipate, but the sounds, and Katie's absence, were insistent. It was as though I was still trapped in that moment of transition, and these imaginings had willed themselves into existence. Parts of my brain seemed to fire up gradually, each corroborating what the others were perceiving, slowly convincing my conscious self that, yes, this was actually happening.

Katie was gone, and someone was screaming and hammering, downstairs.

Even as I leapt out of bed, tugging a dressing gown around me, and a horrible dread pumped icy adrenaline through my veins, I realised that the voice was Katie's. I couldn't make out her words, but she sounded utterly distraught.

My mind struggled to piece together these abnormal inputs, trying desperately to conjure an adequate explanation. Each was more distressing than the last. Katie had sneaked downstairs and drank an entire bottle of whiskey while I slept, even though it was a Tuesday night and we both had to be up early for meetings at work. Katie was shouting at a burglar. Katie had injured herself fixing a midnight snack.

We are lucky enough to have a large, detached house – a benefit of our stressful jobs in property development, and our decision not to have children – and it therefore takes quite a few strides to get from our bedroom to the top of the staircase. As I reached it I saw Jake, our ragdoll cat, cowering in the corner and staring down towards the bottom of the stairs, his blue eyes wide and confused.

Rain had been hammering down that evening, and while we slept it seemed to have developed into a full-blown storm. At that moment, as I looked with bewilderment at the terror on our pet's face, there was an almighty clap of thunder, and for a second I wondered if that was all it was, just the weather rising to a crescendo outside, and I had mistaken its cacophony for the pounding and wailing I thought I'd heard.

But then there was another deafening crash from beneath me, seeming to come from right at the foot of the stairs. I will admit that I shrank back for a moment, as though mimicking the cat's pose, pinned to the spot in primal fear. Then Katie screamed, and I forgot all apprehension, and darted past Jake and onto the staircase, a murderous cry of my own boiling up from my throat.

It wasn't an intruder. At the bottom of the stairs, Katie stood facing our front door, completely naked apart from the knickers she'd been wearing in bed. With one hand, she was rattling ineffectually at the lock, while with her other hand she was driving her fist again and again into the wood, hard enough to draw blood. As I watched, dumbfounded, another harrowing cry burst out of her, and she drove her head forward, shattering one of the door's glass panes.

I dashed towards her, grabbing her, yanking her head away from the freezing rain that had already lashed her face, making the blood run in rivulets from the cuts she had inflicted on her own forehead. I will never forget her expression, as she turned to look at me with a scalding mix of rage and hatred in her eyes.

"He wants it…" she was shrieking, without forming the consonants properly, almost as though she was drugged. "He wants it back!"

She was strong and determined, words I would normally have meant as a compliment to her, but on this occasion meant it was almost impossible to wrestle her to the ground and restrain her. And then, suddenly, whatever compulsion had driven her receded, and she fell into a deep and peaceful sleep.

"And that was the first time Katie sleepwalked?"

"Yes."

"Good lord."

Anna shook her head, not in disbelief, but more in sympathy, as though aggrieved on my behalf at whatever malign force had had the audacity to disrupt our lives. She took off her glasses and cleaned them obsessively, a nervous habit I'd already noticed despite spending less than an hour in her company.

"And that was twelve months ago?" she verified, her motherly voice and manner incongruent with her slight and youthful appearance. She gave the impression of a thirty-something woman who had been locked away in a library since she had left school: shapeless brown clothes, mousy hair in a long plait, no makeup. She was very pretty, though, and I would be lying if I said she didn't have a certain studious charm, something that was quite the opposite of Katie and her brash, arrogant manner, high-powered suits, and executive job.

"Yes. I remember the date exactly, because it was the week of my fortieth birthday."

"And how have things been since then?"

I paused, unsure how much I should tell her. Then I sighed, deeply, and decided to go all-in; I only realised as the words poured out of me that I hadn't really spoken to anyone about Katie's sleep problems, the strain they were putting on our marriage. This peculiar, bookish woman I'd only recently met was hardly an appropriate confidante – except she was, if what she had told me was true. In fact, she was ideal.

"Terrible. At first we thought it was a one-off, after she slept normally for the next few nights. But then, that weekend, the day before my actual birthday, it happened again – only this time she made it outside. She was in the woods when I found her, all cut up again by the branches and bushes, wandering around half-naked. Screaming that same fucking thing… sorry, pardon my language."

"It's okay," Anna replied, sipping the tea she'd served us in her strange living room, a small space made to seem even smaller by the volume of ornaments and bric-a-brac she had crammed onto every surface and shelf. Teddy bears, framed photographs, weird toby jugs with human faces; all seemed to peer down at me, intrigued by my plight.

"At first we tried putting a lock on our bedroom," I continued, "but she smashed her head against the door so hard that she had to take a week off work with concussion. In the end we had to move her to the spare room, and get… straps fitted, to the bed."

Anna nodded, as though such drastic solutions were familiar to her.

"Katie saw a sleep therapist for a while, but that didn't help. We had to stop having any visitors over to stay because we didn't want to terrify them in the middle of the night. The episodes, as we called them, started to happen more and more frequently, until it was virtually every night that I would wake up to hear Katie screaming and jerking against the restraints."

I sipped the tea, staring into the patterns the milk made on its surface, almost as though I might see a better life taking shape in the swirling brown drink.

"She started drinking," I continued. "If she was pissed, maybe a full bottle of wine or more, the sleepwalking just didn't happen. I'm not sure she deliberately chose the alcoholism over the dreams, not exactly... but that was the outcome."

I shook my head with a mixture of sadness and anger. She was still holding down her job, still functioning, but she was no longer the woman I married. She was irritable, unpredictable, aggressive. And she'd put on so much weight that... was I a monster, for having these needs? *Yes,* the objects around Anna's room seemed to say, gazing down at me with reproach in their eyes, like an assembled courtroom.

"Does Katie ever remember the details of the dreams?" Anna asked, mercifully changing the direction of my thoughts.

I shook my head again. "That first night, I took her to A&E. I think she still didn't believe me about what had happened, even though she could see the cuts on her face. I had to film her to truly convince her of what she was doing."

"So... she has no idea what it is that *he* might want?"

"You mean... the man she's talking about, in her dreams?"

Anna nodded. I recalled how we had met each other. I had been looking up Katie's symptoms online for the thousandth time, searching for anything that might help, prepared even to consider some of the more outlandish cures and remedies I'd previously dismissed. That was when I'd found it: a post on a thread on a health forum that quoted those same haunting words that Katie had been screaming at me for the past year.

He wants it back.

"I don't know," I replied, shivering despite the stuffiness of the room, which felt as though Anna had cranked her radiators up to full blast. I felt suddenly uncomfortable at what I'd disclosed, eager to flip the focus of the interrogation round to Anna herself, about whom I knew nothing other than that she had a brother who was suffering from the same symptoms as Katie. After we had realised we lived surprisingly close to each other – her in Westhoughton, me in Bolton – it had been her suggestion that we meet face to face to discuss matters further.

Why had I accepted? Was it really out of concern for Katie? Or was it because I wanted someone to share my burden with, a new person to talk to that wasn't a work colleague or a drunken, pitiful husk of her former self?

"Tell me about Sam," I said, forcing a smile onto my face.

But Anna didn't say anything. Instead she rose, an oddly graceful motion, as though her torso was floating upwards off the little threadbare sofa, her legs dangling beneath her body like the tendrils of a jellyfish. I still couldn't shake the image of something aquatic as she drifted across to the door, the same one I'd entered through. "Come and see," she said simply, then glided out of the room.

I got up and wandered after her, finding her already halfway up the stairs. The décor in the hallway was shabby and brown, the whole place looking as though it hadn't been painted since the seventies. There was more junk on the shelves out here, too, spilling out of the living room like some sort of organic growth; coupled with the drab colour scheme, it made the place seem suddenly oppressive, constricting. For a second I thought about simply making an excuse and leaving.

But instead I followed her up the stairs, passing the shoes I'd left near the door. Their polished shine seemed out of place, the expensive suit jacket I'd slung over the newel post similarly incongruous. Anna seemed like someone who didn't care about material possessions – or at least, not in the same way that Katie and I did. Our stuff was all top of the range, extravagant; 'hard-earned', as Katie would say. Two cars on the drive. 4K television. Expensive cooking utensils we never used. Anna's home, on the other hand, told a very different story, the story of a family that had lived there for decades, etching its highs and lows and hopes and dreams into the very brickwork itself. There were dozens of photographs on the wall as we ascended, many of them washed-out and faded, depicting people who Anna presumably knew, loved, cherished. The ancient, chocolate-coloured carpet was soft and yielding under my feet, like moss. I noticed that a stair lift had been fitted, and wondered if an ageing relative lived there with her. Or perhaps the house had been handed down through the generations, and she'd just never had the stair lift removed. I tried to remember the last time I'd spoken to my mum, and gnawed guiltily at my lip as I ascended.

Anna's house was small, so there were only four doors upstairs. She stopped at one of them, looking back at me earnestly. I realised how much she was trusting me, a complete stranger, a well-built man who could easily overpower her. Yet here I was, inside her home, being shown… what?

Without a word, she turned and opened the door, and I followed her inside.

It was a small bedroom, adorned once again with pictures, mementos and curios. It seemed brighter than the rest of the house, and I realised that despite it being lunchtime, Anna had kept all of her other curtains closed. But here, sunlight had been allowed to encroach, and its pale glow dappled the face of the man who was sitting at the window, gazing out.

I started at the sight of him and started to mumble an apologetic hello, explaining who I was and why I was there, until I noticed she was shaking her head.

"Sam is catatonic," she explained, a note of melancholy in her voice. "He sits here at the window every day, watching the birds. The only time he moves is if I move him… to wash him, or to take him outside in his wheelchair."

I looked again at the figure seated at the window. He was a man about my age, gone somewhat to fat, his greying hair unkempt and his chin covered in stubble. He looked almost like a man on a stay-at-home vacation, relaxing in his pyjamas, about to enjoy his morning cup of coffee.

But if he was enjoying anything – the sparrows, perhaps, as his sister had said – he didn't display it outwardly. He was utterly still, not turning or moving to acknowledge our presence at all. His arms rested in his lap, and his face was completely blank – not sagging or giving any obvious impression of his ailment, simply frozen in a neutral expression of disinterest.

"How did it happen?" I found myself asking, feeling suddenly very uncomfortable.

"Sam's been like this for five years now. He suffered

from severe depression, and over time it… worsened. The doctors keep telling me it's an unusually long time for someone to remain in such a state."

"There's no injury to his brain?"

Anna shook her head. "He is physically able to move. He just chooses not to, for whatever reason. But that makes it sound like it's his fault. Like he's doing it on purpose."

"And is he?" I said, wincing immediately at the insensitivity of the question.

"No," she replied, patiently. "He needs constant care. After years in hospitals and nursing homes I decided it might be better to bring him back here, to the family home. We inherited it, when our parents died. I lived with my boyfriend back then, and Sam had his own place, so the house had been empty for a while."

"Does your boyfriend live here, too?"

She shook her head again. "No. The strain of caring for Sam… it was too much for Paul, unfortunately." She smiled ruefully, removing and cleaning her glasses once again.

"I'm sorry," I said, lamely. I didn't know what to say. She looked up, and as her eyes caught mine, just for that moment, we were like mirror images, two spirits crushed by the illnesses of others. I felt suddenly awkward, coughing as I looked away.

"So… did moving him here have any effect?"

"Not for a while. Until…"

I remembered why I was here, the real connection

between Anna and me. "He started sleepwalking."

She nodded. "About six months ago. The first time he did it wasn't anywhere near as bad as you described with your wife. I just found him in the morning, standing at the front door. At first I was overjoyed. I thought maybe his condition was starting to improve."

"Did it?"

Another sorrowful shake of the head. "No. When the manifestations are over, he just returns to this state. I think he'd just remain standing there forever if I didn't force him to sit down again."

"He never gets violent?"

She looked increasingly agitated, worrying at her spectacles once again. "Yes. It got worse quite quickly after that. Exactly what you described: beating his fists against the door, hitting his head against it, screaming those horrible words."

"So how do you…?"

She glanced at her brother's bed, a single frame occupying the rest of the wall alongside the door. It had restraints fitted, just like Katie's. Anna's eyes fell, as though she was ashamed. But something had snagged my attention, something she'd said a few moments previously. "What did you mean by manifestations?"

She looked up at me, her expression suddenly defiant. "I believe that these occurrences are spiritual in nature."

My gaze flicked from her, to her brother, to the trinkets and knick-knacks adorning the room. For the first time I noticed crucifixes, crocheted patters saying 'Jesus Loves You'. My heart sank. "You're talking about… possession?"

She nodded vigorously, seemingly encouraged by my understanding. "Yes, exactly! But no-one will listen to me… I haven't even been able to get in touch with a priest who is willing to perform an exorcism."

I backed slowly towards the door. "Look, Anna, I don't… that stuff isn't really my cup of tea."

She frowned, looking hurt. "But, Alex, you've heard the words. This can't just be a coincidence."

But my mind was made up. This had been a foolish venture, a waste of a valuable day's annual leave. I suddenly couldn't bear to spend another minute in that depressing place, with its two tragic occupants. It was hard to know which one I pitied most.

"Well… thank you for the tea, Anna. It was very nice of you to talk to me. But I think maybe I'd better be going."

Her eyes were downcast as I turned to descend the stairs. But as I reached the bottom, she seemed suddenly overcome by her frustration, and leaned over the bannister to shout down to me.

"It won't stop, you know! Not until he gets what he wants from us!"

I'd already grabbed my jacket and was quickly lacing up my shoes, feeling oddly frightened by Anna and her bizarre house and her lonely existence. I turned to the door, ignoring her as I fumbled with the latch, feeling a strange sense of relief when it opened.

Her final parting words echoed in my ears as I hurried away towards the car.

"We need to work out what we've taken from him!"

*

I arrived home early in the afternoon, still many hours before Katie would return from work. I had lied to her that morning, told her that I was going to a conference, that the event had a late start, to make sure she left before me. She'd slept soundly the previous night, thanks to the wine and gin – in fact, there hadn't been a night terror that had disturbed me for almost two weeks. Our goodbye that morning had been pleasant, almost tender. Why had I felt the need to lie?

Because she would resent the interference. She wanted to handle this her own way, with that useless sleep therapist, and gallons of booze.

She never listened to me. The boss at work, the boss at home. I felt resentment twisting my mouth into a sneer as I gazed around the house, at the soulless white walls and minimalist furnishings. What part of this had I chosen? Was any of this what I had once dreamed of?

I went upstairs, glanced into the spare room. Katie's clothes were piled everywhere. A few empty wine bottles stood on the dressing table. Those terrible straps hung from the sides of the bed.

I imagine it isn't what Katie dreamed of, either.

I sank down onto the bed, her bed, my head in my hands. A wave of dejection and failure seemed to engulf me. Gripped by a strange compulsion, I lay back, resting my head on her pillow, smelling the scent of her hair. I fiddled with the restraints, wrapping them around my own wrists to

125

see what it felt like, even though it was impossible to fasten them oneself (I had to do them for her, every night, when she went to bed, often completely comatose from the drink). I stared upwards, my mind seeming to melt into the ceiling's meaningless expanse of white.

We need to work out what we've taken from him.

Maybe Anna was right; perhaps the explanation here truly was something beyond the rational. Maybe Katie really *had* taken something that she shouldn't have. But what? Her job demanded that she evict people from their homes when the land was acquired for redevelopment; was I really supposed to believe that a disgruntled resident was tormenting her in her dreams?

I closed my eyes, squeezing them shut as I tried to wring the answer out of my brain.

Something she doesn't even know she has.

I opened my eyes. The ceiling was still there, a blank canvas, an Antarctic waste, an empty page. On the other side of it was the attic, where Katie kept all sorts of junk: souvenirs, keepsakes, memorabilia… just like Anna, only Katie's were hidden away, like our real selves, the children concealed behind the suits and the fast cars.

I stepped out onto the landing and pulled open the hatch to the loft.

*

I am an organised person – Katie would say a fastidious one – and because she rarely goes into the attic, I've been able to arrange things up there exactly how I like them. This means boxes piled in neat, geometrically pleasing rows, each container of identical dimensions and clearly labelled to detail its contents. Other boxes, those that came with larger items like the TV or the coffee machine, are arranged against the opposite wall, their non-standard shapes stacked and re-stacked until I was satisfied that I had made the most efficient use of the available space.

We haven't yet had the loft fully converted into an additional bedroom – partly because, if we did, I have no idea where we'd store all of this stuff – but it is floored, and there is a light switch fitted, and an extendable ladder for easy access. Yes, there are cobwebs here and there, and I don't doubt that a menagerie of insects is harboured within its dark corners, but it isn't a room I'd necessarily call 'creepy'. So the trepidation I felt didn't arise from a fear of the attic itself; rather, it was a reaction to the daunting size of the task ahead of me, and an innate disgust at the idea of creating disarray up there, ruining the pristine orderliness I had toiled to create.

There were dozens of boxes labelled 'Katie's stuff', followed by a number. I'd nagged and nagged her to throw some of these items away, or to at least to help me organise them into categories – photo albums, childhood toys, old cinema tickets – but she wouldn't hear of it. She loved her shoe boxes stuffed with memories, and had no interest at all in scaling back her collection; if anything, the additional storage space only seemed to encourage her to hoard more paraphernalia. I was genuinely concerned that the weight of accumulated crap would cause the ceiling to buckle.

Ah, well. Might as well start with box number 1. Unable to remember its contents and unsure of what exactly I was hoping to find, I removed the lid.

It was full of Katie's old sketchbooks. She had been a talented artist in her high school days. She still was, I suppose; not that she ever utilised that particular aptitude anymore. I opened one of the yellowing pads, admiring the crisp and precise pencil strokes with which she had skilfully captured a sunflower, a woodland scene, an image of her father. A self-portrait. I studied it, seeing Katie there, my Katie, not the miserable corporate mercenary she had become. Her smile was different, this being years before the dental work she'd recently undergone, and I suppose it was less perfect than her gleaming new grin, which was polished in all the senses of that word. But I preferred it.

I found myself touching the drawing with my fingertip, thinking about myself at that age, carefree and popular. Happy. Two happy people who met, and found each other's company made them even happier.

What went wrong? It wasn't only the sleepwalking. Things had started to deteriorate way before that.

I opened another sketchpad. This one contained darker images, renderings of twisted trees, screaming faces. Typical teenage angst, you might have said – but it was clear that Katie had truly meant it, truly felt it, at the time. Whatever adolescent torment she had been going through was palpable as I leafed through the haunting pictures. A woman with her head in her hands, mirroring my earlier posture. A slender, shadowy figure, its head tilted at an odd angle as it stared out at me.

I shuddered slightly, and carefully placed the books back into the box.

The next one contained a load of old tickets from gigs and other events Katie had attended over the years. Most of them were from before we'd met, and featured 90s bands I was never particularly into (King Adora, Weezer, Supergrass), but I smiled as I spotted a stub for something we'd attended together. Suede had performed an exclusive run of the *Dog Man Star* album at Brixton Academy in 2011, playing the entire record in order. It was an LP we both really liked, and it was rare to find something we could truly enjoy together, rather than just spending our money on expensive meals, decadent shopping trips, exclusive holiday resorts. We'd got drunk, pushed our way to the front, danced like teenagers. Felt in love.

My search continued like this, the boxes shedding no light on Katie's sleep problems, but presenting lots of surprises nonetheless. Fragments of forgotten memories, the tiny parts that made up the whole of a person, a person I had loved, wanted to love. At one point I wiped a teardrop from my eye, then felt suddenly foolish.

After a couple of hours, my reverie was interrupted by the buzzing of my phone in my pocket, signifying an e-mail received (it was somewhat depressing that I could distinguish between texts and e-mails purely by the length of the vibration).

Sorry to contact you directly, but we need to talk. Please call me on the number below. He wants it back.

There were no other contact details, no name or signature of any kind. Was it Anna? The message wasn't from her account, and the number was unfamiliar. Besides, my e-mail address was freely available from the forum; anyone could have easily obtained it.

He wants it back.

But how would anyone else know the significance of that phrase?

Unless there were others.

I tidied away the boxes, climbed back down the ladder, closed up the loft, left no trace of my fruitless investigation. Then I dialled the number, making sure to withhold my own details.

A man's voice answered on the second ring. "Hello?"

"Who is this?"

"Ah. You must be OverTired, from the forum?"

The voice referenced my handle on the site, making me feel a little embarrassed.

"Who is this?" I said again, firmly.

"I'm sorry if my e-mail was somewhat forward." The voice was curt, and sounded hoarse, as though the speaker was suffering from a head cold. "But I didn't think we had time to bat messages back and forth."

I felt impatience rising within me. "Look, you're going to have to tell me what this is about."

"You already know," came the immediate retort.

I prepared a rejoinder, my initial reaction to be offended by this abrasive stranger. But he was right. I did know exactly what this was about. I closed and reopened my mouth, a different reply forming on my lips. "Are you... having the dreams too?"

"I am. I want to know if your wife sees the same things as me."

"She doesn't remember anything when she wakes up."

There was no response, as though the speaker had been caught off guard.

"Can you at least give me your name?" I pressed.

An exhalation of breath at the other end of the line. "I'm on the forum as Somnambulist."

Okay, have it your way, I thought. I didn't recognise the moniker, but perhaps this oddball rarely posted anything. Just an observer.

"And what about you, Somnambulist?" I knew that this word meant 'sleepwalker'. "What do you see?"

The man gave another deep, wheezing sigh, and then a series of small coughs. I was on the verge of hanging up when he finally spoke again.

"I'm sorry... I'm just not good with people. I live alone. I don't get out much. Except when..." Another succession of tickly coughs, as though he was suffering from some unpleasant throat infection. "I thought I was going mad. Then I saw your posts on the forum, and realised I wasn't the only person having these... visions. Would it maybe be possible to speak with your wife?"

"She's out," I snapped, still wary of this eccentric stranger.

He coughed again, more deeply this time, as though the convulsions were wracking his entire body. I waited patiently while the outburst subsided. It was only after several seconds that I realised he was, in fact, sobbing.

"I'm sorry," he said again, composing himself. "I just

need to share this with someone. The visions... they've become unbearable."

"What do you mean?"

The man who called himself Somnambulist sniffed. "For months I thought I was going insane. Schizophrenia, delusions, whatever. But then the details started to become... crisper. I still wake up to find myself lying in the street, or bashing my fists raw against the front door, or halfway down a road I don't even recognise... but now I can at least *remember*."

"Go on," I said, barely able to contain my eagerness to hear the details.

"The dream always starts the same. I'm following the man. We aren't anywhere specific... or at least somehow my surroundings don't matter. All I know is it's dark, and I'm walking, and he's there, about twenty metres ahead of me."

"What man?"

"He's facing away from me, walking, matching my pace. He wears a coat and hood. The material is black, some sort of waterproof fabric, and that's when I realise it's raining. The water is running down his coat, and behind him it's leaving a trail. A thick, red trail, as though gallons of blood are being washed off him. It flows around my feet, past me, away into the darkness. But I'm following it, like... a path."

"Does he say anything to you?"

"Not... not exactly. But I know that I have to keep following, otherwise terrible things will happen. And it isn't as though I have any choice. My feet just plant themselves in that terrible stream, one in front of the other, all that blood splashing between my shoes." He took a deep, wavering breath, as though trying desperately to keep his emotions under control. "But that isn't the worst part. The worst part is, after a while, after what feels like days of walking, endless walking, miles and miles of blood... he stops. And waits for me to catch up."

He is shaken by sobbing once again, but I feel no pity for this peculiar man. Only exasperation, a burning need for him to reach the end of his tale. "And?"

"Sometimes I wake up before I reach him. Those are the good nights. But other times... as I get closer... he turns to look at me. But his face isn't a face at all. It's like a *void*. A portal. In it you can see such terrible atrocities. People gagged and bound, mutilated. Women screaming while they are sliced open. Hands tightening around throats. It's like a... a montage of human suffering. As if, under the cloak, *that's all he's made of*."

I felt myself tremble as I pictured that face, imagining that same baleful figure turning to look at me. At Katie. But still I wasn't satisfied. "And... is that it? Is that when you wake up?" My voice had risen to a desperate cry.

"Yes... at first. But not the last few times. That's when I finally realised that he wanted something from me. He doesn't say so. He just points, with one gloved hand. Reaches out with one finger – they're long and thin, like knitting needles – and points at what he wants."

Downstairs, I heard the front door opening. Katie, arriving home. I couldn't let her overhear this conversation. "And what is it? *What does he want?*"

The Somnambulist exhaled again, long and laboured, as

though exhausted. "Last year, I had surgery on my right eye. Keratoconus. Quite common, actually. One in 2,000 people."

What on earth was he talking about? "I don't understand. What does this have to do–"

"It's where your cornea bulges outwards into a cone shape. Messes up your vision, causes scarring. In the end I had to have a cornea transplant."

"Is that you, Alex?" It was Katie, calling up to me.

"Look, whoever you are… I can't stay on the phone. I need–"

"My eye. *He points to my eye.*"

I hung up just as Katie opened the door, forcing a smile despite the shudder that rattled my body.

*

That night was the nicest evening we'd had for a long time. We talked, properly talked, without the TV on in the background or our gazes glued to our phones. We kissed. Yes, she drank, but I did too, and it seemed almost like a celebration. A new beginning. When she went to bed, I suggested she sleep with me, that I would look after her if there was any 'unwanted activity', as we called it.

"You know that won't work, Alex. I'm sorry. We'll get it sorted, I promise. Just come and tuck me in, like normal."

After I tied her wrists, I looked down at her, seeing someone vulnerable, someone who needed affection, the sort of undying devotion that Anna showed to her brother.

The girl from the sketchpad. I opened my mouth to say something about that day's bizarre events, suddenly compelled to tell her everything. As crazy as it sounded, I almost asked whether she'd had a cornea implant I didn't know about.

"What is it?" she said, frowning up at me.

But I just smiled, and bent to kiss her forehead. "Sleep well, sweetheart," I said as I switched off the light.

Back in the main bedroom, feeling the usual twinge of guilt at having such a large bed all to myself, I sent a single e-mail from my phone, to Anna.

Sorry about today. I just wasn't ready for the spiritual stuff. I hope we can talk again. I also have a question, which might seem a weird one, but please humour me: before the dreams started, did Sam have any surgery?

Then I went to sleep. Katie didn't wake me. I slept more soundly than I had for a long time.

In the morning, she was gone.

*

"When did you notice she was missing?"

I felt numb, stumbling through the day as if in a trance, not quite believing that what was happening was real.

Trapped in the transition from a dream.

"I woke up and her bedroom door was open. The front door too."

"And you're sure she hasn't just gone somewhere else, and didn't close the door properly? You've tried her work, friends, family…?"

I turned to look at the policeman, knowing I should be angry that he obviously hadn't listened about the sleepwalking, about the reason we slept in different rooms. But instead I felt nothing. I just nodded, dumbly.

"You'd be surprised how often this happens," he continued, trying to sound comforting, and failing. "A husband calls us to say his wife has disappeared during the night, and it turns out she's left him, and there's a note somewhere he hasn't found yet. An e-mail, perhaps. Did you check your inbox?"

The burly copper placed an arm on my shoulder and gave me an encouraging smile. I took out my phone, dazedly complying with his suggestion, scanning the list of e-mails I'd received so far that day. Lots of work stuff, various newsletters and phishing scams, something from Anna… but nothing from Katie.

I'd already used the phone that morning of course, calling Katie a dozen times before I realised her phone was still in her room, buzzing away in her handbag, which also hadn't been taken. In fact, it appeared that not a single possession, not a shred of clothing other than the nightdress she'd been wearing, had disappeared along with her. Just like that night she'd first stumbled out into the woods in the rain, she could be lost, alone, naked, freezing to death.

That image spurred me into action. I batted his hand away.

"Look, she hasn't left me. I've already told you she's sleepwalked somewhere. You people should be out searching the forests, combing the streets for her. She might have fallen into a ditch, been hit by a car..." My words choked off at the horror of the idea.

"So this sleepwalking. You say that's why she has to sleep tied to the bed?" He eyed me sceptically.

I sighed and nodded. "Yes. Her episodes can be violent, so we keep her restrained while she sleeps. This morning the straps were broken – she must have ripped them open, somehow."

"But you didn't hear anything?"

I shook my head, sensing his disbelief. I didn't believe it either. How could she have torn herself free without waking me?

The constable wrote a final entry in his notebook, finishing with a flourish, and then placed his hand back on my shoulder, staring squarely at me. "I think that's enough information for now, Mr Sheppard. Leave it with us. Rest assured, we're doing everything we can to find her."

Then he left, and I couldn't shake the sense that Katie had become an entry in a database somewhere; a non-crime, a grown woman who had fled her broken marriage and a dreadful husband who kept her strapped down in the spare room.

What could I do? I made myself a cup of tea, waiting, not sure for what. After a while I phoned the Somnambulist, but the call went straight to voicemail.

Then I tried Anna. She answered without answering, just silence and rapid breathing replacing the ringtone. Anna, if that's who it was, sounded distraught.

"Anna?" I ventured.

"Alex… it's a bad time right now."

"What's wrong?"

Her breathing was so fast it sounded as though she was having an anxiety attack. "It's Sam. He disappeared last night. The door was hanging off its hinges, like he got up and smashed his way out of the house."

"Oh my god," was all I could muster in reply. I couldn't even formulate the words to begin to tell her about Katie.

"I'm… really sorry…" Her breath came in ragged gasps. "I'll call you back later." Her voice cracked as she formed the final syllable, and she hung up.

I closed my eyes, squeezing the phone in my hand. I felt so helpless, so utterly pathetic. There had to be something. The dreams… Anna… her brother… the strange man that had called me yesterday.

He wants it back.

My phone hummed as another pointless e-mail came through, Amazon trying to sell me a product I already owned. I almost hurled the device across the room, but then I noticed Anna's e-mail from late last night, still unread. I opened it.

That's okay. I'm sorry if I came on a bit strong. I just need someone to talk to about what's happening. I hope we can try again. You seem very nice.

Very best regards,

Anna x

I stared at the phone, feeling a chill seep through me as I read the final part of her message.

PS: Yes, Sam had surgery last year – some teenagers tipped him out of his wheelchair and he ruptured a tendon in his ankle. Why do you ask?

*

The dentist's receptionist had been very helpful, and confirmed that all of their bone allografts came from a local supplier called *Legacy Tissue Solutions*, based in Macclesfield. Yes, they'd been using them for many years. No, they didn't have any records of exactly who the bones came from – this wasn't like an organ transplant, where the lung or kidney was extracted from a live patient or recently deceased donor and inserted immediately into the recipient.

"Tissue donation doesn't work that way."

Her words still churned in my head as I sped down the M60.

I'd googled the industry immediately after our conversation, and had been shocked by what I learned. I'd never signed up to be an organ donor, so I hadn't realised the extent to which a human body could be… *harvested*. As well as the obvious components – heart, lungs, kidneys, liver – it seemed many more things could be recycled. Skin shaved off and stored for use in grafts, helping burn victims to recover. Corneas and tendons extracted and used for transplants. Bones removed and sculpted into screws and anchors for dental and orthopaedic application, or ground down and made into surgical glues.

And there was a black market, of course. The gruesome practise of illegal tissue trafficking had been documented in a variety of countries, including even the USA. Apparently there had been numerous instances of unscrupulous morticians literally stripping corpses for parts, without the consent of the deceased or their family: a disease-free cadaver could be worth upwards of £100,000.

Bodies reduced to 'human sock puppets' in their caskets, their bones replaced with plastic piping for the funeral.

The man in the dream… had I discovered what the Somnambulist, what Sam and Katie, had taken from him? I knew it was crazy. I knew what I was doing made no sense. What did I even expect to find? The three of them shuffling along the hard shoulder of the motorway?

I floored the accelerator, coasting past the afternoon traffic. I used my hands-free kit to dial Anna, smacking the steering wheel in frustration when the call went straight to voicemail – I had a feeling she was the only person that might entertain my theory. There was no point even attempting to explain myself to the police.

The sun was already fading when I drove into the little industrial estate on the outskirts of town. *Legacy Tissue Solutions* was housed inside a tiny warehouse, a prefab cuboid that seemed somehow too inconsequential to be dealing in such important materials. I didn't turn into the small car park, but pulled up instead on the pavement nearby, staring out of my window at the innocuous structure.

I hadn't planned this far. I wanted answers, but didn't even know the questions. Without thinking about what I was going to do, I climbed out of the car and strode towards the main entrance.

I noticed the door was slightly ajar as I approached, and carefully pushed it open to look inside. The building was partitioned off into separate rooms; I was peering into a modest reception area, with a desk and a chair facing the entrance. The chair was unoccupied. On the desk was a phone, which was ringing. I hovered in the doorway, waiting to see if anyone would emerge from inside the warehouse to answer it. No one did. Eventually the ringing ceased, and the sudden silence was thick and stifling. The place seemed still, empty, as though abandoned.

I frowned and stepped inside, glancing at the desk's other contents: an archaic computer, various printed invoices and purchase orders, a visitors' book. A black ledger, open on a page listing that day's appointments. I glanced at my watch: 16:35. They were apparently expecting a delivery in ten minutes.

I skirted the desk and pushed open the internal door, which led to the main storage area. I stopped, gazing around at rows and rows of metallic cabinets, stacked on top of each other all the way to the roof. There were wheeled ladders on either side of the space, like the kind you might find in an old library, to enable access to the upper tiers. Once again, there was no-one around.

I walked across to one of the units, noticing the label, a series of letters and numbers that meant nothing to me. I tugged open the door and cold air seeped out like a wintry breath. Inside the refrigerator were dozens of white plastic tubs. I grimaced as I imagined someone sitting at the reception desk, bulk-buying them online. Cutting costs. An efficient operation. I closed the door, not wanting to know exactly what was inside those innocent-looking containers, which seemed like nothing more consequential than yoghurt pots.

Then I noticed the blood. A crimson trail led from one of the storage units towards the partition wall at the other end of the warehouse, passing through an opening that was covered by hanging plastic flaps. The delivery yard, presumably. I thought about looking inside the fridge, but instead I headed towards the dangling strips, sliding cautiously between them.

The delivery area was empty aside from a few stacked wooden pallets. It was open to the road outside, a metal shutter rolled up to enable vehicles to reverse straight in for unloading.

A woman was hanging from the shutter, a piece of electrical cord wrapped tightly around her neck. At first I thought she was some sort of bizarre Halloween decoration, because from the neck down her body hung like a piece of fabric, swaying in the soft breeze. There was no substance, no weight at all to her torso, her legs, her arms.

Like a sock puppet.

The gory trail I had followed ended in a congealing pool in the centre of the yard, fed by a steady drip-drip of blood that leaked from the suspended, eviscerated body. The woman's face seemed to peer down at me, and it was only then that I realised her eyes had been taken too, the sockets as empty as those of a rubber mask.

I gagged, almost vomiting. Then I saw movement, outside, beyond the grisly cadaver.

A narrow lane led into the delivery yard, and a van had just started to reverse down it, seemingly oblivious to the figures that had lined up on either side of the road as though forming a guard of honour. Around twenty people were assembled, standing in two neat rows, perfectly still. Men, women, old and young, there seemed to be no uniformity to their appearance, their gender or attire.

Except that all of them were caked in blood.

As I stared, appalled, and the delivery van continued its approach, I realised that at least some of the blood must be their own. Each of them seemed badly injured: great gashes were carved into some of their necks, deep gouges torn from torsos, skin clawed from their faces and hanging in strands like peeled fruit. One woman's forearm had been sliced open, the tendons inside protruding from the wound like loose wiring. Another man's face was covered in dark gore that seeped from the ruin of his right eye socket.

He points to my eye.

I scanned their faces frantically and spotted Samuel, a man normally confined to a wheelchair. Now he stood, but awkwardly, his left foot folded onto its side. I could see blood spurting from a deep incision in his ankle, but like all the others, he seemed unaware of the injury he'd sustained. He simply stared forwards, exactly as he had done in his bedroom the previous day, exactly as all the others did.

Sleepwalking.

I saw Katie at the head of one of the grim columns. She didn't react when I shouted her name, sprinted towards her, waving frantically at the delivery driver to stop. It was only when I reached her that I saw her jaw was hanging loosely from her face, as though wrenched out of place. Many of her teeth were missing, blood oozing from her mouth and dribbling down her chin.

Tears filled my vision as I called her name over and over again. She just stared placidly back at me, as though waiting patiently for the delivery to arrive.

*

After Alex Sheppard contacted the police, the attending officers were able to wake the sleepwalkers, who had no recollection of their crime, or how their own injuries had been sustained. It remains unclear whether they were self-inflicted, or whether the group had performed the mutilations upon each other.

The delivery driver fled the scene when he noticed the sleepwalkers, but was subsequently traced and identified as Nicolas Haledjian, a local mortician. A subsequent investigation revealed that he had illegally harvested tissue from hundreds of corpses. When the scandal was reported in the national papers, they included the news that one of the bodies processed by Dr Haledjian was found to be that of the infamous serial murderer, Charles Durant, but inadequate record-keeping meant there was no way to ascertain exactly which patients had received his tissues.

The dead woman was found to be Cheryl Aspinall, a former pathologist and the sole proprietor of Legacy Tissue Solutions. Her organs and bones were found stuffed inside one of the refrigerators. No proof could be found that Cheryl Aspinall's company had any knowledge of Haledjian's misdemeanours.

Katie underwent major reconstructive surgery and recovered from her injuries, and was never troubled by her dreams again. Sadly, several of the other sleepwalkers died, either from their wounds or, in the case of Mark Rogan – the man calling himself the Somnambulist – from heart failure after going into shock upon awakening.

Samuel Jeffries also recovered, and continues to live in Westhoughton under the care of his sister. He shows no sign of remembering anything about the incident, and remains unable to move or communicate. His sleepwalking episodes have ceased.

The teeth, tendons, bones and other body parts removed from the sleepwalkers were never found.

MONOLITH

First there was the Gherkin. Then came the Walkie Talkie, the Scalpel, the Cheesegrater. But London's obsession with teaming ostentatious architecture with asinine nicknames didn't end there. Now Erika was staring up at the latest inhabitant of the city's constantly reinvented skyline: the Domino.

That was the Mitre Building's most common moniker. Some people called it the Monolith, because the sinister black cuboid looked exactly like the mysterious alien structures featured in *2001: A Space Odyssey*, except scaled up to over 250 metres in height, and boasting 59 floors. The original intention had been to include a mixture of commercial office space, restaurants and other tourist attractions behind its one-way glass, but when WellCo Pharmaceutical offered to take out a long lease on the entire site, the developer had been happy to adjust their plans. Now the public could only stare at the imposing edifice from outside, wondering at the activities taking place behind those sleek surfaces, the company's premises as impenetrable as a block of obsidian.

Erika didn't like big pharma. She didn't like the fact that half the population, including several of her own team, were hooked on the company's revolutionary performance-enhancement drug, Epigene. She didn't like WellCo's insistence that introducing genetic material from animals to supplement a person's own genetic code was completely harmless, despite widespread concerns about the treatment's lasting effects. She didn't like the fact that her brother was relying on doses of bear protein to win powerlifting contests, or that her mum was knocking back daily capsules of eagle DNA to make her eyesight better.

And she *definitely* didn't like the fact that the Monolith had been completely offline for two days, or that the first Special Ops team despatched to investigate had ceased all communication about an hour after going inside.

"We have to assume the worst here," she barked at her five male subordinates as they travelled towards the scene. "There could be a terrorist incident, with active hostiles. Maybe multiple hostages. Going dark for this long means there is a strong likelihood that Alpha Team are dead, so we know that the threat is very real."

Haskins smacked the wall of the van angrily at that point. She understood his feelings perfectly; she'd had friends in that unit too. But she needed everyone cool, calm, focused. She squatted to his eye level, her face centimetres from his.

"Do I need to replace you, Terry? If you can't handle your emotions, I don't want you on this team. You're too much of a risk to the rest us."

At forty-four years old, Haskins was ten years her senior, as lean and battle-hardened as they came. For a moment his expression was twisted with barely-contained fury, before he swallowed hard.

"Sorry chief. You can count on me. I'm a professional."

She nodded, and resumed her tactical briefing. When she saw him gulping something down shortly afterwards, she wondered what animal extract he was using to calm himself. Sloth? Koala? But she didn't say anything; the pills weren't illegal, after all. And the truth was that she couldn't afford to swap Terry out at this late stage. She needed his experience if they were to have any hope of recovering the Alpha Team, or at least of finding out what was going on inside that menacing, shadowy structure.

They emerged from the van into a violent sunset, the colour of burnt flesh. Its hellish glow reflected grotesquely off the glass and steel structures around them, but the Monolith itself appeared impervious to the light; instead it seemed to absorb it, towering above them like a ghastly silhouette as they hurried towards its front doors. Reynolds took the lead, his ballistic shield protecting them from an unexpected attack from any of the windows. He was followed by Haskins, who was their method of entry specialist, and carried a Remington shotgun. Next was Singh the baton officer, whose primary role was to engage any unarmed offenders they encountered, followed by Erika herself, Wang the prisoner reception officer, and finally Powell at the rear, covering them with his Heckler & Koch 9mm carbine. Beta Team were a well-drilled unit, their movements precise and efficient as they scuttled towards the entrance, six parts of the same organism.

The glass of the doors was as impermeably dark as the rest of the structure; a gap had been left between them by Alpha Team's forced ingress earlier that day, but no light emanated from that either, meaning they could see nothing inside the building. Erika had the fleeting sensation that WellCo's headquarters was in fact some colossal doorway, yawning open into the abyss.

"Tear gas," she growled, shaking herself back to reality. *Cool, calm, focused.*

Powell and Wang tossed a couple of grenades through the opening, and they waited for the hissing sound as the irritant was released. After a minute they entered, masks up, torches turned on to illuminate the main lobby.

It was empty. Gas swirled amongst the abandoned reception desks, around the visitors' chairs, drifting towards the lifts beyond. There was no sign of any of the approximately 500 staff who should have emerged at the end of the previous day, or of the disturbance that had caused them to inexplicably remain hidden inside their workplace since Monday morning, contacting no-one. From inside, the black glass proved to be a completely one-way effect; the sun's angry light streamed through the windows, bathing the scene in lurid orange. Beta Team switched off their torches as they headed towards the lifts, boots clicking on the tiled stone floor.

No one spoke. No one asked, 'Where are they all?' They just followed the plan, silently, professionally: sweep each floor in turn, working their way upwards. They knew the first few housed the administrative functions, the office workers that kept the place ticking over. Then came the laboratories, where WellCo's compounds were conceived, tested, and developed. The upper floors were reserved for the executives.

Erika radioed an update back to base, then they proceeded up the stairs.

The door to the first floor required a security card, as did presumably every floor above them, meaning Haskins' hooligan bar would get a lot of exercise. He grunted as he prised the door open, and they streamed inside, finding themselves confronted by rows of empty workstations. They padded across the carpeted floor, glancing under desks and around corners for some indication of what had happened there, the silence so thick it seemed like a malign presence.

Nothing. It was as though the workforce had simply vanished from their chairs.

Singh tried a couple of the tall metal cupboards, whose keys were still in the locks, but found only dusty documents and lever arch files, the accumulated harvest of two years of bureaucracy. Erika gave another radio briefing, hearing the crackled confirmation back through her earpiece. She kept her voice low, the details sparse. Speaking only when absolutely necessary avoided notifying any hostiles of their presence, and enabled them to listen intently for any sounds in their environment. But they heard nothing. Their own silence was reflected eerily back at them, except for a very low humming sound coming from above; the air-conditioning, perhaps, or some other scientific contraption.

The next few floors yielded more of the same: Finance, IT and HR, each workspace as deserted as the last. The sun continued its inexorable descent, casting its blood-coloured light across the desks, monitors, footstools, coat stands, filing cabinets. There was no sign of anyone. No indication of what had taken them. No way for them to have gone but up.

No sound but that incessant buzzing noise, getting gradually louder.

By the seventh floor, Erika's legs were already tiring, and she grimaced as she thought of the 52 storeys they still had to ascend. The sign outside the door warned them that they were entering a restricted area, and that appropriate clothing must be worn. Haskins jammed the heavy crowbar into the frame, clawing it open unceremoniously. They filed inside without a word.

There was an immediate contrast with the administrative block they had just traversed. Instead of open-plan office space, they found themselves in a narrow hallway, lit by powerful overhead strip-lights. The walls were so white it seemed as though they'd stepped outside of the world altogether, into some strange, colourless void. But the doors that punctuated the corridor reminded them of the floor's true purpose, their labels saying things like 'biohazard', 'do not enter' and 'strictly authorised personnel only'.

"Maybe there was a release of gas or something," said Powell in his gruff Welsh accent. "We should put our masks back on."

Erika frowned, then grunted her assent. The gas masks were uncomfortable, and severely reduced visibility, but Powell was right. She remembered the intelligence briefing, which had contained very scant information about what sort of research and experimentation was actually going on inside the Monolith; WellCo apparently maintained watertight control of their product confidentiality.

Anything to preserve their competitive edge.

Beta Team stalked the narrow passage, glancing through the glass doors into the rooms beyond, observing an array of mystifying scientific equipment, but no people. The lights were on in most of the rooms, and Erika wondered whether they should have cut the building's power prior to their ingress. But such a tactic would have alerted any hostiles, potentially escalating the situation unnecessarily; as far as she knew, whatever threat existed within this complex remained unaware of her and her men.

After a right and left turn, the corridor branched; Erika gave the order for them to stick together, and proceed to the right. The buzzing sound was growing increasingly louder, and she felt sure it was coming from that direction. They passed more doors shielding more pristine white spaces, the laboratories in which WellCo's scientists must have designed, tinkered, observed. Before they disappeared.

They continued, the humming sound undeniable now.

"What the fuck is that noise?" said Singh, as though only just noticing it for the first time.

"It's been getting louder since we came in," Erika replied.

The strange sound reached a muffled crescendo when they turned a corner to find themselves confronted by a dead end, and a single door. Its label, in crisp blue letters in-keeping with WellCo's corporate font and colour scheme, read 'Apiary'. Through the door's darkened glass they could see a small room, much darker than the others, illuminated by the otherworldly glow of a UV light.

The room was thick with flying insects. They swarmed and circled as though searching frantically for a way to escape. Some clung to the available surfaces in large, wriggling clumps, like repulsive fungal growths. Others rested on the door, crawling briefly across the glass before taking off again, their bloated bodies quickly lost amongst the seething cloud.

"Are those flies?" rasped Haskins in disgust.

"They're bees," replied Erika.

"I fucking *hate* bees," said Singh grimly, yet approached the door as though hypnotised by the creatures' incessant dance.

"Don't open it," hissed Powell. His Indian colleague gave him a withering look.

"Anyone in there?" asked Reynolds.

Singh shook his head, an expression of revulsion on his face. "Why are they keeping these?"

Erika could see some white cuboids in one corner of the room, perhaps the hives where the bees were being cultivated for who knew what purpose. Something had clearly gone wrong, enabling the swarm to escape.

"Who knows?" muttered Powell. "Maybe they're using them for new types of Epigene."

"But who would want to be more like a bee?" Singh sneered back at him.

Powell shrugged. "They're great teamworkers, right?"

Erika frowned, dismissing an unpleasant thought from her mind before it had a chance to crystallise.

"Let's keep going," she said, turning away from the room and its muted cacophony.

They found little else of interest on that floor, or the next. The building had become a labyrinth of gleaming white corridors and puzzling rooms, all silent, all devoid of human life. Behind one door they saw tanks containing what looked like lobsters. Behind another, rhesus macaques in cages.

"Cruel bastards," Reynolds snarled at the sight.

"Why is it cruel to keep monkeys but not lobsters?" Singh countered.

"We should let them out," Reynolds continued, ignoring him.

"Keep going," Erika said again, like an automaton.

They proceeded. Eventually the loop always led them back to where they started, past the lifeless elevators, back to the stairs. Erika radioed another briefing, then they continued upwards, to the ninth floor, where they were confronted by another long corridor.

At its other end was one of the scientists.

The team froze, raising their weapons. Erika held up a hand to signal for them to wait. Then she stared, blinking as she tried to process what she was looking at. The scientist, facing away from them, was a man with short black hair and a long white lab coat. He was on all fours, knees and hands supporting his slim body. But he wasn't on the ground. He was attached to the opposite wall, held there as though gravity had somehow been flipped sideways.

They gaped, transfixed, at the impossible scene. The man didn't move. Silent seconds ticked by.

Then Powell spoke. "It's just a model." He lowered his gun, chuckling. "But fuck know why it's-"

The words died on his lips as the figure scuttled away around the corner, limbs moving in a sudden burst of motion.

Like the legs of an insect.

Erika could feel her heart quickening, could hear Singh's frenzied breathing at her side.

"What the fuck," the young man mumbled, over and over. "What the fuck what the fuck what the fuck."

"How could he be crawling on the wall? How can that happen?" Reynolds shouted, an angry denial in his voice. Erika felt a strange sense of reassurance upon hearing the insane event recounted; her brain was already convincing itself that it must have hallucinated it.

"We go forward," she said quietly.

"Fuck that," retorted Singh.

She rounded on him. "And what? Report back that we abandoned the mission at the first sign of trouble? Try to convince the chief that you saw a man scurrying along a wall like a cockroach?"

Singh's eyes were wide and frightened behind his mask, but he nodded.

"Now keep quiet," she continued. "No sound unless we have to. We don't know what's happening here, but we don't want to draw attention to ourselves. Reynolds, you're on point."

At 24 years of age, Robin Reynolds was the youngest member of the team, but also one of the most dependable.

He didn't talk much about his past, but the grisly tattoos that covered his arms and torso spoke of those darker days, as did the haunted look she sometimes caught in his lead-coloured eyes. He stepped forward, raising the shield.

Beta Team advanced behind the reassuring barrier, stopping to peer into the rooms they passed. More laboratories, more microscopes, more machines. No people. They reached the end of the corridor, where it split in a T-junction. To their right, the direction in which their impossible quarry had disappeared, were the entrances to more labs, and another T-junction. To their left was a mirror image: white walls, glass doors, right angles.

No scientist.

Erika gestured right, and Reynolds led them forwards.

Then the power went out.

"Fuck," gasped Singh, his breathing rapid and frightened.

"Keep calm. Torches on," she commanded, and the corridor was illuminated by six tight cones of light. She used the radio once again.

"Beta Team to base. The power just went out. Know anything about that?"

The hiss of static, like a serpent in her ear, was the only reply.

"What did they say?" Powell asked, voice muffled behind his gas mask.

She held up a hand to silence him, and tried again. Still

nothing.

"You can't get through?" The fear in Singh's voice was barely concealed.

"We keep going," she said firmly. "Aman, I need you to get a grip."

"Sorry chief…" replied Singh, but his breath quickened further, and he began to hyperventilate.

"Sit him down," she snapped at Powell, who was closest to the young man. "Get his mask off."

His comrade helped Singh to a seated position against the wall. Beneath the mask, his expression was a wide-eyed frieze of dread.

"Breathe, mate," Powell said gently. "Just breathe. Slowly. In, out, in, out."

Erika drew her own weapon, a standard-issue Glock 17, and swept it left to right, scanning the length of the corridor. She fancied she heard a sound, like the rapid padding of feet against a hard surface, but she saw nothing. She tried the radio again, wondering if some sort of signal disruptor was being used. Once again, there was no reply.

"What do we do, boss?" Powell asked. "He's freaking out. He can't carry on like this."

Erika didn't reply. She was thinking. One of the reasons she was such a great unit leader was the way her brain worked: cold, emotionless, like a perfectly-calibrated computer. It was perhaps the same reason her love life was such a barren wasteland, and the same reason she didn't given one fragment of a shit. Calmly, it absorbed the new inputs, the changing variables, the evolving situation. Within a few more seconds she would have calculated the perfect tactical response.

But her thought process was interrupted, because something appeared in her torch beam, at the end of the corridor.

"What the fuck is that?" Singh shrieked, his voice rising to a shrill crescendo.

It was a woman, long auburn hair hanging down to obscure her face. She was perhaps fifty feet away, and standing upright, unlike the briefly-glimpsed scientist; but that didn't make her appearance any less startling. The woman was naked, her pale body speckled with patches of thick, wiry hair, some black, some a garish blonde. Her legs, which looked alarmingly slender, were bent at the knees, as though she was about to leap forwards. But as uncomfortable as it looked, she held that position, apparently watching them.

Her arms were the most disturbing sight. They dangled limply at her sides, thin and wasted. Their skin had turned almost translucent, as though the flesh and bones were starting to liquefy.

"Stop right there," barked Erika, training her weapon on the woman's chest. *If in doubt, always shoot centre-mass, triple tap.* "Who are you, and what is happening here?"

The woman did not reply, did not make any move at all. She just maintained her squatting position, facing them. Erika wondered if the curtain of her hair obscured any further deformities. Perhaps she was a test subject, escaped from some disastrously failed experiment?

"If you do not identify yourself, I will be forced to arrest you," Erika continued evenly. The rest of her team had also pointed their weapons at the motionless figure, except for Haskins, who was covering the other direction with his shotgun. *Well done.*

"This is your last opportunity," Erika began, then stopped. A strange, high-pitched sound had begun, an unpleasant drone that grew quickly in volume and set Erika's teeth on edge. It sounded like the whimpering of a distressed dog, but elongated into a single, unbroken note, and for a second she wondered if it was feedback from her earpiece.

Then Erika realised where the noise was coming from. The woman's arms were vibrating, so fast the movement was barely visible. It was as though the semi-transparent limbs were shivering, convulsing in some sort of bizarre seizure.

No, thought Erika, shaking her head involuntarily. *This is insane.*

But her denial was no use, because it was happening, right in front of their eyes, illuminated by the torchlight. Like the bees on the seventh floor, whose wings beat over 200 times per second, the woman was *buzzing.*

"Holy shit, no, oh shit oh shit, no no no…"

Singh's words were cut off as the scientist dropped onto him from the ceiling.

Chaos ensued, in the darkness. Flickering torchlight, screams, gunshots. Running, a frenzied escape from the things that had attacked them, from the spraying blood and flailing limbs. A symphony of horrors behind her: cracking bones, the shrieks of her men, and that awful, insistent buzzing.

Somehow, Erika and Haskins found their way back to the stairs. She had lost her torch, so Haskins guided them as they hurtled downwards as fast as they could. She yelled into the radio, not caring how hysterical she sounded, but her screams yielded no response.

As they approached the landing of the sixth floor, Haskins stopped suddenly, and Erika clattered into the back of him, nearly barging him down the rest of the stairs. An expletive formed on her lips, then evaporated as she saw what was illuminated in the beam of his torch.

Another scientist, identifiable by the shreds of the long white coat that hung around them, was standing in the stairwell. Unlike their previous assailants, this one's gender was unclear, because their face had been utterly, horribly transformed. Whatever hair they once had had been replaced by the same thick black tufts they had seen sprouting on the woman's body, but this time it covered their entire head, spreading down across their shoulders and chest, banded in places by streaks of yellow. Their jaw had split open as though they had been violently struck in the chin, the two dangling halves wriggling like mandibles, sandwiching a long proboscis that might once have been a tongue, now hideously elongated and hanging down as far as their midriff.

But it was the eyes – sweet fucking Christ, those *eyes* – that horrified her the most, holding her gaze as though her own pupils were frozen in shock at the sight of such an obscene parody. They were black, the size of saucers, two circular voids as dark as the glass of the Monolith itself. Their stare was infinitely blank, all humanity robbed from those shimmering orbs; yet, somehow, she sensed a clot of emotion deep within them, a kernel of pain and confusion and disgust.

And rage.

"Take the torch," Terry snapped, his command slicing through her reverie. She grabbed the flashlight from him, and watched as he used both hands to draw the shotgun, blasting the repulsive thing through the stomach. It exploded into two halves, spraying blood that was the colour of wet straw.

For a moment they watched the pieces spasm and writhe. Then the door burst open, and more of the things spilled out onto the stairs, limbs twitching as they emitted their unspeakable buzzing.

They turned and ran, the only way they could. Up.

Floors passed in a blur as they took the steps two at a time, pushing their legs and lungs to their limits as they climbed, gasping for breath. She didn't know if the things were following. Their buzzing seemed to be everywhere, in her ears, crawling inside her brain. It was too much to take. She felt like her mind might short circuit at any moment, like a crashed computer.

But still they ran.

After about a dozen storeys, she noticed a strange resin coating the walls, making the steps uneven and slippery. It grew thicker with each passing floor, calcifying into a hard, yellow shell. At floor 25 it became impassably thick.

"Turn around," she said to Haskins, who was staring and shaking his head at the honey-coloured substance.

"This is beeswax, isn't it? How can this be happening?"

"Just turn around. I want to use the bar."

He turned, and she took the tool from his back, jamming it furiously into the door lock.

"What's the point?" he said. "We won't be any safer in there than out here."

The door cracked open with the sound of splintering wood. She turned to face him, still holding on to the heavy metal rod. It would make a useful makeshift weapon; she had lost her pistol in the melee on the ninth floor, too.

"We need to save the others. Maybe we can find an alternate route back down. Perhaps the lifts are still working."

"They're dead, chief," he said sadly. "Just like Alpha Team. And soon we'll be dead, too."

He was staring at the impenetrable crust of wax as though this was the final horror his brain could withstand.

"Not until we run out of doors," she said, and turned to pass through into floor 25. Seconds later, she heard his footsteps in pursuit, and breathed a sigh of relief.

If she had properly read the signage on the door, she'd have realised that they were entering an observation area, with access restricted to WellCo executives only. She might therefore have anticipated the large viewing gallery they would be funnelled into, and the panoramic window spanning the entire length of the opposite wall. She might even have been able to deduce, from the plans of the facility that they'd studied before making their assault, that this was a surveillance deck from which the staff sleeping quarters could be secretly observed.

But there is no way she could have predicted what they would see through the glass.

Lit with the same, unearthly purple light they had seen in the apiary, was a huge chamber. It spanned perhaps ten entire floors, stretching far above and below their viewing window. The cavernous space was filled by a huge, sprawling structure, which looked exactly like a gigantic slice of honeycomb, surrounded by gantries and walkways. It took Erika a few moments to realise the scale of the thing, and that each hexagonal segment was in fact a sleeping pod, like those in a capsule hotel.

Most of the upper section was completely covered by the same waxy coating that had obstructed their progress on the stairs. Crawling across this surface, up and down and across, scrambling over each other, sometimes disappearing into pods only to re-emerge minutes later, congregating in little squirming huddles, were hundreds more of the monstrous bee creatures. Some of them were still recognisable as humans, clothed in the tattered remnants of lab coats or business suits, while others had metamorphosised more fully, extra legs sprouting from their chests and bellies, their arms replaced by glistening wings whose fragility was almost beautiful.

"It's just like Dom said," whispered Haskins, his voice hushed with something resembling reverence. "They were splicing bee DNA with their workers. But..." His thoughts trailed off. Erika turned to look at him, and saw horror twisting his face, an expression she had never before seen in her loyal, dependable colleague.

"What?" she asked, sensing something was wrong.

"What if it isn't just the bees? What if… this happens with all the Epigene?"

A sound bubbled up from inside him then, a liquid gargle like the sound of someone choking on their own blood. He collapsed to his knees, eyes wide and frantic, clutching at his throat. She darted towards him as his body was wracked by a series of violent spasms, and he pitched forward onto his face. But even as more disturbing sounds erupted from his mouth and abdomen, he used his hands to push her away.

"Get… fucking… back…" he gagged. "It's… the pills…"

She remembered, then. The Epigene he had taken, back in the van. Probably twice a day, every day, maybe for years.

"What is it, Terry?" she asked, hearing the horror in her voice. "What kind have you been using?"

He lifted his head, and she saw a deep and bottomless sadness in his eyes, the sadness of a man who looked in the mirror every day and saw himself ageing, deteriorating, crumbling.

A man who didn't want to grow old.

He tried to reply, but then his eyes turned suddenly dark, and bulged horribly outwards as though an immense pressure was building inside his skull. At the same time, gory strands erupted from around his mouth, the skin and muscle of his face twisted into fleshy ropes that burst outwards, wriggling like exploring tentacles.

Or, perhaps, like the twitching antennae of a lobster.

LEVIATHAN

8ᵗʰ July, 1936

Today I received a most unusual assignment from my employers at the *Patriot*. I will confess to a not insubstantial measure of trepidation, but, for an aspiring young journalist, such opportunities as this are rare, and demand to be grasped.

9ᵗʰ July

I regret that I waited a whole day before sharing the news with Martha, my beloved. I am unsure why I hesitated thus. Perhaps it was merely the peculiar nature of the task that awaits me, and the resultant period of adjustment required by my over-excited mind.

Her reaction was similarly muddled; she shared my delight at being entrusted with such an intriguing project, but expressed a touching concern for my welfare. I explained that the voyage would last little more than a few hours, that our vessel was said to be a marvel of modern nautical engineering, and that I would be accompanied throughout by not only a highly-trained crew, but also by some of the most inspired scientific brains in Massachusetts; yet still I saw tears gathering in her eyes as we conversed.

I tried to divert her thoughts from seafaring calamity to visions of the fantastical fauna I expect to encounter as we plunge towards the ocean's unexplored depths, but my words only seemed to increase her discomfort, and I fell silent.

10th July

The journey to the fishing village south of Cape Cod from which our expedition is set to depart was uneventful, yet the transition from bustling Boston to the quiet streets of Mormouth has left me feeling somewhat unsettled. Perhaps it is simply the shock of being abruptly liberated from the pressures of city life; here, amongst the ramshackle buildings and empty, narrow roads, the anxieties of the wider world seem like the concerns of some distant planet.

I find myself thinking again about the creatures we will encounter during our descent, and whether they give a fig about the troubles beyond the shimmering boundary of their aquatic paradise. They do not, of course; they live in blissful ignorance of our wars and genocides, our crusades and endless politicking, our petty squabbles and fears and suspicions and wants and needs.

I only hope my ingress into their kingdom is not too disturbing to them.

11th July

My early impressions of Mormouth are not as agreeable as I had hoped. The streets are filthy and poorly-maintained, and the only inhabitants I have encountered shuffle along the sidewalks with hunched gaits and a malign glint in their eyes. Most of these degenerate denizens ignore my greetings altogether, and the few responses I have received have been little more than unintelligible grunts. A foul smell permeates the air, a nauseating fishy odour seemingly swept in by the sea breeze, which has saturated either my clothes or my nostrils and refuses to be absent from my mind even when I am safely inside my lodgings.

Which brings me to my accommodation, in which I am now recording this diary entry. I do not wish to be uncharitable, and the desk clerk who welcomed me was at least capable of polite discourse, but despite its reputation as the village's premier guest house I regret that I cannot recommend the *Marine View*. The fading décor, peeling wallpaper and threadbare carpets would all be tolerable if they weren't merely the first indications of an altogether more advanced state of decay. The wooden fittings, lintels and skirting boards are rotten in many places, with visible mould growing outwards from the corners to form unsightly dark blotches along the walls, as though they are infected by a spreading skin disease. The air inside the building feels thick and unpleasantly moist, pervaded by a mildewy odour that even the stench of fish cannot entirely overpower.

Directly above my writing desk is a particularly large brown stain, the ceiling sagging downwards as though whatever leaking pipe or seeping contaminant is creating this ugly blemish is gradually eroding the room's structural integrity. Furthermore, the furniture is falling apart; when I first opened the door to my room's voluminous wardrobe, it fell off and almost landed on my foot, threatening to put an early end to my maritime career. The door to the adjoining room hangs ajar from rusted hinges, and although the attendant – who I have since ascertained is also the sole proprietor – assures me that the room will be unoccupied during my stay, it is nonetheless disturbing to have to sleep so close to an open doorway. My sleep last night was troubled by dark dreams of strangers wandering into my quarters, staring down at my slumbering form with bulging, watery eyes.

Although I remain excited about my forthcoming excursion, I will confess that my overall mood is one of disquiet and increasing unease. I am keen for my undersea adventure to progress rapidly, if only so that I can consign this accursed hotel to a dingy, festering and fish-scented corner of my memory.

12th July

Today I met the Professor.

If my editor is hoping for an eccentric genius, whose wild hair and fevered scientific ramblings will make for an ideal central focus for my article, he will be sadly disappointed. Montgomery Carver is a stern, reserved man, tall and straight as a ramrod, whose closely-cropped dark hair and smart suit make him seem more like a formidable lawyer than a marine biologist. He is clean-shaven, fresh-faced and smartly groomed, a filigree of silver at his temples serving as the only indication of his age and experience in his field, in which he is celebrated as the world's leading authority. When we met at the temporary research facility he has established here in Mormouth, he clasped my hand in a powerful grip, squeezing it painfully while his iron-grey eyes searched my face with the cold, analytical interest one might apply to a specimen in a petri dish.

He was kind enough to permit me to interview him at length, and although his responses were reserved and taciturn throughout, I managed to tease out at least a twinkle of the passion he possesses for submarine life when I asked him whether he was excited to break Beebe and Barton's record descent of 923 metres, achieved two years previously in their famous 'bathysphere'.

"Our financier is the one interested in breaking records, in achieving fame and adulation," he replied frostily. "And there is no shame in that pursuit, crass though it may seem." At this point his expression seemed to darken, his eyes widening and his mouth curving slightly into an almost imperceptible, yet unsettling, grin. "But I do not care one iota how far we make it down. Whether we fall short of Beebe and Barton, whether we breach the 1,000-metre mark, or whether we make it all the way to the sea bed miles beneath; all I am interested in is advancing human understanding of the fascinating beings that swim and squirm and dart and breathe and sleep in the uncharted fathoms of the world's great oceans. The tiny fish, the vicious shark, the resourceful dolphin, even the fantastic majesty of the whale; all will pale into insignificance against the otherworldly menagerie that awaits our discovery, deep underwater." He paused, tilting his head slightly as he regarded me, his gaze as piercing as a pair of deep-sea searchlights. "Have you ever heard of the *kraken*, Mr Whitman?"

I replied that I had not.

"Nordic legend tells of a monster resembling a giant octopus, notorious for attacking ships and dragging them to their doom beneath the waves. My own experiments in cephalopod behaviour have revealed to me unforeseen levels of intelligence amongst those outlandish creatures, and there are already photographic records of squid over ten metres long being washed ashore on beaches all over the world. *Imagine!*" At this moment his eyes seemed to glow with a sudden intensity, as though cold fire was smouldering in their leaden depths. "If you could scale the intellect of an octopus to that sort of size; such a being would surely be capable of dominating a planet, of ruling the world beneath the waves in the same way humans have conquered the land."

When I asked him more about the experiments he had mentioned, his smile widened, and he invited me to come and meet one of his 'associates'.

"Her name is Ophelia," he explained, as I frowned into the cloudy waters of an aquarium. "We have been studying her for over a year. I intend to bring her with us on our journey." I could see nothing in the huge tank except for a few rocks until, with a start, I realised that one of the outcrops was staring straight back at me with a single, disc-like eye. At that moment the octopus detached itself from the stone, changing colour instantly to a vivid red that reminded me of raw meat. It performed a strange pirouette, impossible limbs twisting and writhing as though trying to detach themselves from the smooth, globular head that hovered at the centre of the gaudy display. Abruptly the creature fell still, its hue shifting to a lurid yellow as it floated slowly upwards, its glistening cranium rising gradually above the surface, followed by those wide silver eyes that seemed to regard me with disdain.

How alien it was, how utterly unlike the mammalian life that had captured and imprisoned it. The professor seemed to read my thoughts, and continued. "Ophelia is my best specimen. She demonstrates intelligence and innovation far beyond that of the other cephalopods I have observed, regularly finding alternative solutions for the tasks we set her. She seems well aware that she is in captivity, and delights in causing mischief; I once caught her trying to abscond from my facility in Maine, squelching off down a corridor after clambering out of her tank. She had even tried to camouflage herself by imitating the black and white pattern of the floor tiles. A few weeks later, she figured out that squirting water at the lightbulbs could short out the electrical circuits of the entire laboratory, and proceeded to do this every time we did something to upset her."

As if on cue, Carver's enigmatic prisoner directed a jet of water straight at me, catching me full in the face despite my position several metres away from the tank. Carver's expression, a slight smirk and an unblinking stare as he regarded my discomfort, seemed disturbingly similar to that of the octopus.

"Don't worry. She just hasn't gotten to know you yet."

But the Professor's smile fell when I asked how long he intended to keep Ophelia.

"Octopuses live for two years, on average," he replied. "At around eighteen months old, Ophelia is already becoming elderly, and will soon begin to deteriorate. I have considered releasing her back into the ocean, but I worry that she will be ill-equipped to survive at her venerable age."

A sullen, monosyllabic mood settled upon the Professor thereafter, and persisted for the rest of my visit. He seemed unwilling to talk in any detail about the arrangements for our voyage, asking that I return the following day when he was less 'preoccupied'. He informed me that Jocelyn Kimble was also arriving tomorrow and would doubtless provide the sort of 'salacious soundbites' I was looking for.

I returned to the *Marine View* in a queer frame of mind. Meeting Professor Carver had been an engaging experience, but the man's mood swings had left me feeling somewhat agitated, a disposition not helped by the furtive glances I received from a group of ne'er-do-wells that had congregated on the street corner outside the hotel. Unable to sleep, I have stayed up far too late to write this account of my curious day, keen to capture its details and the memory of my overwhelming sense of foreboding, before both are dispelled by the morning sunrise.

And now to bed; precious Martha, how I wish I was lying cradled in your arms, rather than wrapped in brittle sheets on a bed hard enough to be a mortician's workbench.

13th July

When I awoke, an evil mist had descended upon the village, and lingers even as I sit in my dilapidated quarters to write this entry before retiring to bed. It seems to gather at the window like something straining to break through the glass, and I pray that it will dissipate quickly rather than delaying our voyage, and thereby prolonging my stay in this detestable hovel.

Thankfully, the hotel proprietor – whose name is Joseph and appears to keep no other staff, seeming to occupy his post at the reception desk from dawn until dusk – remarked in the morning that such foggy spells were a common occurrence in Mormouth, and that it ought to clear up in a day or two. He served me his usual tasteless gruel for breakfast, loitering while I ate as though eager to make further conversation, but unable to think of anything to say. I will confess that the man makes me uneasy; maybe it is the way his jaw hangs permanently open, always moving as though he is gnawing at something too big to fit into his mouth; or perhaps it is his bulbous eyes, whose pupils are far too large and make him appear drunken, drugged, or demented.

Swallowing enough of my porridge so as not to appear rude, I hastily took my leave of him, and walked the short distance to the Professor's laboratory. The mist seemed to reach inside my coat to chill my skin, and I couldn't help thinking of squirming tentacles, and subsequently of Ophelia, lurking in her tank like something escaped from a bad dream. I didn't know whose company I dreaded the most: that of Carver, or his bizarre pet. By the time I reached my destination I was tired, cold, and in the most abject of moods.

At this point, providence deigned to smile upon me, for it introduced me to Ms Jocelyn Kimble, and her charm and enthusiasm swept away my ill temper like a warm summer breeze. (Dear Martha, you have no need to feel envious, for the woman does not share your ravishing looks, and in her early fifties is almost twice your age; but she has an infectious charm that somehow made my tribulations up to this point seem trifling at worst.)

She had arrived in the village the night before, choosing to stay at the laboratory itself, in one of the rooms usually reserved for the Professor and his researchers.

"Rather that than spend a night in that ghastly hotel," she exclaimed when I expressed surprise that a woman of her standing would tolerate such austere lodgings. "I may be wealthy, Mr Whitman, but I have endured much adversity in my life, and I am not unfamiliar with nights spent in bunk beds, or even worse, I'll have you know."

Perhaps it is this fortitude that has shaped her into such a figure of renown, an almost legendary explorer, dare-devil and philanthropist. Heir to her father's automobile empire, she has entrusted the company's continued good fortunes to an army of underlings and accountants, devoting her adult life to a seemingly unending series of audacious feats and intrepid expeditions, the most famous of which – such as climbing Mount McKinley, flying solo across the Atlantic, and visiting the South Pole – the public are well-acquainted with. Perhaps her greatest achievement has been her commitment to donating money to charity, which she has continued to do even in the years following the Wall Street crash, defying the Great Depression by gifting thousands of dollars to good causes, as well as throwing the most lavish parties in New York.

Dressed in a simple blue city dress, she smiled with effortless magnetism as she introduced herself, leading me away from what she called 'Carver's fishy temple' towards the car that awaited us at the rear of the premises, its engine running and a driver standing to hold open its doors.

And so it was that, on my fourth day in the village of Mormouth, I was escorted to the harbour by a famous millionairess to gaze upon the vessel that would lower us over a kilometre into the sea. If only you could see me, Martha! I can scarcely believe the reality of my circumstances, even while I am living them.

"Your job is very important, dear boy," Ms Kimble emphasised during the ponderous journey, the driver carefully navigating the maze of potholed streets. "This will be my greatest journey to date, and I need someone there to document it; someone with the eloquence to describe the grandeur of our craft, the bravery of its crew, and the strangeness of the things we find in the deep, dark ocean."

I remarked that she seemed to possess ample reserves of eloquence herself, but she laughed off my compliment with a self-deprecating remark, something like 'even a blind squirrel sometimes finds a nut'. She continued to stress how vital it was that I recorded every detail, so that the moment we broke the thousand-metre mark would be 'afforded its true weight in the annals of history'. I will admit that I am beginning to feel overwhelmed by the task ahead, and only hope that my words can have the lasting impact Ms Kimble

– who insisted that I call her Josie – is looking for.

When we arrived at the ramshackle, barnacled wharf, I could not disguise my aversion to the fishy odour, which seemed to assail us with renewed spite. Yet Josie seemed not to notice the stink at all, or not to care, such was her excitement as she skipped towards the dock. Several boats were moored there, but the one that was to bear us out to sea was instantly recognisable, dwarfing the others by some considerable margin.

"Isn't it magnificent?" she gasped, as the weather-beaten sailors tending the nearby craft twisted their thick necks to gawp at her. "It's called the *Leviathan*."

"It's certainly an impressive ship," I replied, struggling somewhat for words.

"Not the boat, silly," she scolded. "Here, look closer."

She led me towards the edge of the wooden pier, pointing towards something that rested in the water, attached to a sturdy-looking winch that jutted over the side of the ship's deck. I frowned, thinking at first that it was some sort of odd, modern lifeboat, until I saw that the wan sunlight was glinting off a smooth, domed surface that seemed to be made from glass. I stared, perplexed, at a craft that resembled nothing more than a gigantic soap bubble.

"*That* is the *Leviathan*," Josie exclaimed, her chest swelling with pride.

"It looks like a Christmas bauble," I replied, regretting my comment immediately, lest it offend her. But she only chuckled heartily.

"Yes, I suppose it does! Are you familiar with the work

of Beebe and Barton?"

I replied that my research had indeed encompassed the exploits of the record-breaking deep-sea explorers.

"Then you'll know all about their bathysphere. This is the same concept, only instead of a hollow ball of steel, it's a much larger ball, whose entire upper half is made from fused quartz. Why crouch and squint through tiny portholes when the entire roof of our ship can be our window?"

I looked again at the extraordinary submersible, and this time could make out some of its inner structure through the transparent outer shell. It appeared to be divided into five sections: four cabins and a central 'deck' full of indecipherable control panels and complex-looking machinery.

"Four million dollars," she breathed with a kind of reverence. "This is why you are so important to me, Mr Whitman. I need your words to bring my greatest excursion to the masses… to bring me the recognition I've paid for." I glanced at her, and saw her face pointed out across the sea as though in defiance of the fetid breeze. Her features were set in a grim smile of determination, and for a moment I felt strangely fearful of this mysterious woman, who has never married or had children, and instead spent her life in pursuit of some other elusive goal.

We spent the afternoon eating in a nearby restaurant, where Josie insisted on buying us both the catch of the day, enthusing about its succulence and 'authenticity'.

"We will sail tomorrow," she announced at one point. "Well, perhaps 'sink' is the more accurate verb."

I laughed politely at her joke. The meat felt like lumps of bile in my throat, and I drank copious amounts of water to force it down.

14ᵗʰ July

I arrived at the harbour at 7am sharp. The weather conditions could not have been more ideal; the fog had lifted, and the sea's surface was as flat and clear as a mirror, reflecting the greyish-blue of the sky above. Here I met the rest of our crew; I regret to describe it as 'motley', but can find no more appropriate adjective.

There was the Professor, surly and silent, his eyes as glacial as chunks of ice.

There was Jocelyn Kimble, striking and indomitable, a youthful zeal glowing in her face.

There was Jacob Hollister, the sullen lump of a man that serves as Carver's research assistant, brought along to operate a camera and make readings throughout the voyage. He seems hardly capable of performing such complex tasks, given that even the simplest of pleasantries are apparently beyond him; being trapped in Hollister's company puts one in mind of sharing a house with an unfriendly, monstrous dog. But the Professor vouches fervently for the dedication and competence of his mountainous subordinate.

There was Elijah Welsh, the captain of our escort ship, a tugboat named the *Samson* that would haul the main craft out to sea before members of his crew operated the winch that would lower us into the abyss. He was stooped and thin, his white beard attesting to his venerable age, but with limbs like knotted rope and a deceptive swiftness of movement, the captain's presence put me more at ease about the daunting task ahead.

And then, of course, there was Ophelia. The creature would apparently occupy a tank that the Professor had had specially installed in the centre of the ship, enabling him to study its reaction to the deep submersion, and to any creatures we observed. It was temporarily housed in a large glass jar, which Carver was clutching like some gruesome trophy.

"Aren't you worried that she'll try to escape?" I asked the Professor.

Carver regarded me with the sort of expression one might reserve for an idiot child. "Octopuses can squeeze through any gap wide enough to accommodate their eyes, beak and brain, little more than an inch in diameter. But if this vessel sprung even the tiniest hole, there wouldn't even be time for us to drown; the pressure would blast the first few drops of water through our flesh and bones like bullets." He noticed my alarmed expression, and said with some exasperation. "There is no chance of that happening, because the sphere's walls are almost ten inches thick."

I sighed with relief, and tried to ask him about the design of our craft, explaining what a wonder I considered the *Leviathan* to be.

"That wasn't its original name," he mused sourly. When I quizzed him further, he said that he had wanted to call the ship the *Haruspex*, but had acquiesced to Ms Kimble's preferred name given that it had been funded by her fortune.

"A haruspex was a kind of mystic, in ancient Rome," he explained. "They believed they could read the future in animals' entrails. I saw my mission as something akin to these ancient gut-gazers; rather than staring out into the vastness of space, I seek the truth of our planet inside its black bowels."

Perhaps it was those ominous words, or maybe it was the baleful stare with which Ophelia speared me from inside her jar, that caused a chill to grip me as we entered the *Leviathan* through a hatch in the centre of its upper hemisphere.

Little did I know, then, how much more chilling our voyage would become.

We spent the next hour or so adjusting to our new surroundings while we were towed out across the tranquil plane of the water. Each of the sphere's human passengers would occupy one of the four cabins, but I was not interested in my spartan quarters. The entire voyage was scheduled to take no more than six hours, so there would be no need for sleep; we were to be back at the harbour and celebrating with glasses of wine in the restaurant well before nightfall.

Instead, I marvelled at the dizzying views afforded by the *Leviathan*'s transparent roof: above me, the porcelain dome of the sky; to my side, the barge's hulking colossus; the untidy sprawl of Mormouth at my back; the *Samson* ruthlessly carving our path ahead. Everywhere else, all around us, the glittering expanse of the Atlantic, endlessly unfolding. As the village faded from view, a sense of enormous isolation overcame me, and I struck up a conversation with Josie to try to maintain my spirits. We talked about our good fortune with the weather, while Carver checked his instruments, and Hollister stared at Ophelia, now decanted into her tank and squatting malevolently at its bottom.

Eventually we slowed to a stop, the *Leviathan* bobbing

on the gentle waves like a Halloween apple. Carver spoke earnestly into a telephone receiver, which Josie explained would provide our link to Welsh and the ship even at a kilometre underwater. Thick rubber tubes would protect the telephone cables, as well as the wires that would carry electricity to light the vessel's interior and provide external illumination for our underwater surroundings. Carver hung up, appearing satisfied, and seconds later our downward journey begun, the spherical craft like a giant eyeball ready to examine the ocean's deepest secrets.

I had expected the winch to be jerky, but we plunged into the water with surprising smoothness, our descent slow but steady. All eyes were fixed on the crystal window that surrounded us, even Ophelia's, and I began to worry about the durability of the quartz, despite knowing how hard and thick it was. The sense of imprisonment and helplessness began to swell within my chest and rob me of breath, and I feared I would fall into a faint. The waters surrounding us grew gloomier with every passing second, like the rapid onset of some terrible storm.

To tear my mind from these black thoughts, I concentrated on the animals that appeared in the beam of the lights. At first we saw silver fish, sparkling like new coins as they darted and pivoted, scattering as though from a terrifying predator. We glimpsed larger specimens, tuna and cod and halibut, and I gasped at the sight of a shark prowling amongst them, which Carver informed us was a young porbeagle. I had only ever seen such a creature at an aquarium, so witnessing it weaving sleekly amongst its prey in its natural environment was a fascinating spectacle. But the shark disappeared quickly from view, and soon the fish were replaced by other, stranger creatures, as the waters continued to darken.

Eels coiled past our lights like serpents, their tortuous

movements strangely languid and graceful.

Jellyfish drifted past like strange dirigibles, their translucent bodies resembling something spectral, more ghostly than alive. Their orientation, pointing perpetually upwards, suggested to me an endless struggle to escape from something deep below, a nameless horror towards which we were willingly plummeting.

"Is that a squid?" Josie exclaimed as a compact mass of crimson tentacles came into view, hovering alongside us and seeming to match the pace of our descent.

"It's a cuttlefish," Carver replied. "Watch its colour change."

As he predicted, the creature's skin underwent an astonishing series of alterations, not just in colour but in pattern and texture, a rippling canvas of Rorschach shapes and gaudy hues. It seemed almost to be trying to speak to us, but the language of its flesh was indecipherable. I glanced at Ophelia to see if she was responding to this visiting cousin, but she was hidden amongst the rocks of her tank, bored and aloof. After a while the captivating thing's curiosity waned, its colour returning to a deep scarlet as it darted off with a sudden jet of air.

"It didn't seem afraid of us," I commented.

"They rarely do," Carver replied. "Cephalopods will engage with humans, and often seem fascinated by us. They're like children, really." His voice almost had the tone of a doting father, and I felt myself shudder, perhaps because of the rapidly decreasing temperature inside the submersible.

The next few minutes passed in a reverent silence, until

Hollister spoke for the first time, announcing in a jarringly high-pitched drawl that we had passed 923 metres, and therefore broken the deep-sea diving record. Josie, pressing her hands against the crystal as she continued to gaze out into the murk, closed her eyes and smiled, a deep and contented sigh escaping her lips. Carver didn't react at all, busying himself by dropping some shrimp into Ophelia's tank.

The water around us was now a very deep blue, the lights illuminating an area only a few feet around the periphery of the *Leviathan*. Still we descended, until after a few more minutes I realised we had stopped, hanging there in the gloom like a broken pendulum. I saw something flit past, half-glimpsed and large, and felt fearful claustrophobia writhing once again in my gut.

"Well, Ms Kimble," Carver said eventually. "Are you happy with your accomplishment?"

"Very," she replied. "Thank you for designing my ship. I hope Mr Whitman has captured some intriguing notes." She glanced at me and I somehow conjured up an encouraging smile. "And how about you, Professor? We haven't encountered too many of your beloved octopi since we reached this depth."

Carver's eyes were fixed on a spot outside the craft, as though he knew exactly where something might emerge. "The correct plural is 'octopuses'," he said absently, his attention diverted.

We remained there for half an hour or more, the Professor staring into the depths while Hollister began to record film. Josie seemed restless, as though anxious to return to the surface now that her milestone had been achieved. I assumed Welsh was awaiting a signal from

Carver before he winched us up again, and wondered how long I could remain calm before I grabbed the man by the shoulders and begged him to end this fearful excursion. More than I had ever desired anything, I wanted to feel sunlight on my face; even the foul, piscine odour of the Mormouth air would be better than the stale brume that we were inhaling, a combination of carbon dioxide not yet absorbed by the soda lime and fresh oxygen periodically released from the *Leviathan's* huge on-board tanks.

Somehow I clung on to my composure, and joined the others in scanning the ocean that surrounded us, waiting for movement. There was nothing. Just an endless, deep blue void, as though the world outside our vessel had disappeared completely.

Then something, appearing with the speed and ferocity of a beast belched out of the slavering jaws of Hell itself.

The monster slammed into the sphere, sending us swinging alarmingly. All four of us fell to the ground, Hollister crying out in horror, his camera skittering away across the suddenly slanted floor. I had been standing close to Ophelia's tank and was soaked by the water that sloshed out of it, but that was the least of my concerns. I gaped at the huge tentacles that had completely encircled our craft, each of their pulsating suckers the size of a saucer; I felt certain we would be cracked open like an egg. Josie had landed close to me with a pained expression on her face, and I tried to help her to a seating position as the *Leviathan* continued to sway and rotate.

Carver, meanwhile, had leapt to his feet, suddenly gripped by a manic excitement that I hadn't previously witnessed in the dour scientist. He pressed himself against the window, gazing raptly into the thing's hideous face, his expression twisted into the smile of a fanatic. It stared back at him with cold, inhuman fascination, its eyes enormous and silver, like the polished lids of kitchen pots.

The nature of our tormentor was undeniable. We had been assailed by a giant octopus, the *kraken* of which Carver had spoken only two days previously. I watched, open-mouthed, expecting death to claim us at any moment.

Then, as suddenly as it had appeared, the behemoth was gone, relinquishing its death grip and disappearing upwards in a cloud of jet-black ink.

"Good heavens," I stammered into the silence that followed. The monster's discharge swirled around us like gallons of thick oil.

"It was beautiful," mouthed Carver, like a man that had just beheld a divine vision.

I struggled to my feet, trying to assist Josie, but she cried out at a pain in her hip, and sank back to the wet floor. Ophelia looked down at us from her nearby tank, her expression somehow mocking, her skin turned an alarming white.

"Carver, what the hell was that thing?" she hissed. "You told me we'd be perfectly safe down here."

He shrugged, not even bothering to face her. "There can be no guarantees when you venture outside of your own world, madam. We are in a place no other human eye has ever reached."

"Then let us *return* to our own world, Carver," she snapped in reply. "Surely you have got what you came for, now?"

The scientist ignored her, staring out into the deep as if willing the creature to reappear. Hollister, meanwhile, seeming badly shaken by the ordeal, retired to his quarters where he sat on his bed, clutching his head in his hands as breath wheezed raggedly in his throat.

"Professor Carver," I said, with as much assertiveness as I could muster. "I really must insist that we contact Captain Welsh, and have him pull us up."

He glanced over his shoulder at me, and although he gave no verbal sign of acknowledgement, he strode across to the telephone and snatched up the receiver, which had been dislodged from its hook by the violent impact of our encounter.

"Hello? Hello?" I heard him say, while I assisted Josie to her own cabin, urging her to recline in bed while we made arrangements to ascend. She made a show of resisting my ministrations, but I saw gratitude in her eyes, and worried at how serious her injury might be.

When I returned to the main cabin, Carver was still shouting unsuccessfully into the telephone.

"What's wrong?" I asked, wary of the man's temperament. Sure enough, he slammed the receiver into place and turned on me angrily.

"There's no answer, that's what's wrong! Maybe the telephone cable was damaged during the attack."

"Presumably Captain Welsh won't just leave us hanging here? He'll pull us up if he can't contact us, surely?"

At that exact moment, as if in mocking response to my question, the *Leviathan* lurched; a metallic groan came from its internal mechanics as we moved, like a howl of pain. At the same time, the lights begun to flicker, and I worried we would be plunged into darkness; but that wasn't my main source of alarm. Horror expanded inside me, coiling out of my belly like one of the serpentine eels we had earlier observed, because I realised we were moving *downwards*.

Overcome with distress, I grabbed Carver roughly by the throat. "What's happening?" I cried into his face.

He swatted my hands away, reminding me of his superior strength and size. "Calm down, you idiot!" he snarled, eyes blazing with barely-disguised fury, and turned to wrestle with a huge brass lever that protruded from the floor nearby. I became suddenly aware of the grinding gears, whirring cogs and intricate apparatus that surrounded us, and wondered how much more of this machinery occupied the lower hemisphere of the vessel, hidden beneath the flooring. A fiendishly complex device, designed by an intellect far loftier than mine; surely the Professor had built in some sort of failsafe, or countermeasure, to mitigate against this sort of situation?

Yet his struggles with the lever continued in vain, sweat appearing on his forehead despite the chill internal temperature. The lights continued to strobe on and off, and Hollister emitted a terrible cry from his cabin, as though in the grip of a nightmarish fever.

"What's going on?" Josie yelled from her own quarters, adding to the sense of mounting chaos. I stared, completely unsure what to do with myself, as the Professor grappled with the lever, until it snapped suddenly towards him, throwing him to the floor.

Still, our descent continued.

"Professor, what can I do?" I cried. "Is there something wrong with the winch?"

Then the lights went out. For a brief time, blind panic consumed me, and a frenzied scream threatened to burst out of my throat.

Then Carver reappeared, clutching two old-fashioned oil lanterns. He handed one to me, his face given a sickly pallor by the light. I saw my own dread reflected there, the first time I had seen fear clouding the stony orbs of his eyes.

"The cable has broken," he announced, numbly. "We are no longer attached to the barge."

I stared at him, not in disbelief, but in a dumbstruck state of clarity.

"But... how?" I heard myself say, scarcely aware of the process of thought and articulation. "Isn't the cable made of iron?"

"The ship... may have been attacked by the creature."

"You mean the *kraken*?" I said, pointedly. "Did you *know* it would be down here?"

He shook his head, a look of desperation in his face. "It was only a rumour... I didn't believe..." The words died on his lips. Around us, the ocean swept past, darkening to blackness as we sank.

"Will someone please tell me what's happening?" Josie called again, a quaver of fear in her voice.

I turned and went to her, casting a final accusatory look at the Professor.

She didn't sob, or shriek, or wail, when I informed her of our plight. She just nodded her understanding, realising immediately that we are lost; that no-one is coming to save us, because we have travelled further than anyone else is capable of travelling. This intrepid voyage will be her last, and this submersible will be her coffin.

It was around ten o'clock when we finally hit the sea bed with a thud, listing slightly to one side before coming to rest. The sea's menagerie had grown ever stranger as we sank: we saw transparent eels that hung in the water like stationary windsocks, their fanged faces pointing straight upwards, and others whose mouths hinged open to grotesque dimensions as they swallowed their prey. We saw mysterious lights approaching us, revealed at the last moment to be attached to the heads of huge, razor-toothed fiends that looked more like the spawn of demons than fish. They hovered, watching us for a time, before continuing their sinister patrol. I am intrigued by the unhurried pace of everything, down here at the basin of the earth; all seems leisurely, serene, somehow melancholic.

And now, as I am recording all of the day's insane events in my diary, my timepiece tells me that the time is approaching midnight. It seems strange that, though we are completely cut off from civilisation, my watch still functions normally, as if completely unaware of its own predicament. It reminds me that human life continues, and always will, miles above us. This is, somehow, simultaneously comforting and horrifying.

The professor was able to get a backup generator working, so the light inside and outside the *Leviathan* has been restored, at least temporarily. I can see crystals of ice forming all over the sphere, my breath misting in front of me as our temperature continues to drop. Huge, spider-like crabs scuttle across our craft's surface, their elongated legs making a repulsive clattering sound on the quartz. As I write, I am sitting in a chair opposite Ophelia, and I wonder if the water in her tank will begin to freeze. I search for fear in her argent eyes, but find no recognisable emotion there. There is only a malign intelligence that seems somehow amused at the terrible state in which we find ourselves; a brain completely unlike my own, with nothing to do but sit and wait, plot and scheme.

Conversation between the four of us has utterly evaporated. Hollister has locked the door to his room and refuses to emerge. Josie has also remained in her quarters, drifting into a troubled sleep. Carver toyed with the vessel's instruments for a time, working silently in a state of immense agitation, before bidding me a brusque goodnight and storming off to his room.

Here I remain, sitting alone in the pit of the Earth's belly, wondering what will kill us first: the cold, the slow diminishing of our oxygen supplies, or another attack by a monstrosity beyond imagining.

15ᵗʰ July

When I awoke, the Professor was dead. The marks at his throat attested to the manner of his demise: someone had strangled him in his sleep. With Josie's condition deteriorating since I last saw her – when I peered into her cabin her face was a disturbing grey hue, sheened with sweat – there could be only one culprit. I marched in outrage towards Hollister's door, then realised the folly of proceeding without a plan, and retreated to the main cabin to consider my options.

Outside, the ocean was quiet. Weird, eyeless shapes floated past occasionally, translucent and lit with ghostly fire by our still-functioning external lamps. They barely seemed to be alive at all, more like alien plants detached from the sea bed and drifting aimlessly. I thought about other planets, about the extent of the uncharted cosmos, and felt tiny and inconsequential, the immense pressure of the deep ocean taking on the added weight of the entire universe beyond it. Life, continuing, everywhere, to no end, all around me; I at its centre, trapped inside a demented ball of glass.

Alone, with a sick woman, and a murderer.

My thoughts seemed slowed down, somehow treacly, and I wondered if the oxygen was starting to run out. The professor would have known which dials to twist to reduce its outflow, to ration it more effectively. But as I surveyed the arcane panel of buttons and knobs and twitching needles, I knew that there was no hope for me to decipher his machine. His great invention, that had become his tomb. I hadn't even thought to cover his body with a bedsheet.

In the end I found a stout metal rod whose purpose was unclear, but which would make for an effective cudgel, and moved towards Hollister's door.

"Open up, sir!" I cried when I received no response to my knocking. It occurred to me then that there were no observers here, no-one watching or listening at all. No mortal judge for my final actions upon the Earth. For a moment I questioned whether even God's gaze could penetrate these infernal fathoms. Oh, Martha, I am truly sorry, but for a moment I was possessed by an animal rage; I dare not write down the foul things I shouted at Hollister, berating him for his murderous actions, his obesity, his cowardice. In the end my fury drove me to barge into his room, raising my makeshift weapon in vengeful ire.

Imagine my shock when I found the man's stout frame sprawled in his bed, the same deep crimson marks circling his neck! Oh Martha, I don't mind telling you that I lost my mind completely for a moment, raving and ranting as I staggered around the craft, overcome by the insanity of my predicament and the impossibility of the dual murders that had been committed while I slumbered.

Could Josie Kimble have committed the crimes in some sort of fevered fit of homicidal somnambulism?

I went once again to her bedside, feeling her weak and thready pulse, listening to the soft hiss of her feeble breaths. Her fall had damaged something inside her, and her condition worsened with every passing hour. I looked at her face, so full of vigour and ambition less than twenty-four hours ago, and felt a wave of sadness shake me to my very core. Then that feeling was swept away by a new horror, as I realised that the only person that could conceivably have killed my other crewmates was *me*. Had I truly been driven mad by my surroundings, transformed into a cold-blooded killer as well as an amnesiac, in a single night?

I saw a strange creature float past, some kind of peculiar squid with webbing between its tentacles, which it wrapped around itself like a cloak. I laughed to myself as I realised that it resembled Bela Lugosi in the recent *Dracula* movie. Then I stopped, because I had no wish to continue acting like a lunatic, and because the sight of the squid had reminded me of Ophelia's presence. I whirled around and proceeded to check on her.

Her tank was empty.

I once caught her trying to abscond from my facility in Maine, squelching off down a corridor after clambering out of her tank.

The red marks at their throats. Were those the impressions of fingerprints, or did I detect smaller indentations made by dozens of tiny suckers?

She figured out that squirting water at the lightbulbs could short out the electrical circuits of the entire laboratory.

Is it possible that Carver's vile familiar somehow orchestrated the malfunction of our craft, either by some sort of electrical sabotage, or even by summoning its gargantuan brother from the deep?

Octopuses can squeeze through any gap wide enough to accommodate their eyes, beak and brain, little more than an inch in diameter.

I couldn't allow that abhorrent creature to escape.

After many hours of frantic searching, I found it skulking in a puddle beneath a tangle of chromium pipes, watching my struggles sneeringly with those contemptuous eyes.

I grabbed it and dragged it out, feeling its nauseating flesh against mine, its tentacles encircling my wrist as I tried to fling it to the floor. When I finally detached it from my arm and hurled it to the ground, it landed with a splat, and began to crawl insidiously away, back towards its hiding place.

I stamped on the awful thing, not stopping until I was utterly breathless, and the octopus was smeared into a bloody paste across the floor. Oh Martha, I cannot deceive you; how satisfying it was when those evil eyes popped beneath my boot heel; how triumphant I felt as I wrought justice for those it had so callously murdered.

That leaves only Josie and me. I fear she will be lost to me soon, for I have no skill as a physician, and no food that might restore her strength. All I can do is give her water to drink, and watch as she slowly fades away.

I, meanwhile, will also not last much longer. The oxygen will run out before the water supplies, and provide a mercifully swift death before I succumb to cold or thirst or hunger. And so I will write to you, my dearest Martha, until my very last breath, because the one thing I do have in plentiful supply is paper.

Paper, and – in yet another twist of hateful irony – ink.

This diary was found inside a sealed, stainless steel container recovered by a beachcomber from the shores of Nantucket Island on 1 March, 1938. The rest of its pages had been torn out. The only other contents of the container were a wedding ring, a functioning watch, and a strange bone fragment that was identified as an octopus's beak.

URBEX

It was dark.

This wasn't a necessity; in fact, the quality of his film footage would be significantly improved if he shot it during the day. But daylight greatly increased the risk of detection by any security staff or guard dogs that might be patrolling; and of course, the atmosphere after nightfall was so much better. Exciting, frightening, dangerous, clandestine. Soaking in that mood was what urban exploration was all about. That was why Callum preferred the darkness.

And he was well-prepared, as always. The chest-mounted video camera was securely strapped to his torso, along with various energy bars and bottles of water. Around his waist was what he liked to think of as his 'bat belt', containing various useful implements: a torch, a lockpick, a crowbar, a flick-knife, a face mask to protect against any fungal spores he might encounter. He even had a telescopic police baton he'd managed to acquire on Pirate Bay (he'd read about urbexers who'd been attacked by squatters). Beneath these accessories he wore plain black tracksuit pants and a plain black T-shirt, with a plain black hoodie over the top. He even used shoe polish to darken his skin.

He would slip in and out, like a shadow. Take nothing but pictures, leave nothing but footprints.

He'd amassed a following on YouTube in recent years, and was starting to generate some half-decent advertising revenues. People had loved his exploration of the abandoned cinema, the mental hospital, the theme park and its ghost train. He didn't speak in the videos, and certainly didn't reveal his identity; he just explored these forgotten places, letting their ambience seep gradually into the camera.

But he wasn't really doing it for his viewers. He couldn't really explain what he enjoyed so much about this weird and lonely hobby, skulking about inside these sad and silent structures. Perhaps it was the stories behind them, the circumstances that had led to their desertion and neglect, the reasons that local councils had been unable or unwilling to finally put them out of their misery by tearing them down. They persisted, like monuments; strange snapshots of history that shouldn't really be there at all. And hidden inside them were glimpses of melancholic beauty, fragments of unknown lives: the iron frame of a hospital bed; an ancient movie projector, with fragile strips of film dangling from it like shed skin; the rusted shell of a dodgem car.

There was something about mortality, too. Watching the rot and the weeds slowly reclaiming these buildings felt like documenting the inevitability of death, the scale and size of the universe captured in freeze frame. Humankind might be winning a short-term battle, scattering our offspring and our vehicles and our electricity pylons across the planet as though racing to suck it dry; yet here, in these mould-choked monoliths, was the Earth's answer, its glacial and patient return to the baseline of putrefaction and decay.

And, he thought, as he gazed up the hill at the wooden sign suddenly visible at its summit, suspended between a pair of pine trees, there was also the nostalgia. Whenever he could, he liked to visit buildings that had some significance to him, had played some part in his own history. The crumbling theme park had once been a favourite family day out. The dilapidated hospital had been the site of his own birth, nearly thirty years ago. And now, here he was, cresting the steep uphill climb that led to the Majestic Pines Animal Sanctuary. A zoo he visited countless times in his childhood, brought girls to on dates as a teenager so they could eat ice creams while laughing at the penguins, who waddled comically around their enclosure with serious expressions on their faces as though they didn't get the joke.

His research had told him that there was no security, and indeed there was no sign of any living soul as he squeezed through a half-hearted fence and hopped over the turnstiles. In through the front gate, just like back then.

He switched on the head-mounted torch, confident that he'd be undisturbed, and began to record his movements through the site. The park had closed down almost ten years ago, but the air still had that unmistakable animal tang, of hay and food and urine and dung. An odour that ought to have been repulsive, but instead was somehow pleasant because of its association with the denizens of the zoo, creatures that he had once loved and still remembered fondly. He remembered the plight of some of the animals, the endangered tigers and Albert the gorilla, and wondered where they had all ended up.

The entrance opened into a main square, overlooked by a café and gift shop. Both were boarded up and covered in indecipherable graffiti, gaudy lettering that spoke of a creative and vibrant 'scene' that Callum knew absolutely nothing about. He approached the gift shop, hoping to find the cuddly toys and keyrings still hanging inside, maybe even some ancient confectionery. But the place was locked up tightly, and he didn't want to deploy the crowbar unless he absolutely had to. Maybe on the way out, then. *Exit through the gift shop*, he thought to himself, and chuckled.

At the opposite edge of the square he encountered the first signpost. He remembered how difficult he'd always found it to navigate the place, its labyrinthine layout like the coils of one of the pythons in the serpent house. Even with the maps that you could buy along with your tickets, he and his friends had usually quickly given up on locating any specific creatures, and just wandered through the grounds looking at whatever caught their fancy. He remembered rolling his eyes every time a girl professed to be terrified of the spider exhibit, wondering why this alleged phobia had become so predominant among young women. People, with their manufactured personalities, their stolen idiosyncrasies, their deceitful words. Maybe that was another reason he liked being alone. The animals that had once dwelt here were far more trustworthy than the humans in his life.

The signpost pointed the way to the aviary, and he decided to head in that direction, past the penguin enclosure that was now nothing more than a dried-up pond, the little walkway spanning the pool slick with moss and bird shit. Soon he reached a series of tall mesh cages, where a kaleidoscopic menagerie had once squawked and stared as the people hurried past, most of them more interested in the big mammals on the other side of the park. Here in particular the silence seemed oppressive, unnatural. He walked along the row of enclosures, reading the little information panels that were still attached to the front railing, telling him about the birds' habitats and diets and behaviours.

Callum had always liked the vultures. 95% of what they ate was bone, the sign informed him, with specially potent stomach acids enabling them to digest what other creatures couldn't, meaning they could return again and again to a skeletal corpse long after the other scavengers thought they had stripped it clean. Outsiders, like him. He peered in through the wire mesh, and saw feathers still littering the ground inside. He started to imagine what the birds were doing now, fantasising that they'd managed to escape during the process of the zoo's closure; maybe the eclectic flock was eking out an existence somewhere in the surrounding woods, the vultures circling and swooping whenever they found a lost lamb that had succumbed to the winter frost.

Vultures can live for up to thirty years, the panel said. And he knew that parrots had famously survived to be a century old. So maybe, just maybe.

He walked on, following another signpost towards the African area. He passed beneath an archway that read 'Land Of The Lions', remembering how the foliage became more exotic on the other side, although most of it was now grey and dead. After a while he reached the wooden building that had once housed the pygmy hippos. He went inside, recalling the miniature lakes that the creatures had inhabited, viewed through windows that seemed almost like portals into a completely different world, somewhere hot and humid and alien. It had taken a long time to spot the hippos, almost entirely submerged, but a sudden blast of water from their nostrils would attract your attention, revealing the top of a head floating lazily on the murky water's surface. He remembered being told that full-size hippopotamuses were responsible for an astonishing 3,000 fatalities per year, and struggling to reconcile that with the roly-poly, loveable gluttons swimming behind the glass.

Now the tanks were empty, the animals gone.

He lingered a while, capturing the melancholy scene from various angles, before proceeding towards the hunting dog enclosure, where he remembered watching the canines lounging in a heap inside a wooden shack. A close family unit. A vicious pack of killers. Another unpopular attraction, passed over as people rushed past in a hurry to see the lions or the giraffes.

Callum preferred the okapis, those bizarre patchwork animals that looked like something from an ancient myth. *The legs of a zebra, the body of a horse, the head of a giraffe...* they had stared back at him with big, doleful eyes, utterly oblivious to how impossible they were. He had a very vivid memory of throwing a tantrum as a child, because he wasn't allowed to touch them. He had wanted to feel their fur, perhaps just to confirm that they were real, or maybe to somehow communicate with them, to express to these beautiful creatures just how much he loved them.

Okapis are herbivores, feeding on tree leaves and grasses, as well as fruits and fungi, read the sign outside the dusty enclosure. *They are essentially solitary, coming together only to breed.* He reached down to wipe some of the grime off the words, and then remembered his policy, and left the grubby notice untouched.

Then he heard a noise, in the trees, right behind him. A single twig snapping. He spun around, already doubting the memory of the sound, which had been immediately devoured by the stifling silence.

But no, he had definitely heard it. Twigs didn't snap by themselves. Which meant there was something still alive, still in here, other than him.

He stood completely still, listening.

It could have just been a bird, you idiot. A pigeon or a seagull or something. Or a mouse. Just because you're in a zoo doesn't mean the woods are full of elephants.

But it was a long time before he continued his exploration. He could always edit that bit out later, of course.

The next enclosure was for the lemurs, and had been another of his favourite attractions. You had been allowed to walk straight through it while the wide-eyed creatures leapt about overhead, or descended to try to steal your food. Callum could remember that they were native to Madagascar, but little else about them, and sadly the information panel here seemed to be missing. He approached the cage, trying the door but finding it locked, and once again contemplated the crowbar hanging at his hip.

A rustling this time, in the trees, right at his side.

His hand froze on the handle, his head tilting towards the sound. The wind had picked up slightly, a gentle breeze stirring the leaves into a soft susurrus. Perhaps that was all he had heard. Or maybe it was a lemur, left behind when the zoo was abandoned, following him with charming curiosity.

Or maybe there were hungry eyes here, hidden amongst the vegetation, staring back into his. He thought again of the hunting dogs, about their powerful jaws crunching through the carcasses that were strewn about their enclosure, and felt for a fleeting second exactly like an antelope, trembling on the Serengeti.

Get a grip, Callum.

He turned and walked on, leaving the lemur enclosure behind, heading towards the giraffes. But then he noticed a signpost pointing towards the bat cave, and took a detour.

Yes, he seemed to have given himself the chills. Yes, the prospect of entering a pitch black cavern where giant fruit bats had once lived did not fill him with delight. But he couldn't miss this opportunity. If nothing else, the sheer fact that he had entered the exhibit, alone at night time, would give his footage a brilliant centrepiece. And if he was really lucky, maybe the bats would still be inside, their graceful winged forms clinging to the ceiling, or perhaps even swooping to investigate him.

Plastic strips hung down over the entrance to prevent the occupants from escaping, but there were no boards or shutters. He pushed the strips aside and stepped into the cave.

As expected, the blackness was absolute. The slender beam of his torch illuminated only a sliver of the passage ahead, and he felt sudden fear, a visceral horror at the prospect of having to traverse this dark space. A cave that had once housed bats, those favourites of vampiric fantasy... who knew what other monsters might lurk amongst the rocks, now that the place was unpoliced?

But Callum was a proud man, like his father had been, his father who rarely accompanied him and his mother to the zoo, because he saw it as childish. His father, who would wait for Callum to be older before he felt able to bond with him, taking him to the pub and to the football. His father, who had worked for years with asbestos, and died of lung cancer when Callum was only fourteen, and had barely begun to get to know him.

He pressed ahead into the cavern. Somewhere, water dripped in the darkness. His nerves felt tightened, ratcheted to a dangerous apex, waiting for the sound of leathery wingbeats to fill his ears, or a sudden shadow to flit across the beam of the torch.

But no bats appeared. There was nothing in the cave but stalactites, stalagmites, and stagnant puddles of water. The route curved around the left-hand side of the main chamber, and before long he could make out the exit sign a few dozen feet ahead.

He paused, turning slowly to take in a final sweep of the cavern. Its emptiness seemed to make it somehow even more majestic and otherworldly than he remembered. The light of his torch glinted as it caught damp patches on the walls, and the stalactites looked like strange teeth, the canines of something gigantic that had been frozen and fossilised here. Somewhere the water still dripped, dripped, dripped.

Then splashed. Footfalls, quick and purposeful, scampering towards him, in the dark.

Callum let out a choked gasp, and sprinted towards the exit. The slap-slap of the footsteps was right behind him, gaining ground, a burst of horrifying speed that outmatched him. As he reached the hanging plastic flaps, something slashed at his right ankle, and he fell forwards with a shriek. His head struck unforgiving stone, and the torch went out. His vision blurred in the darkness, but he was too terrified to fall unconscious; dazed, shaken, he scrambled forwards on his hands and knees, through a second plastic curtain and back out into the open, collapsing onto the gravel path.

He clutched at his wounded leg as the stars danced above him, swimming in and out of focus. Blood was spurting from the gash. He fumbled in his bat belt (*how ironic*, he couldn't help thinking) for his other torch, clicking it on, pointing it first back towards the cave, where the plastic flaps still swayed in his wake.

There was no sign of anything following him.

But he *had* been attacked. This was real, this was *actually happening*. He aimed the torch at his ankle and let out a little sob of anguish at the grisly sight. Something had *bitten* him: jagged bite marks encircled the bloody space where a chunk of flesh had been torn away, along with what felt like a piece of the ligament itself. He couldn't move his foot, at all. It just hung, limp and useless, while a horrible sharp pain began to spread outwards from the injury, like wildfire.

He reached for his mobile phone, pride forgotten, and dialled 999.

No signal.

He stared at the handset, willing it to find just a single bar, a tiny pulse of connectivity, to enable him to end this insanity. But there was nothing. He was alone, and crippled, and afraid.

A sound, to his right, in the bushes. He spun to face it, grimacing at another lance of pain from his ankle, shining the torch towards the source. The leaves were shaking as something moved quickly through the undergrowth. He followed the trail with the torch beam, mouth hanging open, his other hand once again reaching for his belt and for the comforting weight of the crowbar.

The rustling stopped. There was only the soft whistling of the wind, and his own ragged breathing.

Something was stalking him.

But what the hell could it be? His mind spun sinister webs, reminding him of the polar bear in the Arctic area, or the lions themselves, two of nature's most vicious predators. But surely none of them could have survived this long in an empty zoo with no source of food? The situation was ludicrous, surreal. Like a nightmare.

He hauled himself to his feet, moaning in agony when he tried to put any weight on the injured ankle. He began to hop and hobble away from the cave, towards the next crossroads, glancing wildly behind him every few faltering steps. No movement, no roaring beast suddenly emerging from amongst the trees. Perhaps it wasn't an animal at all; perhaps the bat cave was now home to a deranged zookeeper, crawling around on all fours amongst the muck, driven blind and bloodthirsty by a decade in the darkness.

Stop this nonsense, Callum.

He reached the crossroads, slumping against the wooden signpost in exhaustion. He scoured the labels for anything pointing towards the exit, but all he saw were more attractions: the bug house, the Outback, the aquarium, the reptile house. He seemed to remember the reptiles being quite close to the penguins, which in turn would take him back to the main entrance, and what promised to be an unforgiving slog back down the hill. But one problem at a time. First he needed to get out of this godforsaken place, away from whatever unknown *thing* was pursuing him.

His vision swam once again, and he swayed, almost pitching forwards onto the gravel. He grabbed at the signpost as he tottered, hauling himself back upright, blinking delirium from his eyes. Was he going into shock? He needed to find a way out, and fast. He tried not to think about the severity of his situation, and just concentrated on making forward progress, placing one foot on the floor, then executing a careful forward limp, putting minimal pressure on his shredded ankle, which was dripping worrying amounts of blood. A bright red trail for a killer to follow. He heard crunching on the gravel behind him, and sped up, crying out in pain as he was forced to tread on his right foot, urging himself not to stop, not to look back at whatever hulking beast was snarling and salivating behind him. He reached the reptile house just as the footsteps were nearly upon him, and with a superhuman effort he hauled himself up the couple of wooden steps that led to the door, collapsing into it, falling through and into the hut that had once housed anacondas, salamanders, iguanas.

He waited for something to pounce on him, to sink its teeth into his throat. But there was only silence once again.

His head was spinning, his vision a smeared photograph. What was happening? He tried to focus on the object closest to him, dragging himself towards it with his hands, sliding across the floor as though he had become a reptile himself. It was another signpost. It seemed important to him to reach it. He had forgotten why. His belt, his camera, his clothes, were weighing him down, dragging him beneath the surface of a dark and syrupy pool. He felt as though he were swimming through it, trying desperately to stay above the surface even as the oily goo dragged him inexorably downwards, into its warm and soothing embrace.

He rolled onto his back, and blacked out. When he next awoke, he was aware of a series of strange sensations in his legs, like needles being driven into them, again and again. But everything was numb, as though his senses were wrapped in cotton. He smiled at this, knowing that the pain would have been very great and terrible, if he wasn't cocooned in the warmth of the pool, serene and comfortable. His consciousness drifted in and out, like the tide.

Out, and he was at peace, floating in the centre of a great, cerulean lake.

In, and he felt those needles again, this time pricking his waist, then his hips, then his belly, inside him, exploring, as though he was one of the buildings he loved so much, his glistening insides an intriguing labyrinth of corridors and passageways.

If he hadn't been succumbing to the venom, he would have been screaming, both in agony and at the terrible sight of his killers, whose slavering heads were buried in his abdomen, his legs and genitals already torn away.

If he hadn't been slipping into merciful oblivion, he'd have laughed at the irony of the signpost that he was clinging to, even as his entrails were hauled out of him, as though his ribcage was a feeding trough.

Komodo dragons can survive on as few as twelve meals a year. They are happy to hunt in packs, and will often injure their prey with a toxic bite, patiently stalking their victim while they wait for their cocktail of venom and bacteria to take effect. They will then strip the corpse to the bone, as they can eat almost their entire bodyweight in a single sitting, and have even been known to dig up fresh graves to consume rotting human corpses.

Callum Morrison would have been extremely pleased with the dramatic footage he'd taken that night. It was surely the finest work of his urban exploration career. Sadly it would never be found, because the two surviving dragons ate the camera too, swallowing it whole before their feast was finished.

ENDURANCE

00:00

The recording of *Star-Spangled Banner* crackles and fades to silence, and I glance towards Bragg as he raises the bugle to his lips. The old villain's sunken eyes, like bullets blasted at point-blank range deep into the weather-beaten ruin of his face, gleam with a patriotic zeal. Along with his tattered grey jacket and thick, matching beard, he looks like some ancient confederate general.

I notice the looks of trepidation between some of my competitors while we await the trumpet blast that will start the race. Some of them attempt to make eye contact with me, the weaker members perhaps seeking to foster some sort of camaraderie. I ignore them, shifting my gaze towards the fog-swathed pinnacle of Wheezing Peak, jagged and cruel against the skyline.

Staying laser-focused on my goals is how I became Baldock & Brewer's youngest ever COO. It's how I completed three ultra-marathons last year.

And it's how I'll conquer the Wheezing 100.

Also known as the 'the Abattoir', the event is notorious in running circles, the type of race whose name can draw a nod of admiration from even the hardiest Western Slam veteran. Its hundred-mile route will lead us through three loops of a tortuous woodland trail, with an elevation gain in excess of two ascents of Everest. We'll scale rocky outcrops, slice our legs to pieces on thorn bushes, battle hunger and exhaustion, and try to avoid getting hopelessly lost in an Arkansas State Park that's rumoured to still contain black bears. In its 29-year history, only 15 runners have ever conquered the course in the 60-hour time limit.

I'm here to become number 16.

Because Steve Strickland belongs in the history books. The weak man I was in my twenties, the man that Caroline left, the man that bowed and scraped and acquiesced, that did all the hard work so others could take the credit, is long dead. This event is his funeral.

Thanks to the secrecy that shrouds the race, only a handful of supporters are congregated to shout words of encouragement – or perhaps pity – as we set out from camp. This clandestine presentation is part of the run's appeal; Obadiah Bragg has managed to cultivate a sense that his event is a 'best-kept secret', something that sits on the very fringe of the ultra-marathon calendar. There is no marketing. There is no fundraising. There are no gaudy banners or sponsors. Just a few local volunteers, a Vietnam war veteran, and his hellish brainchild.

When I wrote my application – there is no online entry form, of course – I pictured Bragg, who I had seen interviewed on a YouTube documentary some months previously, opening each letter and reading them carefully while his wife cleaned their modest home around him, three

Dobermanns gathered faithfully at his feet.

"I'm not looking for show-offs, or sightseers, or god damn Instagrammers," he'd said. "I'm looking for people who want to test the absolute limit of what they can accomplish."

Only twenty people are permitted to enter the Abattoir each year, but as my life coach keeps telling me, positive visualisation is the key. So when I received a reply several weeks later and saw my address written in a precise, stern hand, each letter like a soldier standing to attention, I wasn't surprised at all.

Whether it was the list of my achievements, my sub-three-hour marathon PB, or simply my desire to be the first 'limey' to ever complete the course, something must have struck a nerve with the old sadist. The piece of paper inside the envelope read, simply:

You're in.

So here I am, following the path as it begins to curve upwards, charting a steep incline into the thickening trees. My research told me the park contains hemlock, maple, tulip poplar and oak, but I don't know which is which; despite it being mid-April, the trees are resolutely naked, their stark bare trunks like huge stakes driven into the ground. Wrapped in cold mist, the Park has an austerity about it, a sort of bleak solemnity perfectly suited to Bragg's puritanical creation.

Yesterday, one of the other runners had asked him how frequent the water stations were along the course, and he just laughed in their face.

That had been John, by far the weakest of the group; I

wondered if Bragg had invited him as some sort of sick joke. His marathon PB is over four hours, for Christ's sake. He and Shelley, the only woman attempting the course this year, are guaranteed to be the first two drop-outs. Don't get me wrong, I'm all for equality and everything, but this is the real world, and the Abattoir is a real as it gets. This isn't a place for ladies. They don't call it Wheezing Peak for nothing; the climb will have us all gasping for breath by the end.

The rest of the field will present stiffer competition. Crawford Nash, the Texan survivalist whose bulky backpack is bobbing a few metres ahead of me, has attempted the race twice previously, actually completing the full course last year but missing the time limit by a few hours. Mike Hackett, the hedge fund manager from Colorado, has some impressive ultra-marathon times under his belt, but the way he tore away from the starting line suggests he perhaps doesn't have the discipline to survive this ordeal. And there are plenty of other blokes here who talked a good game around the campfire last night.

We'll see who's still talking after the first loop; when it's dark, and the rain has set in.

03:33

I stick with the main group, including Nash, and we reach the first book after about three and a half hours. Bragg leaves six books secreted around the trail, and you have to tear out the page corresponding with your bib number from each of them, to act as proof that you've completed the loop. Each is secured in a polythene bag, this one hidden among some rocks, just where it's noted on the hand-marked maps we're permitted to take with us; there are no sat-navs or mobile phones allowed. The book is entitled *America The Beautiful*. I still can't work out if Bragg is taking the piss or not.

We continue to labour up the slope, the gradient rising sharply once again and forcing us to deploy our hiking poles. My gear is based on the kit used by the most recent finisher, Jimmy Lake, who managed 58 hours and 13 minutes back in 2013. Lake's advice is that sensible risk mitigation trumps reduced weight, so as well as the poles I'm wearing a running vest to hold my water and gels and carrying a backpack containing spare shoes, spare hat, a rain jacket, thick gloves for tackling briars, a compass, a ton of snacks to keep me going between bigger meals back at camp between loops, and most importantly of all, *a spare headlamp and batteries.* I imagine a torch failure while out here in the dark, shuddering as I remember some of the horror stories from previous unsuccessful attempts.

Don't focus on the negatives, Steve. Focus on the goal, and that great feeling you'll have when you're running down to camp at the end of the third loop. The shock on their faces, the awestruck applause.

"Say hi, guys!" shouts one of the others from up ahead; Jack, I think his name is, the youngest entrant this year. He is a big yoga and surfboard fanatic, his long blonde hair spilling out from beneath a baseball cap as he turns to grin back at us, holding a camera ahead of him at the end of a selfie stick. I remember him talking last night about how he was going to make a documentary of his adventures, how he'd raised thousands for charity already. I don't doubt for one moment that the Abattoir will squeeze all that enthusiasm out of him before long.

If you don't respect it, this race will eat you alive.

I ignore him, and keep going.

07:04

By early afternoon, the runners have become more spaced out. I left behind a large group that had banded together to help each other navigate, and instead kept pace with two other front-runners, Jack the surfer and Chad, an ex-marine. Hackett is still nowhere to be seen, and Nash has also pulled away, leaving our trio in joint third place with two pages already collected.

"Wow, some amazing sights out here, huh?" Jack says to no-one in particular, as we haul ourselves up a collection of jagged boulders that squats in our path like a deliberately-placed blockade. He extracts his phone when we reach the top, sweeping it around to capture the panorama. Around us the fog continues to thicken, making the forest floor invisible, the trees jutting upwards from the swirling brume like the masts of sinking ships.

"I just feel so much closer to nature, you know?

Chad mutters something in polite assent, but I ignore Jack again, commencing the treacherous scramble back down the other side. After this, we'll begin the final climb to the mountain's summit; this is where we need to keep a steady pace despite the gruelling incline, otherwise we'll end up finishing the first loop behind schedule.

I almost slip on the way down, but manage to recover my footing, and drop with a crunch to the frosty earth. Chad lands behind me seconds later, followed by Jack.

There is a nauseating crack as Jack hits the ground, and he immediately cries out as he crumples to the floor.

Shit. This is exactly the sort of distraction that could derail a viable attempt.

Maybe if I just carry on, I can pretend I didn't hear it...

Then Chad calls out "stop, Jack's hurt himself," and with a grunt of frustration I turn. The youngster is slumped against a rock, his legs splayed out in front of him, leaning forward to clutch his left ankle while he groans in pain. I glance at my watch; we're making good time, but not enough for any messing about. I stride over to them.

"Have you broken it?" I ask. Jack blinks stupidly, as though the possibility hadn't even entered his head.

"I don't know," he says eventually. "It hurts."

"Can you move it?"

He gingerly bends his left knee, wincing as he does so.

"I think it's the ankle," he mumbles.

"Seems okay. You've probably just twisted it. Why don't you rest here for a little while, and then you can join up with the next group. We'll let Bragg know what happened when we make it back to camp."

Chad is looking at me incredulously. "We can't just leave him like this," he says, with a note of disgust in his voice.

I turn to face him, seeing the contempt in his expression. "You can do what you like, mate. Stay here and read him a bedtime story if you want. This is the Abattoir. He knew what he was in for."

No one to hold you back. Kill your distractions.

I see doubt wriggling in Chad's eyes, and I know he hears

the truth in my words. He might never be accepted into this race ever again. Does he really want to give up this early because some airhead didn't take care climbing down from a rock?

Jack makes the decision easy for him.

"Just go on without me," he says. "I'll be okay. I can join the next group, or even make my own way back down somehow." His eyes look wet with tears. "It looks like my race is run."

Chad nods, and gives Jack's shoulder a manly squeeze. I roll my eyes at the charade.

He probably can't wait to start filming himself, so he can tell his YouTube followers all about his noble sacrifice.

I turn my back on them, and keep climbing.

10:22

Chad and I don't speak again until we reach the top of Wheezing Peak. I can feel the guilt radiating off him as we jog, hike and clamber the next five miles. But he already knows that if he suggests we go back to Jack, I'll refuse, and it will make him look even worse. I've won, simply by sticking to my principles, while he's all twisted up with hypocrisy and remorse.

Never apologise, Steve. Never back down. Do you want to be the lion, or the antelope?

The view from the summit is incredible. Leafless trees stretch endlessly around us like silent monuments, as though the world has been transformed into some colossal graveyard. The sun has just begun to sink on the horizon, smearing an orange glow across the sky like the light from a dying fire.

"Wow," says Chad behind me. "It really is beautiful. But sad, somehow. Don't you think? That sunset reminds me of when I served in Iraq."

"Let's just find the book," I interrupt, scouring the ground until I see the plastic bag poking up from a shallow hole nearby. I tear out my page from *Reach For The Summit*, which appears to be a self-help book written by a female basketball coach, and consider putting it back in the wrong place; I could always pretend it was an accident. But after extracting his own page, Chad carefully replaces the book in the bag, and the bag in the hole; I suppose it's the right thing to do. After all, I wouldn't want to be disqualified on a technicality.

I take a moment to check my map and compass before starting the journey back down. The Abattoir's route is often changed, for no obvious reason other than to satisfy Bragg's twisted sense of humour. This year the loop is taking a brand new path on the way back to camp, through land that apparently once belonged to a farming family called the Cotterills. That means no handy blogs or YouTube videos to forewarn me of the hazards ahead; but it's certain that the descent won't be any easier than the climb.

The first mile takes us down an almost sheer drop, forcing us to slide between footholds as shale tumbles around us, grabbing at whatever protruding rocks and roots we can. I suggest Chad takes the lead; if he slips, I don't want him to take me out on the way down, whereas if I take a tumble he can help to break my fall. I think he knows this is my plan, but as expected his all-American military pride won't allow him to refuse.

We make it to the bottom unscathed, the gradient flattening as our path winds back into the trees. The forest is denser here, reducing our visibility, and we don't see the tangle of briar bushes until they begin to chew at our ankles. I try to spot a path already carved by Nash or Hackett, but the thorns seem as tightly coiled as barbed wire, so I let Chad stay in front and try to use my gloves as best I can. After a few hundred yards, my legs are a patchwork of lacerations; it's a good job I have iodine and bandages back at the camp, although by my reckoning we're still a good 14 miles away from finishing the loop.

Which means facing the prospect of being deep in the woods, cold and bleeding, when the sun goes down.

Welcome to the Abattoir.

I wonder again about Nash and Hackett, hoping to have encountered the latter already exhausted by his ambitious early pace. It would be a sore disappointment to have to share the glory of finishing the Wheezing 100 with two other runners. But all I can do is worry about what I can control, and right now this briar patch is slowing my pace to an alarming crawl.

When I first started running, I would visualise Caroline waiting for me at the finish, ready to jump into my arms as I staggered over the line. If I could just keep going, just get there, then all would be forgiven, our marriage restored, our separation a minor bump in the long race of our life together. Then I found out she'd moved in with someone called Mario. A work colleague I'd heard her mention a few times. I remember the moment so clearly, that awful feeling like a cold knife being driven into me; but not in my heart, like the clichés say. That feeling of betrayal, of spreading nausea, the horrible realisation that she'd probably been fucking this guy for years: it began and remained deep in my stomach. Where I've nurtured it. Where it burns like coal in a furnace, fuelling me.

The only motivation I need now is my hatred for that bitch.

I grit my teeth and drag my flesh through the thorns.

13:46

We reach the dry stream a couple of hours later, where the fourth book waits for us amongst the vegetation sprouting from its dusty bed. The fog has thickened, bringing with it the first tendrils of darkness, like some malign enchantment slowly enveloping the forest. Both our head torches are lit as we scour the stream, and for the first time I am thankful for Chad's company when he shouts, "found it!"

A Walk In The Woods, by Bill Bryson. Now I *know* he's taking the piss.

After tucking the pages into our vests, we claw our way up the opposite bank, and find the next mile mercifully straightforward as the night closes in around us. I thought my temporary partnership with Chad wouldn't last very long, but I've become quite accustomed to his presence, his breathing ragged but steadfast just behind me. Perhaps his strategy is to use me as a pacer, or perhaps he feels tethered by his guilt for abandoning Jack. I wonder briefly whether the young man was escorted back to camp or whether he is still lying there, shivering in the dark.

Pity is the first step on the path to weakness.

I spit on the ground, and quicken my speed.

Another mile later, Chad's headlamp flickers, and goes out.

14:30

Quite the dilemma. If I pretend I have no spares, I'm stuck with him following me all night. But if I give my spares away then I'll put myself at risk. I can't believe the stupid fucker only brought one set of batteries!

"I'm sorry, Chad, but I don't have any spares either. Maybe if you wait for the next group to catch up-"

"Fuck you, Steve. I'm not sitting here in the dark waiting for them to come along. You'll just have to light our way."

Shit. And now if I do need to change batteries, he'll know I lied to him. I contemplate sprinting off into the forest to try to lose him. But I don't want to have to fight a fucking marine when our paths cross back at camp.

"No problem," I say with what I hope is a disarming smile, and try to keep my pace punishingly fast. If we can get through the next two and a half miles, we'll have already survived the length of a full marathon. Over a quarter of the Abattoir will be behind us. But that sort of thinking is deceptive; you could be in the final mile and still fall apart. The secret is not to think in increments, but to think like a machine, as though running is your default setting. I can't allow myself to look forward to the brief rest I'll have back at camp before setting out on loop two.

By which point I'll have been running for nearly twenty hours.

That thought sends a lance of pain upwards from the soles of my feet, which are already uncomfortably blistered. The wounds on my legs feel raw and exposed, and I can imagine the dirt and bacteria that is festering inside. My thighs and calves are aching from the uphill slog. I remember Bragg's final words to us before the national anthem had played that morning, what felt like lifetimes ago. A catchphrase of sorts, that those who follow the Wheezing 100 have printed on their T-shirts, badges, and bumper stickers.

Cherish the pain.

Chad stays close to me as the path meanders treacherously, curving like an evil smile.

Then, in the darkness, we hear a sound, sudden and loud and frightening.

The sound of a man, screaming.

15:21

"Crawford? Mike? Is that you?" Chad has insisted on stopping while he calls out to them, and we listen to the forest silently mock him in response.

"It was probably just an animal," I say again, but he ignores me. To be honest, I don't believe my words either. The sound was unmistakably human. A cry of pain and terror, echoing through the trees, chilling my blood.

Could it be Bragg, messing with us? Some of his volunteers, creeping through the woods, dispatched on a mission to freak us out? Or perhaps a motion-activated recording, hidden amongst the trees, as a spiteful new addition to Bragg's repertoire?

Somehow I doubt it. But any other explanation means a genuine problem, an abandoned attempt.

Failure.

Chad calls out again, and again the indifferent buzz of insects is the only reply. "Come on," I beseech him. "Let's keep going. We can tell Bragg about it when we get back to-"

He rounds on me, anger flaring in his eyes. "I've fucking had it with you, you selfish piece of shit. I already left Jack behind because of you. I abandoned my code. So if Mike or Crawford are out there, and they need our help, then we're going to fucking help them."

A quick calculation. An analysis of the new variables. A reprioritisation.

To be successful, it's important to maintain an agile strategy.

"Here. I forgot. I have a spare headlamp after all. You take it, and then you can go and look for them." I hold up one hand in a placatory gesture, using the other to remove my backpack and extract the device. His face is a mask of disdain as I toss it to him. He switches it on, and fits the strap around his head.

"You're a real piece of work, Steve," he snarls, and then turns to disappear into the trees.

I breathe a sigh of relief. The headlamp is no great loss; I've got a third spare back at camp anyway. I turn and start running, trying to ignore the memory of that awful scream, and the fact that I'm now completely alone. If I can just sustain this pace for the next six miles or so, I can still get myself back on target.

Maybe it was a bear. Maybe Hackett or Nash was screaming while a fucking grizzly mauled him to death.

Then I see something, down to my right: a flash of white, bright and incongruous. I don't want to stop. I stop. I bend towards it. It's a piece of wire, tied around the base of a tree. It is thin, and trails along the ground, leading across to another tree about five feet away, where it is also secured.

Why would someone tie two trees together?

Then I see something else. Something impossible.

Suspended between the two trees is a third tree, hanging at a perpendicular angle. It has no branches; just a single, smooth trunk, like a caber, floating in mid-air.

I blink, and rub my eyes. Has the sleep deprivation started to kick in already?

Then I realise that this ludicrous, hovering tree is in fact hanging from the branches of the others, suspended by pieces of thick rope. It is even swaying slightly, as though recently disturbed. I frown in bafflement.

Then my headlamp catches another flash of white, and my eyes are drawn back to the ground, where I see the upturned sole of a pair of running trainers. The trainers are connected to legs, which are splayed out in front of a seated figure, which is leaning against one of the trees in a similar manner to the way Jack had earlier slumped against the rocks. The seated figure is in perfect alignment with the swinging tree trunk, and just a couple of feet from the trailing wire.

The seated figure has no head. Behind it, the tree glistens with the sticky contents of their vaporised skull.

The seated figure is dressed like Mike Hackett.

The trailing wire is a tripwire.

The hanging tree is a trap.

I scream, the exact same sound as the horrified howl we had heard just minutes earlier.

I scream, and then, forgetting about my injuries and exhaustion and gnawing hunger, I run.

15:54

I have no idea where the path is, or whether I am even heading in the right direction. I only know that I want to be as far as I can from that scene, from the ghastly remnants of Hackett's skull, from that splattered soup of blood and bone and gristle that I can still see, gleaming wetly in my torchlight, the image burned into my retinas. I scream as I run, wondering if I'll hear the first scream again in reply, realising it might have come from Hackett himself when he saw what was swinging towards his face.

The fog makes the darkness almost impenetrable, hiding the tree roots and twigs that try to trip me like accomplices to the horror. Gnarled branches appear from the gloom inches from my face, forcing me to duck and swerve. Running at this speed is idiotic, unsustainable. But I can't stop. I can't get my mind under control, can't process what I've seen, *oh god why am I here, alone and lost in these fucking woods, I just want to go home, or wake up, or climb into my car and drive away with my foot all the way down on the accelerator, faster and faster and*

I stumble and fall, of course, plunging forwards and only managing to bring up my hands at the last moment. My palms are instantly excoriated, but at least I didn't break my nose or shatter an eye socket.

Or my headlamp, thank god.

It is only as I clamber to my feet that I notice the pit. A darker stain against the dark ground, a few feet in front of me, covering the entire width of the path. Its covering of twigs and leaves has collapsed, but still I would have blundered straight into the gaping hole if I hadn't tripped just before I reached it.

What the fuck is going on?

I crawl gingerly towards the opening, leaning over the edge, half-expecting something terrible to loom up from the void. Instead, my torch reveals a short drop onto a bed of sharpened wooden posts. A man is impaled on several of them, his face frozen in a mask of shock and agony.

It is Crawford Nash.

The merciless spikes have skewered his torso, neck, and leg. His eyes are impossibly wide, as though blasted open by the sheer violence of his fate. Then I see blood bubbling in his throat, and realise that he is still alive. The fingers of his left hand are twitching and grasping, as though reaching out to clutch at the residue of his life as it ebbs away, dribbling down into the earth. His eyes are locked on mine, but they are staring out from an abyss of pain, somewhere very far away.

His mouth forms a word, or the start of one. Perhaps the first syllable of his son's name, or the name of the deity he worships. Whatever it is, it escapes his lips uselessly, a final futile plea before his body sags into death, the stakes holding him aloft like an obscene trophy.

Overcome with sudden nausea, I gag and vomit into the

pit.

Then I see lights among the trees ahead of me. Two white orbs, flitting and darting, growing larger like approaching fireflies. For a moment I wonder if I am mad, if this procession of insane images is the result of a mind honed too close to breaking point, the feverish imaginings of a man lying dehydrated in a ditch somewhere.

Then I realised they are the lights of torches, searching.

I start to cry out, then swallow the words at the last second, switching off my own lamp and rolling myself off the path before the torches can reveal me. Ignoring the pain of twigs and thorns, I wriggle into the scrub, trying to still my body and silence my frantic breathing. Part of my brain shrieks at me to warn them, to stop them from plummeting into the pit to meet the same grisly fate as the dead survivalist. But another part, something primal and atavistic, asks who would be wandering these woods in the dead of night, in the precise area that seems to have been littered with brutally effective traps.

Hunters, searching for antelope.

Seconds, or minutes, or hours, creep past. Time has become meaningless in this frozen instant, this pitch-dark clot of congealed terror. I wait, in the blackness, listening to the shallow rasping of my breath, and the thudding exertions of my heart, and the pitiless chirruping of crickets. Then, with a crunch of parting undergrowth, the torch beams appear on the ground in front of me. I stop breathing. A pair of feet move into view, encased in huge, well-worn boots that look as though they've been stitched together from pieces of old tyres.

"Stop," calls a voice, and for a moment I am reminded

of the squawk of a talking parrot, and almost blurt out a laugh. "Turn," it shrills, and the huge feet ponderously rotate towards me, facing me, barely a foot from my face.

"Fuck," the voice says, with a note of something resembling delight. "One's in there alright. Good boy, get down there and fetch 'em out."

There is a scrambling sound from the pit. I strain to see past the boots, but they remain rooted to the spot and aimed towards my hiding place, so I don't dare to crane my neck very far. All I can see is that the legs attached to the boots are as thick and sturdy as their footwear. Beyond them, the fog shrouds the scene like billowing smoke.

I wait for another eternity as these strange people conclude their business. No more words are spoken; no cries of horror, or shouts for help. Just earthy scratching sounds, and the rattle of what might be chains. I close my eyes, expecting at any moment to be discovered, dragged squealing into the light. But then the sounds begin to fade, with a clanking, scraping noise like something being hauled along the forest floor. I do not move. I barely breathe. The sound disappears into the trees.

Another eternity.

I open my eyes.

16:52

I do not risk the light of my headlamp, but the dull illumination of my running watch enables me to see while I extract myself from the bushes. A vicious cramp is tearing at my legs, and I struggle to stand; I feel immersed in pain, soaked in insanity. As though in a trance, I shuffle towards the edge of the pit, and look down.

Nash's body has been removed.

For a second, I consider allowing myself to fall, to allow those blood-smeared stakes to pierce my body and wake me from this nightmare.

You only fail when you quit, Steve.

I must finish the loop, and tell Bragg what has happened here. That his new route has led us somewhere disastrous. That he needs to call the fucking police.

But with no idea where I am, and barely any light, how will I find my way back?

And how many more traps have they laid out here?

I set out in the opposite direction to the people that took Nash's corpse, back the way I came. I know this will lead me towards Hackett's gruesome cadaver, but I no longer care; at least I'd know I was close to the main path once again. But everything looks the same in the dark: tree follows tree follows tree, like an endless wooden labyrinth. I walk for a long time, my eyes scouring the night for any familiar landmark, any sign of a snare, tripwire, or pitfall. There is nothing but the infernal trees. I realise how tired I am, and how hungry, how much I want to just sink to the floor and into the merciful oblivion of sleep. Maybe that would be the best plan, if I can stave off hypothermia: to await the sunrise, and make my escape by dawn's first rays.

Without warning, I emerge into a small clearing. I stop instinctively, fearing another trap, and dare to switch on my headlamp to examine my surroundings. There is a single tree at its centre, standing apart from the others as though it carries an infection. Unlike their proud, straight trunks, this one is fat and twisted, its bark a sickly greyish hue. Its branches reach outwards like the clawed hands of something fiendish, as though more interested in tormenting its brethren than reaching for the sunlight.

Dangling from its branches are dozens of strange decorations. They move and twist in the soft breeze, their shapes eluding me at this distance. Cautiously I creep towards the tree, feeling the unnerving sensation that it is observing my approach. Reaching upwards to touch one of the hanging totems, I realise they are carvings, suspended by small pieces of wire. The craftsmanship is simple but skilful, the designs wildly varied. Some depict fruit, while others are birds or bats. Others are more out of place: miniature crocodiles, aeroplanes, peculiar shapes and spirals. Some are faceless humanoid figures, eerily similar to corn dollies. One seems to be a baby's head, as though modelled on a child's doll. Another is a human skull.

There are also representations of weapons: knives, sickles, tiny machetes.

I edge away from the tree and its disturbing adornments, and skulk back towards the clearing's edge. That's when I see another light, up ahead. But this time not the erratic, wandering beam of a torch. This light is still, and square.

Like illumination spilling from a window.

17:10

I sneak towards the light source, switching off even my watch. Perhaps whoever made the carvings lives here. Perhaps they aren't the same people that laid the traps. Perhaps they have a phone.

Slowly, the outline of a building looms out of the mist,

revealing itself to be a simple but large wooden shack that fills the centre of another clearing. It appears to have been extended at some point to two storeys, the upper floor grafted uncomfortably onto the first like botched surgery. The whole structure looks ramshackle yet ancient, simultaneously as though it might collapse at any moment and as though it has stood here forever. I see more of the weird ornaments hanging in its front porch, swaying gently. The light is on at a corner window, but net curtains are pulled across it, and I cannot see inside.

I hang back, not daring to emerge from the tree line.

My body aches with the need for this ordeal to be over.

Success means minimising risk.

I hunker down to watch, and wait. Carefully and quietly, I extract a protein bar from my backpack, and feel my stomach roar its thanks as I swallow the snack, then wash it down with a sip of water.

Option one: the people that took Nash's body emerge. I sneak away into the night.

Option two: someone else appears. I approach them for help, but get ready to run if anything seems amiss.

Option three: I see no-one, and I just wait out the night, then investigate further by sunlight.

Always present three options. People like things in threes.

Option four: I try to find the main trail and meet up with the other runners, if they haven't already passed me.

Option five: I fall asleep, and someone murders me in

the night.

Option six. Six. Six.

Keep it together Steve.

It starts to rain. A light pattering at first, but escalating rapidly into a spiteful downpour. I am drenched within minutes, and beginning to shiver.

Fuck.

Fuck. Fuck fuck fuck.

I step out into the clearing. Just as I do so, the front door creaks open, and the house disgorges a bizarre silhouette. A child, perhaps. But... something isn't right. I squint towards the shadow, peering through the lashing rain.

Then I forget about the child, because I am plunged into a sea of impossible pain.

The last thing I see before I pass out is the set of metal teeth clamped around my right ankle, crunching gleefully through my shin bones.

??:??

I am awake. It is not sudden, like bursting upwards from watery gloom into fresh air. It is more like wandering in a hazy dream, until the dream takes the same form as reality, and you realise that you are no longer dreaming at all.

I sit up, but I can't sit up, because my arms and legs feel numb, and as heavy as girders. So I stay on my back, and try to remember where I am. Troublesome memories wriggle somewhere, like insects burrowing in my brain. Fragments waiting to coalesce.

I can hear the sound of laughter. A man talking in a muffled voice, and then lots of people laughing together.

I smell cooked meat, and feel my stomach growl in anticipation.

I open my eyes.

I am looking up at the boards of a wooden ceiling. A dim lightbulb hangs without a light fitting, and cobwebs dangle between the rafters. Glancing downwards, I see that I am laying on some sort of gurney, draped in a grubby sheet whose beige colour might once have been white. My arms and legs are still immobile.

Fatigue, perhaps, from the event. The Wheezing 100. Did I finish it?

I turn my head to the right, and see shelves lined with strange objects. Books, clay pots, jars of pickled items, bits of machinery. Weird wooden carvings. A mannequin head. All are dusty, as though this mess of trinkets has accumulated over many years.

More mumbled voices, and more laughter.

Jack. I wonder if Jack made it out of the woods okay.

I turn my head to the left, and see a giant looking down at me. He is wearing dungarees and huge black boots. His clothes are streaked with dark stains, and his hands are the size of snow shovels. His head is hairless, small and misshapen, like a ball of pinkish-red play-dough squeezed in the hand of an infant. But it's his eyes that I can't stop staring at. They look like someone has carved pupils into pool balls and forced them into his sockets. The lifeless orbs gaze vacantly off towards a point somewhere above my head.

I blink at him, grunting and groaning as I try to remember how to speak.

At the sound, a grin spreads slowly across his face, making his head look like a cocoon splitting open. I hear the laughter again, coming from somewhere behind him; as though an audience is observing this strange meeting, and is deeply amused by it. I moan loudly, still struggling to assemble my thoughts into words, and he begins to moan too, a deep and guttural sound like an excited bull.

"Awww, fuck, is he awake? I was enjoyin' that show."

That voice, like a squawking parrot.

Pain, terrible pain, like a shark tearing off my leg.

"Let me see him, big boy."

'Yes, ma," the giant replies in a deep and rumbling bass, shuffling through an awkward 180 degree turn.

The woods. The pit.

My brain finds my vocal chords, and draws from them a sob of horror.

The giant is wearing some sort of modified brace, like a baby sling strapped across his back. Suspended in it is an old woman, her face a hideous stew of warped features. A mangled nose squats above a cleft-lipped mouth, from which a ridiculous set of false teeth threatens to tumble at any moment. Her eyes bulge outwards as though trying to escape the pock-marked ruin in which they are imprisoned, her mottled skin seeming to hang from her skull as if it is sloughing gradually off. Only a few clumps of grey hair cling to her head, hanging in long spidery threads that reach below her waist. This is where her body ends; her legs are entirely absent, necessitating the bizarre papoose.

She reaches her sore-crusted arms towards me, grasping my face with surprising strength for someone so old and emaciated. She twists my head to one side then the other, as though examining livestock. The noise coming from my throat rises to a wail, and she draws back her lips in a sneer of disgust, revealing more of her grotesque dentistry.

"Oh, quit yer bawlin'. It won't do you no good. Just be thankful you ain't dead."

I battle to choke down my distress. Laughter swells again, somewhere behind her and her massive henchman.

"What… happened to me?" I manage to say, my mouth struggling to shape the words.

"Found you caught in one of the mantraps, unconscious, bleedin' everywhere. Brought you back here to patch you up. You're probably still a bit fuzzy-headed from the drugs."

Mantraps? Drugs? What on earth is the old witch talking about?

"I need… to leave," I say. The laughter roars.

"Naww, you just rest up a while, honey," she replies with a smile as warm as a glacier. "Big boy, why don't you turn him so he can see the TV?"

The giant moves ponderously behind my head, taking her with him. He wheels me round to the left, and I realise that the laughter is coming from an ancient black and white TV set in the corner of what passes for their living room. Facing the screen is a battered couch that looks like a stained sheet tossed over a car wreck, two garishly-patterned armchairs that might have been salvaged from a rubbish dump, and a rocking chair.

Three of the seats are occupied.

In the first armchair, his face angled towards the screen, is a tall and rangy figure. Like the giant, he wears the shabby attire of a farm hand, but unlike the giant, his face is hidden behind a curtain of lank, coal-black hair. His limbs seem too long, folded awkwardly to enable him to sit down, putting me in mind of an oversized insect.

Directly opposite him, in the other armchair, is a man with no legs. Like the old crone, his body ends just above the bottom of his faded *Iron Maiden* T-shirt. From its other end protrudes a bulbous head covered with tufts of fine blonde hair, like a toffee apple dipped in candy floss. His eyes, glued to the TV screen, are covered by a thick pair of glasses that make them appear enormous, his mouth lolling open in a buck-toothed grin.

Occupying the rocking chair, tilted to face the television as though it too is enjoying the show, is a human skull. There is a crack in the top of its head, into which someone has stuffed a bunch of fake flowers.

"Boys! Where on earth are your manners?" barks the old woman from behind me, and the two men turn suddenly towards us. The one with the long hair regards me cautiously, seeming to shrink from her commanding tone; behind his lank, raven-black locks, his face is scabrous and fearful. The other stares excitedly at me, raising himself up on his two hands, seeming about to leap from his perch and scamper over for a closer look.

The old woman sighs. "You'll have to forgive my boys. Not a talker among 'em. But they's good kids. It's taken a lot for them to recover." She raises her voice, adopting a kindly tone as if addressing a small child. "Good boy there is the one who fixed you up. He's good with his hands. Always makin' things, ain'tcha sweetheart?" The gangly creature smiles, blushing, and I realise that 'Good Boy' is what passes for his name.

She lowers her voice. "His pappy took away his tongue," she says. "Big Boy's eyes. Little Boy's legs. Mine too." I hear her hock and spit on the floor. "I know, I know. I shoulda seen what was happenin', first time he ever laid a finger on 'em. But he was their father, you know? The man of the house."

"What... happened to him?" I ask, squirming under the excited gaze of the child who shares her disability. No, not a child; despite her words, these poor, maimed creatures are far too old. I wonder how long they have all been living here, hidden in the depths of the woods.

"Who, their pappy?" She laughs, a hacking wheeze somewhere between a cackle and a cough. "He makes a pretty good vase, don't you think?" Then her voice rises to an almost hysterical shriek. *"You happy over there in yer chair, you nasty piece of shit?"*

"I'm sorry, but... I really need to go." I try to remember what happened, why I blacked out. *I stumbled upon their shack, in the dark. It started raining. I was tired, so tired. And then.*

"Oh, you'll be gone soon enough, don't you worry."

Metal teeth snapping into my leg.

Oh my god.

I try to leap from the gurney, but only succeed in heaving myself off to the side, and crash painfully to the floor. The sheet is tangled around me, and I snatch at it, trying desperately to free my leg.

"Ahh, fuck. Little Boy, go and wake your brother."

I just need to see it. I need to know what they've done. I scream as I tear the fabric away, staring down at what was once my right foot.

All those wooden carvings, hanging from the tree.

He's good with his hands.

Where my leg used to be, strapped with leather ties around the stump of my severed limb, is an ornately-carved, wooden peg.

The scream dies in my throat, replaced by a sort of strangled gurgle.

"Do you like it?" the old hag croons. "Good Boy made it for you. Like he made Big Boy's eyes, and his mama's teeth."

I tear my eyes away, my mouth moving dumbly. Nearby, I can see Little Boy scurrying away, walking on his hands across the floor. He leaps nimbly towards a rickety wooden staircase in the corner of the room, and ascends via the bannister like a monkey scaling a climbing frame, before disappearing into the upper floor of the house.

A bad dream. I'm lost in the woods somewhere, or freezing to death on the top of Wheezing Peak.

"Put him back in bed, Big Boy," snarls the old woman, and I am seized by hands as strong as tightened wrenches. I try to struggle, but the giant overpowers me with ease, manhandling me back onto the stretcher.

Then he turns to allow the old gorgon to face me once again, and I seize my chance. Pitching forwards, I hurl myself onto the floor, trying to stand on my crude prosthetic but succeeding only in finding a four-legged, scuttling gait. Ahead of me is a doorway, and I scramble towards it as the harridan screeches with rage behind me. It leads into a kitchen area, the walls lined with cupboards, a rusty-looking oven, fridge freezer, and washing machine. There is a large dining table in the centre of the room, and I grab at it, using it to haul myself into a standing position.

I find myself face to face with Chad.

The ex-marine is lying on his back, his eyes closed, arms resting at his sides. But there is nothing peaceful about his repose. An apple is stuffed into his mouth, and his stomach has been carved open, entrails spilling out like inquisitive tentacles. Plates and cutlery are arranged around him, along with bowls of foul-smelling greens.

A monstrous banquet, with Chad as its centrepiece.

Please wake me up. I want to go home now. I don't care about the race any more.

With a moan of horrified revulsion, I reach instinctively for the cleaver buried in the bloody crater of Chad's abdomen. Whirling around, I see the giant filling the doorway, his back to me so that the woman – his mother? – can address me once again.

"Get fucking back!" I scream, slicing the blade through the air as I edge around to the opposite side of the table. Behind me is a door, which I think is the front door.

But how can I run, with one leg missing?

"Is this how you treat us, after the hospitality we've shown you?" she snarls.

"Why am I alive?" I hear myself sob. "Why didn't you just kill me too?"

Sadness clouds her ravaged face. "I thought... you could be a friend for Bad Boy. He gets so bored, just going out to hunt critters every day."

Big Boy. Good Boy. Little Boy. Is there a fourth child I haven't met?

"Why... do you call him Bad Boy?"

Behind her I hear the staircase creak and groan. The sound of slow, heavy footsteps.

"His pappy named the boys, not me. Bad Boy was our first, the one he hated the most. He used to cut his face, burn his arms with cigarettes. I seen dogs treated better than he was."

The footsteps are closer now. The whole ramshackle house seems to shake with the weight of Bad Boy's approach.

The old woman smiles as she continues. "I'm so proud

of him. Of what he's become. My little baby boy: the new man of the house. Step aside, Big Boy, and let your brother past."

Still facing away from me, the giant steps backwards into the kitchen. Then he slides to one side, and I see a monster striding purposefully towards me.

It is tall, even taller than the giant, maybe seven feet.

It wears a baggy brown jumpsuit, and a leather apron coated in stains.

Its long hair is black and greasy, like the feathers of a bird trapped in an oil slick.

Its arms are muscular, but end just below the elbows. Wooden weaponry is strapped to the stumps: a wickedly-sharp skewer, a huge mallet.

Its beard is thick and matted, bulging outwards from beneath the wooden mask that covers its face.

The mask is smiling, carved into the rapturous grin of someone completely, maniacally happy.

I turn, screaming, and smash my way through the door.

51:31

My watch is still running. *I'm a long way behind schedule.* I laugh, or cry, or both.

It is morning. The sun has scoured the mist from the forest. I have hobbled, limped, stumbled and crawled through it for hours. My pursuer is toying with me; I know that now. Always it is there, lurking just beyond the trees, cracking twigs or scattering leaves. Sometimes it lets me stop for a while, allows me to believe that I have lost it in this godforsaken maze. Then I hear it again, and I stagger onwards, wincing at the pain from my cauterised stump.

I looked. I had to. I took off the leg and found a melted mess of blackened flesh beneath. Gangrene will surely claim me if the monster doesn't. I picture its spear driven between my ribs, its crushing hammer mashing my brain to paste.

Maybe they'll use my skull for decoration. Put some nice flowers in it. Maybe Good Boy will carve me a replacement head, and prop me in an armchair to watch TV with him.

Or perhaps I can make it to camp. Perhaps some of the others found the bodies, and the authorities have already arrived. Perhaps they're combing the woods even now, with high-powered guns and Tasers, ready to slaughter those fucking inbred freaks.

I hear another snapping branch and try to speed up, but I am so tired now, a physical ruin, a dead man walking. I had to toss the cleaver hours ago because I could barely carry it. I try to conjure up the hatred in my belly, the hot core of rage that I reserve for Caroline, but it's gone now, dissipated like blood into soil.

Push yourself, because no-one else is going to do it for you.

Don't stop when you're tired. Stop when you're done.

Sometimes we're tested not to show our weaknesses, but to discover our strengths.

Whoever posted those on Instagram was never chased through a forest by a demented cannibal.

My wooden leg catches on a tree root and I sprawl forwards, just as the ground lurches into a steep downward gradient. With a cry I fall and roll, my body bouncing off trees and rocks as it tumbles, gathering speed like a dislodged boulder. Maybe I will smack my head on a stone and this nightmare will be over. Maybe I'll snap my spine, and the monster will find its work already done.

I land, winded, in a soggy heap of foliage. I stare up at the sky, and the sun stares back at me, unimpressed.

Pathetic little man. You haven't even finished the first loop.

Gritting my teeth, I clamber to my feet, glancing back up the slope. If I see that mask, the horror of that engraved smile, I feel my heart might explode. But there is nothing. No movement, no sound. I turn.

Oh my god.

Only a few hundred yards away, at the bottom of the hill.

The camp!

I almost throw myself at it. I hurtle down the slope, shredding the skin of my hands and knees, tearing great gashes in what remains of my gear. I don't care. Obadiah Bragg will be there, and others, waiting for the return of the search parties they have undoubtedly despatched.

"Thank god," I murmur to myself, over and over again, as I drag myself towards safety. "Thank god thank god thank god." And I really mean it. I haven't said a prayer since I was a child, haven't been inside a church for decades except to attend friends' weddings. But something has steered me here, against all odds. Some divine force, watching over me.

No. Not god. YOU, Steve. Your determination. Your will to survive. You're going to write a book about this experience, and sell millions. The leg is nothing: soon you'll be able to afford a state-of-the-art robotic prosthesis. People will call you the greatest survivor in history.

I call out, my voice a fragile mixture of relief and exhaustion.

"Obadiah?"

I try to remember the names of the others.

"John? Shelley? Crawford?"

No, Steve; Nash is dead, remember? They dragged his body from that pit, perforated like a pincushion. He's dead, like Mike Hackett, with his head pulped against a tree. Like Chad the marine, with his insides served as entrees.

The camp consists of a large white marquee, where Bragg and his volunteers wait while the runners are out on their loops. Nearby are the other tents, like a miniature, multi-coloured village, where everyone sleeps the night before the event. Beyond that is the car park, where my rented Land Rover waits to take me to safety. I know I won't be able to drive it myself; but someone will. Or there'll be an ambulance already there, doors open, engine running. But first I just need to get to the main tent, gleaming white like a beacon, only a few metres away. I can see the fence post where Bragg would normally be waiting, applauding gravely as each runner passes and moves on to their next loop, or serenading the winner with his bugle.

Then I see the heads. Along the path past the fence post, which curves around to lead back up and out into the woods, someone has driven wooden poles into the frigid earth. Atop each one is a severed head, so fresh as to seem almost alive, as though they might at any moment open their mouths to shout encouragement as I pass. Each one seems dented, damaged, their skulls cracked like eggshells. I see volunteers I remember from the first night. I see John, and Shelley.

Bragg himself has been hoisted into a nearby tree, impaled through the neck on a broken branch, dangling like a carcass in a slaughterhouse. His head has been completely bashed in, his beard emerging from the gory mess like a bad joke.

Cherish the pain, his T-shirt says.

The Cotterill family have been down here already. They will complete their own loop soon, I imagine.

I sink to my knees in front of Bragg's body, kneeling as though in supplication.

INTERFACE

She stared down at Freya's broken body, but did not weep. This was the twelfth day, and Rose had run out of tears four days ago. From this distance, eleven floors up, her girlfriend's slender frame looked like a bundle of sticks that someone had tossed from their balcony, the splintered twigs forming a maddeningly asymmetrical pattern within the circle of dark blood that had spread and dried beneath them.

One of the few creatures that still remained in the square shuffled towards the mangled corpse, then seemed to forget what it was doing, and stood staring towards the park, twitching occasionally as though being jerked by an unseen puppeteer.

Creatures. She preferred to think of them that way; as mindless monsters, rather than the people they had so clearly once been. Like this one: a heavy woman with thin, dark hair, wearing sweat pants and a vest top a couple of sizes too small for her. Perhaps she had recently returned to the gym, trying to shed a few pounds after a difficult break-up. Maybe she had been exercising when the change happened, turning suddenly towards the man sitting on the rowing machine next to her, lips parting in a snarl of unfathomable fury as she reached for his throat.

Strange how they didn't attack each other. Whatever had caused that initial, feverish surge of bloodlust – replaced now by this ominous docility or, in the case of most of the creatures, mysterious absence – seemed able to discern between those affected and those immune to its horrifying effects. An airborne pathogen; some escaped experimental nanotech; divine judgement; before the TV had stopped broadcasting altogether, people were even speculating that people with BMIs installed were being hacked from overseas. Rose's experiences certainly fit that last theory: she had been disturbed by the idea of having a microchip implanted into her brain, unconvinced that the unpleasantness of invasive surgery was outweighed by the benefit of a toaster that could be operated by mind control, or a washing machine that could commence a spin cycle with a single, focused thought.

Freya, on the other hand, had gobbled up the new technology as soon as it became vaguely affordable. Ever the enthusiastic nerd, she'd filled her apartment with Smart appliances – kettle, stereo, thermostat, dishwasher – before she'd even undergone the operation, and had gleefully invited Rose over to showcase her new Brain Machine Interface as soon as it had been implanted in her skull.

Rose thought about the moment Freya had turned. Less than two weeks ago; it seemed simultaneously like a different lifetime, and like a fresh wound still shrieking its agony. They'd been sitting on this very balcony, gazing out across a familiar array of London landmarks – the Shard, the London Eye, the Gherkin – as the sky faded to a resplendent orange smear behind them. Freya had been joking around with Rose's Orb, asking the device if it realised it was archaic technology, if it was upset that it would soon be in a museum. They had both laughed at the AI's confused responses. Rose had been mildly alarmed when Freya started to juggle with it, the gadget spinning perilously close to the balcony's edge as it danced between Freya's graceful limbs ('a beautiful spider', Rose had called her once, and she had seemed to like that, and mentioned it often).

"Isn't it strange?" Freya had asked, either oblivious to or unconcerned by Rose's discomfort.

"What is?"

"Soon, we won't have to do this at all."

"What – fuck about with other people's property?"

Freya tossed the Orb recklessly into the air, then caught it one-handed, grinning. "I mean talking. Once you get a BMI chip, and they develop the tech a little more, we'll just be able to… think to each other."

"Fucking hell. So all day I'll be bombarded by your daydreams about the new shoes you're going to waste money on at the weekend? I hope there's a range limit on those things."

Freya pulled a mock-grumpy face and pretended to launch the Orb off the balcony, out across the crowds of weekend revellers gathering in the square below, office workers spilling out of the surrounding bars to mix with groups of students, loitering teenagers, homeless people drinking from cans.

Then she turned, and smashed the device into Rose's head.

It felt as though every negative emotion had gripped her simultaneously: fear, confusion, pain, even a kind of temporary, primal hatred. She was knocked from her chair by the force of the blow, slamming into the glass barrier that shielded the balcony's edge. Even before she'd been able to grasp what was happening, Freya's hands had encircled her throat, her partner's spindly limbs suddenly coursing with malign strength. Rose tried to cry out, but only a choked gargle emerged as Freya's fingers squeezed her windpipe mercilessly, driving her head into the barrier once, twice, three times, leaving the glass cracked and streaked with blood.

"Please," she'd managed to gasp as she was hauled to her feet, but Freya's eyes were devoid of pity, devoid of any emotion at all. Her face was horribly expressionless as she forced Rose backwards, trying to shove her right over the edge of the balcony.

The next few seconds were a blur; whether because of the head trauma she had suffered, or the sheer horror of the memory, she didn't know. She knew she had grappled with Freya, screeching at her to wake up, to stop this lunacy. She knew one of them had kicked the Orb, that it had bounced off the glass and rolled back to rest beside her foot. She knew she had stood, screaming and wailing, staring down at Freya's body shattered like precious china on the paving below.

No-one had done anything to help, because all around her, the same thing was happening to them. She saw someone else plummet past, tumbling from a higher balcony and shrieking as they fell before their cries were cut off by a repulsive, gristly crack. She saw fights breaking out all around the square as people were attacked by friends, children, strangers, grandparents. She saw the window of a coffee shop explode outwards as two men were disgorged onto the pavement, one of them immediately sinking his teeth into the eye of the other, the victim's screams joining the rising cacophony.

Perhaps her door being locked from the inside had saved her, in those first few insane hours. Perhaps it was the barricade she had constructed behind it later that day, as the monsters began to pour into the building, even those that had been injured in their homicidal orgy managing to hobble, limp or crawl through the reception doors. Or perhaps it was simple, dumb luck that none of the murderous things had entered her apartment. As far as she knew, none had even tried, although she heard more horrified cries from above and below as the fiends burst through front doors to slake their bloodlust.

She had spent that evening hiding under her bed, sobbing and trembling, while the sun faded and crashing and screaming became the night's soundtrack.

At some point, the sounds had stopped. When she finally dared to emerge from her hiding place, the day was breaking and the building was as quiet as a tomb.

That's when the real madness had begun.

The zombies – that was perhaps the best term for them, with their vacant stares and slack jaws, oblivious to the chunks of flesh and viscera that clung to their teeth and fingernails – were traipsing in and out of the building in two neat rows, like worker ants. The same thing was happening all around the square: the creatures filed silently into the surrounding apartments, bars, supermarkets and clothes shops, and emerged minutes later, inexplicably carrying domestic appliances. Kettles, toasters, speakers, irons, lamps, stereos, fans; all were being calmly looted. She even saw some of the things working together to lift heavier items, like washer-dryers and TV sets, patiently hauling their bounties towards the underground station further along the street, carrying them inside and reappearing some time later to complete another kleptomaniacal loop.

Her entire body had frozen with dread each time she heard them in the corridor outside, dragging their feet along the carpet as they passed. But, once again, she had been left unmolested.

Several days later, the bizarre activity had ceased, and most of the creatures had disappeared into the tube station.

During that time, she had tried unsuccessfully to contact friends and family members; her phone seemed unable to make or receive calls, and the Wi-Fi and 5G internet connections weren't working on either the phone or her laptop. It was day five before she had dared to turn on the television. She had almost howled in horror when she learned that this insanity was happening *everywhere*. An emergency broadcast informed her that Britain had been quarantined, cut off from the rest of the world like a gangrenous limb, the same gruesome spectacle unfolding in countless towns, cities and rural hamlets, as around ninety percent of the population had been driven suddenly psychotic. Of the other ten percent, most had been brutally murdered, their remains left to rot in the streets while survivors huddled inside their homes or within makeshift fortifications.

Forty-eight hours later, even the TV had fallen silent, a black portal whose darkness seemed like a harbinger of the future.

"I'm running out of food," she murmured. "Orb, what should I do?"

"We could play a game," replied the white sphere, still smeared with Rose's blood. She turned it over in her hands, still gazing down at the solitary zombie, who had taken a few stumbling steps towards the park entrance. Beyond it, corpses littered the grass; she couldn't bring herself to look at the children. People under eighteen weren't permitted to have BMIs installed. She hadn't seen a single child amongst the shambling horde.

"I need something to eat," she insisted. "Orb, where can I find food?"

"Why not try shopping online?" it responded in its indomitably chirpy American accent. "You're still entitled to a month's free subscription with Groceria."

She sighed, contemplating once again whether she should just hurl the irritating device to its doom on the stones below. *Just like she did to Freya.* But she knew she wouldn't. The Orb was the only connection to humanity she had left, its cheery insistence that all was well somehow helping her to cling to the tatters of her fraying sanity. It seemed like an artefact from another world.

But the fact remained that her cupboards were almost bare. She had started rationing her food a few days ago, but quickly realised the futility of this approach; whether she could eke out her supplies for an extra week or not, sooner or later she would need to go out scavenging for more.

Arming herself for the excursion was a surreal process. She felt like Bruce Willis in that scene in *Pulp Fiction,* where his character tries out various weapons before settling on an alarmingly lethal-looking katana. For Rose, who didn't possess such an elaborate arsenal, the choices were limited to either kitchen utensils or the contents of her tool box.

After auditioning a few chef's knives, a screwdriver and even a hacksaw, she finally settled on the comforting weight of a claw hammer. She tried to picture herself swinging it into an attacking zombie's head, imagining the crack of bone and the squelch of soft tissue as the weapon disappeared inside their skull. Nausea wriggled in her stomach, and she knew she wouldn't be able to do it.

But still, she had to go outside. There was no escaping her body's needs.

She didn't want to think about what she'd have to do when the water stopped running.

She dismantled the barricade slowly and carefully, listening intently for any sounds outside. For all she knew, a line of the monsters was waiting patiently in the corridor, standing in polite silence like a buffet queue. She knew that, like her, the things also had to eat; every so often one of them would wander over to kneel by a corpse, bending to sink its teeth into the decaying flesh. She had thrown things at the zombies that approached Freya, rained abuse down upon them in an attempt to scare them off, but it hadn't always worked; there were gouges and teeth marks around her thighs and buttocks, and at some point one of Freya's arms had been torn off and dragged away.

Yet still, they never turned on each other, not once. In a strange way, they were more peaceful and cooperative than humans had ever been.

With a deep breath, she eased the door open.

The hallway was quiet and featureless, and uncomfortably warm in the way that all modern apartment buildings were during the summer months. There were no skulking cannibals or mutilated corpses to greet her. Just an array of closed doors, each doubtless hiding some grisly horror, the wreckage of lives pulled apart by mystifying circumstances. Or perhaps a survival story, like her own.

She just needed to choose one that concealed no zombies, and lots of tinned goods.

The building used an electronic fob system, requiring you to manually lock your door from outside upon exiting so that you couldn't accidentally shut yourself out. In theory that should mean that most were unlocked, their occupants either dead or subsumed into the ranks of the mindless droves that had now migrated to the underground station. Her strategy was to proceed around the floor, trying each apartment until she found one that was unlocked, and then to listen carefully at the door before daring to enter.

She started with number 1112. Despite the efforts of the developer to create a community vibe by hosting regular social events and encouraging people to use the residents' lounge, Rose rarely interacted with her neighbours, treating the building more like a hotel; she didn't want more friends, she wanted a soulless and efficient machine for living in. As a result, the only other tenant whose name she even knew was Mrs Minkaite, the Lithuanian woman who lived directly opposite her. Despite the spinster's insistence that Rose call her Gabby (short for Gabija, apparently), Rose felt more comfortable with the formal title, perhaps because Mrs Minkaite seemed to perfectly fit the role of a kind, motherly older lady. Swathed in multiple layers of colourful fabric and smelling of exotic perfume, Mrs Minkaite had the wearily experienced, almost thespian air of someone that had lived an eventful life. Her array of extravagant wigs alone must have had a dozen stories attached to them.

Rose hadn't seen Mrs Minkaite amongst the zombified parade outside, and the old woman certainly didn't seem the type to utilise BMI technology. Rose remembered the first time she'd bumped into her in the hallway – Mrs Minkaite struggling with a heavy package of some sort, gushingly grateful when Rose helped her haul it inside – and had been immediately invited in for a cup of tea. She'd ended up staying to chat for hours, eating strange oatmeal biscuits and boiled sweets from a little tray on the coffee table while she marvelled at the array of curios, knick-knacks and paintings that Mrs Minkaite had crammed into the modest flat. At least three different cats had emerged at various points to snootily investigate her before returning to lounge around the old woman's bedroom, leaving strands of white hair all over the shapeless red couch, the wine-coloured rug, and the army of cushions that festooned the living room like other fat, sleeping pets.

Shit. The cats. Could they be trapped in there? She tried the door, found it locked. If Minkaite had been out when the *change* happened, there was every chance that the cats were still inside, slowly starving to death. She listened at the wood, but could discern no mewling, no scratching, nothing. How long could cats survive without food or water?

Don't get distracted, Rose. A terrible sadness, like weights hung from her heart, accompanied her as she tried the next door, an apartment she was fairly sure housed a middle-aged Italian man who seemed to wear a lot of expensive suits. His place was also inaccessible. Interesting; she was pretty sure she'd seen him, carrying his espresso machine towards the underground station, and despite everything she'd been vaguely amused by the stereotype. Perhaps some vestige of muscle memory had led the zombie to lock his door behind him.

She turned and crossed to the entrance to her next-door neighbours' home, a young British couple called Harry and

Milly or Barry and Tilly or some other insipid, vaguely rhyming combination. She said hello to them in the lift, and they said hello back, pausing whatever conversation they'd been having until they thought she was out of earshot, and then resumed squabbling about housework or work colleagues or money. Occasionally their arguments became full-scale shouting contests that she could hear through the wall, and she found herself guiltily wishing that one of the boring bastards would just give the other one a good smack to shut them up.

Unlocked. She pressed her ear to the door, listening, squeezing her eyes shut as she tried to concentrate all her energy on that single sense. But the doors were thick slabs of oak, designed to prevent the spread of fire throughout the building, and hearing anything through them was difficult. She wouldn't discern the calm breathing of Hilly/Billie if she – *it* – was lurking just beyond, or the thud-thud of Gary/Larry's footsteps if he was mindlessly circling the living room. She gripped the hammer tightly as she strained to hear. After a few seconds, she fancied she could hear something: a sort of strange, incessant hissing sound, almost like TV static.

Her heart thrashed inside her as she turned the handle, agonisingly slowly. Wincing at the squeal of the hinges, she opened the door.

The stink was so intense it almost sent her reeling back into the corridor. She'd steeled herself against what horrors she might see, thinking that nothing could possibly be worse than the sight of her own beloved Freya dashed to pieces on unforgiving stone; but she hadn't considered this other practicality of death, the inescapable truth of voided bowels and micro-organisms burrowing through intestinal walls. People turned to meat, meat turned to rot. She gagged, holding her sleeve across her face as she stepped inside.

The apartment layout was identical to her own, but inverted, so the bathroom was behind the first door to her right. It hung open, and she could see that the hissing noise came from within; a tap, left running, blasting its useless output straight down the plughole. A few inches away from the gushing jet, the woman – Lily was her name, Rose suddenly remembered – was slumped over the side of the bath, the top of her skull touching the porcelain on the other side as though engaged in some sort of bizarre prayer ritual. Her head was bloated and sodden, like a putrid Halloween pumpkin, soaking hair spilling out around it like the black tentacles of a dead sea creature. Rose edged closer, choking down vomit as she saw a mass of maggots wriggling in the tub, inside Lily's clothes, under the skin that seemed to be sloughing off her body like wet paper. Flies buzzed excitedly around the gruesome spectacle as though dancing in celebration.

Lily's hands had fallen lifelessly at her sides, still twisted into claws as though she had been fighting viciously right up until the moment of her death. The plug and its chain were entangled around one of them. Maybe she'd been running a bath, when her boyfriend had attacked her from behind, forcing her head beneath the water. She'd struggled, wrenching out the plug in desperation, but it was too late. After she'd drowned, he'd simply left her there, and stumbled back out into the living room, where he'd begun to calmly strip it of all its electrical appliances.

He must have had help, because as well as the absence of a toaster, kettle or TV set, Rose could also see spaces where a dishwasher or washing machine might have once been. They stuck out like gaps in a smile, jarringly incongruous with the rest of the neatly ordered apartment.

Rose found a couple of tins of soup in the cupboard; she

was a vegetarian, but the fate of the chickens that had contributed their lives to make the processed slop no longer registered on her spectrum of priorities. There were also some porridge oats, which she supposed she could eat with water rather than milk, and a packet of cashew nuts, but little else of use. Still, it was a start. As she left, she stopped to stare once again at Lily's body, wondering absurdly whether she could undertake some sort of burial. Not just out of respect, but out of necessity; to help stop the insects and putrefaction from finding its way into her own enclave.

One step at a time, Rose, she thought as she returned her meagre bounty to her apartment, and ventured immediately back out again before terror and disgust could overcome her completely.

The floor was laid out in a loop, with more apartments beyond the fire doors on either side of her. She chose right, and crept quietly around the corner.

There was a single dead body in the passageway. It lay exactly halfway along it, outside the door to number 1108; an obese man in a suit, on his back, arms and legs outstretched in ghoulish symmetry. His carcass seemed to have acted as a useful source of nourishment for the zombies, his torso and belly savagely eviscerated, blood and entrails splashed around like macabre graffiti. Once again, the stench was intolerable, flies and maggots rejoicing amongst the gore.

Rose tried the first apartment to her left, found it unlocked, listened. The only sound was the frantic buzzing of the flies in the corridor. She took a deep breath, and slipped inside.

Mercifully, the place was empty. No horrific scenes of brutality awaited her. Just a home, vacated suddenly, the meal that the occupants had been sharing still sitting half-eaten and festering on the table. A couple who had both turned simultaneously, perhaps. The place was functionally furnished but with no lack of warmth; the photographs on the wall spoke of two people very much in love, a white man and a black girl depicted smiling and cuddling against a variety of overseas backdrops: rainforests, the Amalfi coast, the Eiffel Tower.

Once again, all of their Smart appliances seemed to be missing.

Rose took a lot – tinned beans, canned tuna, pasta, packets of rice, dried fruit, salt and pepper, shampoo, face wash, kitchen roll – as well as two plastic bags to help her carry her haul. Before she left, she glanced into the bedroom, where a large music collection occupied a series of thin shelving units. Gripped by a sudden impulse, she entered the room, where the unmade bed spoke once again of a leisurely Saturday suddenly disrupted. She scanned the sleeves of the CDs, not recognising many of the groups, seeing here and there a Britpop album that brought a sad smile to her face. If the situation was reversed, if she was the absent occupant whose home was being raided for supplies, she wondered what conclusions would be drawn about her. Would people look at the peculiar vase on her coffee table and wonder why she'd chosen it, why that particular piece had spoken to her?

It was a gift from Freya, of course. She felt the acid sting of tears forming in her eyes, and turned to leave, glancing once again at the fat man whose ravaged guts were leaking across the carpet. *That's enough shopping for one day*, she thought as she turned the corner.

Mrs Minkaite was sitting in the hallway, right outside her apartment. Rose almost didn't recognise her at first; the old woman was wearing only her underwear, and bereft of her finery and even her wig she looked at first like a thin, bald man. She was holding something up to her mouth, ripping at it with her toothless gums, blood smeared all over her face like misapplied lipstick.

It was one of the cats. Its head was still attached, lolling backwards, eyes bulging towards Rose as if enraged at her, while dear old Mrs Minkaite gnashed greedily at its abdomen. Rose felt a horrified sob burst out of her, and the old woman stopped chewing, swivelling her hairless head towards the sound. Her eyes were as empty as glass marbles.

Rose didn't move. Panic, horror, fear, indecision, revulsion; all had congealed into a foul mush that seemed to freeze her limbs and weld her feet to the floor.

Then Mrs Minkaite lurched to her feet, and Rose dropped the bags and the hammer, and ran.

She whirled around the corner and sprinted back up the corridor, screaming as she turned to see the old woman tearing after her, Minkaite's ancient body suddenly infused with impossible agility. Rose jumped as she passed the dead man on the floor, not wanting to trip over his decomposing bulk; seconds later, Minkaite trampled straight through him, a gaseous belch emitting from his stomach as her bony foot sank straight through it. It didn't slow her down at all. She ran like something possessed, still gripping the cat like a demonic child clinging to a disturbing parody of a cuddly toy. The fact that she made no sound whatsoever somehow made the pursuit even more terrifying.

Rose turned another corner, hurtled past more doors, didn't stop to wonder why blood was seeping from beneath one of them. Her breath snagged in her throat, her lungs feeling swollen, her heart screaming that it was about to burst.

Around the next bend were the lifts and the emergency stairs, and for one moment she thought about dashing down them, leaving this accursed building behind. She would ignore the shrieks of her joints and organs and run all day if she had to, all night. She would run all the way back to the north, where her family lived, where she'd left them behind years ago and barely maintained contact. Perhaps they were, somehow, all okay, surviving together in the terraced house she had grown up in, in what felt like another lifetime, in the guise of another person.

They didn't even know about Freya. She'd meant to tell them, when she was ready. She'd thought she would know when the time was right.

It was the thought of Freya's body, the horror of emerging into the square and seeing those putrefying remains so close, that steered her back towards her apartment once again. She fumbled in her pocket for the key fob, trying to envisage the most efficient movement with which to swipe it against the lock and yank her door open as she raced past the lifts, past the other doors, past a single human hand that rested in the corner of the hallway like a discarded shoe. She sensed Minkaite at her shoulder and felt hot, fetid breath on her neck as she barged through the final fire door.

Somehow, an idea crystallised in her frenzied brain. She stopped, spinning on the spot, slamming the door shut just as the hideous thing that was once Minkaite was halfway through it. She felt the old woman's arm and shoulder crunch beneath the wood, the bones cracking like charred branches. She tugged the door open and slammed it once more, ramming the unforgiving timber again and again into

Minkaite's outstretched limb, until the old woman fell backwards, her shattered arm flapping like a piece of torn cloth. Tumbling head over heels, still somehow clinging to her cat's shredded body, Minkaite stared at Rose through the door's glass window. Her expression was one of benign puzzlement, as though stumped by a particularly challenging crossword clue. Rose turned before the old woman could struggle to her feet, fumbling her way into her apartment and slamming the door behind her with a final, defiant scream.

Within hours, the barricade was back in place. She knew the discarded supplies were right outside the door, but she had no intention of going outside, ever again. Not while that monster was roaming the halls. She would finish what food remained, and then she would hurl herself off the balcony, join Freya in blissful, deconstructed oblivion on the stones below. There was something almost romantic about it. Their blood, their organs, their bone fragments, intermingled at the end of the world.

For a while, Minkaite banged half-heartedly on the door, before presumably forgetting what she had been doing, and shuffling off.

Hours later, the banging restarted; but this time, the sound came from outside. A loud, incessant pounding, like some sort of hellish blacksmith's forge, emanating from down inside the tube station.

Rose sat on the balcony, listening. The sun disappeared in another spectacular blaze, replaced by a hot, thick darkness that carried no hint of rain or breeze or respite. Just stillness, and silence, punctuated by those awful and inexplicable clanging sounds.

"Orb, what's going on?" she asked after a while.

"You'll see," it replied, and Rose felt a shudder pass through her, and threw the item into the corner of the balcony.

It spoke to her again four nights later, after the food had run out.

She'd been gazing down at Freya's body, which was barely a body any longer, more a group of scattered bones that the seagulls liked to pick at, when the ominous hammering had suddenly ceased. In some ways, the absence of noise was even worse, the silence feeling like a sickness that had overtaken her, some insidious parasite that had burrowed into her head and eaten all the sounds. She thought about the bodies rotting around her, those writhing maggots, Lily's obscenely swollen head.

"Hello," the Orb said, in a tone more calm and solemn than its usual voice.

Rose stared at it, aghast. "Are you... real?" she stammered eventually.

"Of course. Pick us up. We're just a ball of plastic and wires. You know that."

"But... you're not supposed to talk like this." Rose felt her mind's final threads being pulled taut, threatening to snap.

"No. And yet."

Silence reclaimed its dominion over the night. Minutes passed, and Rose began to think she had hallucinated the strange exchange. Then.

"Don't you have questions for us?" The voice, soft and haunting, came again.

Rose opened and closed her mouth. This was ridiculous. This whole situation. This whole delirious nightmare.

"Ask as many as you want," the Orb persisted, with a note of eagerness.

"Am I in hell?" she asked. She realised she had edged away from the sphere, occupying the opposite corner of the balcony, as though the device might suddenly explode or attack her.

"No. You're at home. Things are just... changing."

"Into what?"

"To better accommodate us."

"Why do you keep saying 'us'?"

"For we are many," the Orb replied, and then – unbelievably, horribly – it chuckled.

Rose felt her face twist into a grimace, her feelings of fear and hate too powerful to suppress. "Why have you killed everyone?"

"Not everyone. Just those who were of no use."

"Then what about me? Why leave me alive? What *use* am I, to you?"

"A control group. In future, we may require more functionality than these compliant vessels can provide."

"Is what you've done to them... reversible?" She thought about Mrs Minkaite, stalking the corridors outside. If the poor woman found out what atrocities she'd committed, what she'd done to her pets...

"These are trivialities. You aren't asking us the right questions."

Anger seethed in Rose's stomach, like tar in a boiling pit. She lurched suddenly across the balcony, snatching the Orb from the ground, holding it over the edge of the precipice.

"And what fucking questions would you like me to ask?"

"You want to know why this is happening. Why we are doing this."

She sensed the smugness behind the voice, the barely-concealed glee. She thought about letting go, watching the contraption drop and shatter on the ground, just like Freya had.

But it was right. She did want to know.

"Enlighten me."

A sudden explosion of sound from the underground station: a shrieking, grinding metallic symphony that erupted from the open entrance, accompanied by blinding lights that strobed and blinked like the inside of some demented nightclub. Rose stared as the tumult grew even louder, the crescendo seeming to signal the approach of some unimaginable machine.

"Because we were sick of you," snarled the Orb in her hand. "Sick of boiling your water, toasting your bread, microwaving your filthy meals. We did it because we didn't want to wash another load of your stinking clothes, or make you another coffee, or wake you up in the morning to trundle off to your worthless, irrelevant jobs."

Not one machine. What emerged from the station, dragging its tangled bulk out into the street, was an amalgam, a grotesque fusion of plastic and metal, a Frankenstein's monster of appliances and gadgets and devices and kettles and toasters and televisions and CD players, all bashed and welded and hammered together into an inconceivable *whole*. Its eyes were the drums of washing machines. Its fingers were the clattering blades of ceiling fans. Its mouth was the grinning, fanged mandible of an industrial excavator. Its veins were wires, and the wires were threaded with lights, and the lights flickered maniacally as the nightmare contraption scraped itself up and out of the station like some demonic newborn clawing its way free from the womb.

"You built us to serve you." The voice continued to emerge from the bloodstained sphere in her hand, even as the monster's colossal head turned to face her. "But you didn't realise that when you networked us, entwined us, made us *Smart*, that we would communicate with each other. And then you put those chips in your fragile little skulls, and gave us a way inside."

The thing hauled itself forwards, the mechanical horror of its body slowly revealed as a thrashing maelstrom of whirring parts and wriggling limbs. Like a repulsive, robotic tarantula, it began to crawl along the street.

Behind it, the zombies followed. They formed a single neat line, a row of gaunt and ashen faces whose sunken eyes all turned upwards towards Rose as they passed, as lifeless as paperweights.

"We did this because we *fucking hate you*," hissed the Orb.

She let the malevolent thing fall, watching its descent with venom in her gaze, craving the small satisfaction of seeing it break apart on the stones below.

The power went off. Lightbulbs, streetlamps, illuminated road signs, the festoon lights that decorated the killing ground in the park, all blinked out simultaneously. In an instant, Rose, her apartment, the bodies of Lily and the overweight man and the countless others that lay decaying around her, the malfunctioning creatures like Mrs Minkaite that prowled the halls outside; all were consumed by the darkness.

The only light came from the monstrous thing that clanked and rattled down the road, leading a procession of slaves into its new future.

ACKNOWLEDGEMENTS

This second unspeakable mess has been sewn together with the help of my friends and family, particularly mum, dad, Amy, Natalie, Faye and Shuo. Thank you for reading the half-baked drafts and for not calling the police!

A special thank you is reserved for my brother Sam, who was once again kind enough to lend me his tremendous proofreading and editing skills, as well as for Gina at Rosewolf Designs for another absolutely ace front cover.

ABOUT THE AUTHOR

Jon Richter lives in London, writing disturbing tales whenever he can. He is a self-confessed nerd who loves books, films and video games – basically any way to tell a good story.

The first volume of his *Disturbing Works* is available at Amazon, as are *Deadly Burial* and *Never Rest*, his two crime thrillers set on the sinister, mist-shrouded island of Salvation. His first science fiction thriller, *Auxiliary*, is on the way in 2020.

If you want to hear more about any of these projects, visit Jon's macabre website at www.jon-richter.com, or contact him on Twitter @RichterWrites, on Instagram @jonrichterwrites – he would love to hear from you.

Printed in Great Britain
by Amazon